THE
LAST
INVITATION

THE
LAST
INVITATION

A NOVEL

DARBY KANE

WILLIAM MORROW

An Imprint of HarperCollins*Publishers*

THE LAST INVITATION. Copyright © 2022 by HelenKay Dimon. All rights reserved. Printed in the United States of America. No part of this book may be used or reproduced in any manner whatsoever without written permission except in the case of brief quotations embodied in critical articles and reviews. For information, address HarperCollins Publishers, 195 Broadway, New York, NY 10007.

HarperCollins books may be purchased for educational, business, or sales promotional use. For information, please email the Special Markets Department at SPsales@harpercollins.com.

FIRST EDITION

Designed by Diahann Sturge

Library of Congress Cataloging-in-Publication Data has been applied for.

ISBN 978-0-06-322556-5 (paperback)
ISBN 978-0-06-327184-5 (hardcover library edition)
ISBN 978-0-06-322558-9 (international edition)

22 23 24 25 26 LSC 10 9 8 7 6 5 4 3 2 1

For every woman who has been ignored, belittled, dismissed, forgotten, overlooked, or abused. This one's for you.

Most people say they want justice. But they
don't really want justice. They want revenge.
They want to see the pain spread around equally.

—DAVID GERROLD

THE
LAST
INVITATION

Chapter One

THE FOUNDATION

SEVEN WOMEN. ONE VOTE.

The Sophie Foundation. To the public, a charitable organization set up by a select group of powerful women to fund special projects relating to women's health and welfare. Very general-sounding in its purpose, and not by accident. Behind the scenes, in private, a smaller group within the Foundation carried out a very different agenda.

"Let's get started." The meeting had been called to order without the need to yell or ask more than once.

Attendees immediately complied. Folders opened. Notepads appeared. They didn't leave an electronic footprint and burned all documents after the meeting. They never wavered from this rule.

"The first item relates to the individual referred to in the documents as Offender C."

They'd wait to vote until everyone had an opportunity to speak and all arguments had been heard and settled. No one dared to come unprepared. The thought was unimaginable. They performed invaluable work. Risky and serious work.

"In light of the facts and history, and the probability of further acts of violence, I'm requesting our most significant penalty." A few members glanced up at the ringing command of the leader's voice. "Death."

Chapter Two

GABBY

GABBY FIELDING HATED talking with her ex-husband. She'd divorced him for a reason. A terrible, still-couldn't-process-it reason that left her with no choice but to get out of the marriage she'd once believed, naïvely so, would last forever.

Back then she'd also considered him her best friend, a man she could trust, which now seemed trite. Today, she thought of him as a gigantic asshole, both relentless in his need to "win" and indifferent to the people around him. A blowhard with an overinflated ego backed up by an impressive bank account he'd built from almost nothing . . . and that "almost" ended up ruining everything.

This morning, yet another fight about their daughter, Kennedy, loomed. She was fourteen and had just left to start her second year away at boarding school in upstate New York, as he'd insisted. He'd argued about her needing a "push" then conflated the high yearly tuition with the guarantee of lifetime success, all while covertly convincing Kennedy she wanted to go. Gabby knew he'd picked the school because she hated the idea of Kennedy being away from home.

The custody arrangement Gabby regretted signing before she'd finished writing her name on the damn paperwork less than three years ago required them to meet by September 1 to discuss and agree on a winter holiday and vacation schedule for Kennedy. The supposed legal genius Gabby paid a fortune to represent her in the divorce insisted this was a good idea. Gabby fought it back then and lost, and she'd been right to be skeptical.

Baines Fielding, self-made and very impressed with all he'd accomplished, did not negotiate. He didn't concede. He did not lose . . . or more accurately, he used the threat of cutting off the money to make sure he never lost.

This round he weaponized Kennedy by refusing to give permission for the summer program she wanted to attend until "your mother meets her obligations." So, fine, Gabby would engage in her agreed-upon yearly grovel for Kennedy's benefit.

Gabby inhaled nice and deep, reaching for the endless well of self-control required to get through this meeting and the expected barbs Baines would aim at her. She refused to fix her hair or take a quick look in the car window before stepping up to his front door. The years of primping, tucking, sucking in, and wearing spiky heels for his pleasure ended with their divorce.

She rang the doorbell. Minutes passed without him showing up, so she rang it again.

Nothing.

She mentally debated walking away but feared he'd lie and

insist *she'd* never showed up. She couldn't risk losing even more time with her daughter. If he wanted to play games, she'd play. Maybe she'd sit on the hood of his pretty little sports car and wait for him to race out of the house, screaming about the paint. Even better, she'd walk in the front door.

After some rummaging in her purse, she found the extra key she wasn't supposed to have. Coming inside without his permission would piss him off, possibly set off an alarm, but so what? The last week in August in DC meant stifling humidity. After a few minutes out of air-conditioning, her clothes stuck to her. She risked melting into a giant overdressed puddle.

She touched the knob and the door opened without the need for the key. No squealing alarm. No yelling about her trespassing in the house she'd picked out and decorated . . . then lost in the divorce.

"Baines?" She called out his name, then, in a much quieter voice, "Asshole?"

The words echoed back to her without a response.

Weird.

Her sandals clicked against the marble foyer. All that shiny white struck her as sleek and pretty when she'd lived there. Now it seemed stark and cold, which fit the current owner's personality.

"Baines, what the hell? Where are you?" Her voice bounced off the two-story entrance as she moved around.

He didn't pop up with his perfectly dimpled cheek and his usual *what's wrong with you?* expression. She assumed her very busy, very important ex was trying to make a point.

She walked across the entry to the paneled library at the opposite side. "Hey, are you on the phone?"

She stepped into the doorway and . . . red. The shocking color flashed in front of her. Bright and out of place. In spots and splashes. Splattered across the painting next to him in a random pattern of dots. Dripping down his white shirt. Oozing from the hole right by his ear.

The panicked screaming in her head told her to run, but she couldn't move. She stumbled. Off-balance, she slammed into something hard. The wall, a piece of furniture—she didn't know or care because every part of her, from her brain to her bones, went numb.

He couldn't be . . .

Baines. She tried to say his name. She thought her mouth opened but couldn't be sure. All that noise pounding in her head, the jumble of thoughts, but no sound came out.

The air in the room wrapped around her, cutting off her breath. The sensation of being hunted and stalked hit her right before the room went dark.

Chapter Three

JESSA

"YOU'RE PATHETIC." HIS rage, usually tamped down and reined in, hidden behind a baby face and black thin-framed glasses, whipped out without warning.

Jessa Hall didn't panic because she'd been called worse. She regularly received comments about her alleged incompetency, or how ugly she was, and how she'd ruined everything. She was a divorce lawyer. Misplaced hate came with the territory.

The issue right now was Darren Bartholomew's unraveling. Forty-six years old, probably objectively attractive to some in a rich-white-guy kind of way, but not to her. He came to court dressed in his usual nerdy, pressed-to-perfection look. He could pass as a college professor, but he was vice president of . . . something in a century-old family business, which meant he didn't do much of anything but collect checks from a trust fund.

She'd known his family for all of three weeks. In that time, he'd never raised his voice. Never showed any outward signs of anger. Never yelled. He'd been a model of calm, practical decency. The smart, reliable one. The one who listened and said all the right things. That he let the mask slip—chose to show the *real* him, the *him* his wife said she feared—in the open area right outside a courtroom, less than twenty feet away from two sheriffs, surprised Jessa.

She refused to show weakness as she turned to face him. "Calling me names isn't going to help your case, Mr. Bartholomew."

She'd hoped the teacher-like snap in her voice would bring him rushing back to reality and click his usual well-meaning façade into place. The discussion provided his estranged wife with the cover she needed to sneak away and make a dash for the elevators behind his back.

Darren didn't blink as he faced Jessa down. "You have no idea what you've done."

"I haven't done anything yet." The judge had handled all the talking during the hearing, but Jessa understood that she'd be the target. In part, that was her job as the guardian ad litem. She'd been appointed by the court to represent the best interests of Curtis Bartholomew, the five-year-old being pulled apart by his parents' very ugly divorce.

Her firm, a boutique family law practice that produced a string of judges to the Montgomery County Circuit Court and the Maryland Court of Appeals, agreed to GAL appointments as a service to the court. She'd been assigned to the Bartholomew divorce, and to Curtis, and she really wished she was back in her office, doing just about anything else right now.

"She has custody," he said. *She*, presumably, being Ellie Bartholomew, his wife.

"Your wife has *temporary* physical custody. You have visitation." Something his attorney should be explaining to him, not her. Jessa stretched up on tiptoes and looked around for the overpriced, business-and-not-really-divorce-attorney good old boy who represented Darren.

"No overnight visits." Darren shook his head. "I'm limited on how much I can see my own son."

"I know that's upsetting." Jessa tried to signal for Darren's attorney, a reinforcement to explain to Darren that physically removing his wife from the house and throwing a duffel bag at her in front of Curtis and his friends had started the custody case off in a very bad way. The judge had not been impressed with Darren's in-court not-really apology for his behavior, which was why they were all in this mess. "But it's just until the psychologist, Dr. Downing, finishes her custody evaluation and—"

"She isn't smart enough to make Curtis's lunch." Darren's soft, nonthreatening tone was back, but it didn't match the heat behind his words.

Jessa assumed he again referred to his wife's perceived failings. But maybe he meant Dr. Downing. Maybe all women. Who knew? But that summed up his entire custody argument—the woman he'd married was too incompetent, stupid, ill-equipped, to even see their son, let alone have custody.

Darren was an all-or-nothing guy who'd already made it clear that his family's influence and money should mean everything when it came to who was best able to parent Curtis. He could give Curtis *things*. Vacations. Private school.

Jessa really didn't like this type of man at all. He seemed

benign. Came off, at first, as caring and devoted. *Completely shocked* that his wife wanted to end the marriage and clearly taken by surprise by her choice after *an unimportant fight that got out of hand,* or so his explanation for kicking his wife out went. But here, today, the real Darren peeked out.

He suddenly smiled, as if they were having a conversation about the weather or some other innocuous subject.

Jessa found the fake-calm version of Darren even creepier than the fury-spewing version.

Darren's voice dropped to a whisper. "You should know if anything happens to my son before I can fix your mess, I will kill you."

The words, so delicately delivered, so cool and unruffled, shocked her. "Excuse me?"

But Darren had walked away. He headed in the direction of the sheriffs, holding out his hand and introducing himself. Politicking, as was his normal state.

His attorney finally stepped in front of her. "Did you want something?"

Some backup, jackass. "Now you show up?" When the other attorney frowned, Jessa tried again. "Your client just threatened me."

"He seems fine to me." He glanced at Darren before looking at her. "He's making friends, as usual. He's a natural. You should know he's not a man who's accustomed to losing."

So entitled. "We're talking about custody of his son, not a business deal."

The attorney laughed. "You act like he knows the difference."

Chapter Four

GABBY

HOURS AFTER SHE'D walked into Baines's library, Gabby sat across from two police officers at the dining room table Baines had fought so hard to win as part of the divorce division of assets. The man hadn't picked out anything for the house, not so much as a napkin, but he'd fought for every stick of furniture, plate, and curtain in the room.

The male officer, the one in uniform, looked at her with concern. "Do you need us to call someone for you?"

Gabby stared into the hallway and watched various forensic and other professionals walk in and out of her former house. Right now, it felt like the whole world was clomping around the property.

This time the woman on the other side of the table tried. "Mrs. Fielding?"

The sound of her voice had Gabby's head snapping back to the conversation at the table. The last few minutes, hours, or whatever amount of time had transpired since she walked into

Baines's office blurred together. Gabby couldn't remember calling the police or letting them in. Her last memory . . . fuzzy. She saw Baines slumped at his desk, and her world stopped.

"I'm Detective Melissa Schone," the woman continued.

"Detective?" For the first time Gabby realized the other woman wasn't wearing a uniform like the officer beside her. Her black suit in sharp contrast to her pale skin and white-blonde hair. The unusual combination came off as striking.

The detective cradled a glass of water, but her hands didn't hint at her age. She could be in her forties or fifties. Gabby couldn't tell. She looked at her own palms. They shook as she turned them over, studying every hard-earned line of her thirty-nine years.

"We know you've had a terrible scare, but could you answer some questions?" the detective asked.

Maybe? The visit with Baines came back to her in pieces. Distorted and uneven. Gabby didn't know if she could trust the flashes in her mind.

Fear. Blood. Baines.

Gabby asked the first thing that popped into her head. "He's dead?"

The male officer nodded. "Yes, ma'am."

Gabby waited for the sadness to hit her, but the haze blanketing her and blunting her emotions, making every memory cloudy, hadn't lifted. She remembered coming here to fight for time with Kennedy . . . *Kennedy! Oh, God.* How was she going to tell Kennedy about her dad? Baines doted on her, gave her anything she wanted. This would devastate her.

An anxious churning moved through Gabby. She gulped in air but still couldn't pull in enough breath. "I need to go to my daughter."

"First, tell us what happened here," Detective Schone said.

Trapped. The word spun around in Gabby's mind. She needed to get through this before she could leave, so she forced her body to sit still. She tried to concentrate on relaying the events even though a few of the words stuck in her throat. "I walked in and saw him slumped in his chair."

"The door wasn't locked?" the detective asked.

"I have a key." A fact Gabby now regretted. "Wait . . . the door was unlocked. I never used my key. Maybe." She shook her head. "I honestly can't remember."

"Okay." The detective continued with what sounded like a preset list of questions. "Why were you here today?"

"Custody stuff." The snippets fell into place and a final, horrifying memory flashed in front of Gabby, nearly cutting off her breath. "All that blood."

"Yes, we believe your husband—"

"Ex." Gabby grabbed on to the one thing that resonated with her. The only thing she could control. "We're divorced."

She forced herself to stop there. She had a habit of babbling when she was nervous or trying to hide something. She didn't want any thought about the latter creeping in as she talked.

The officers looked at each other before Detective Schone spoke again. "Yes, of course. We're wondering if you had any indication that something like this might happen. Maybe in his mood, or possibly something he said to you?"

This? The question made no sense to Gabby. "What are you talking about?"

The detective's hands tightened around the glass she was holding. "We'll get more information later, of course, but initial indications point to suicide."

"God, no." Gabby fought through the confused and conflicting thoughts pummeling her. How secretive he'd become at the end of their marriage. The can't-be-touched showmanship he deployed during the divorce. He'd changed from the man she married until he became this businessman who thrived on being difficult.

The detective put her glass to the side before starting again. "Some people deal with long-term depression. Others have desperate thoughts that are more situational in nature, stemming from a bad business deal, for example. Loneliness or disappointment. Divorce is a loss, even if someone wants out."

Understatement. "Baines would never kill himself." The idea was . . . laughable. It took all the composure Gabby could muster not to give in to her nerves, make a joke, and accidentally make herself a target.

"Do you know if there was a gun in the house?" Detective Schone asked.

But . . . no. Gabby shook her head. "You're not getting this."

The detective sat back in her chair. "Enlighten us."

Gabby had no idea why it was so important to her that they understand the man who right now might be in a body bag, but it was. "I don't know how my life ended up here. That will take years of therapy for me to figure out." *Off track.* Gabby fought to find her way back to the topic through all the fragments of memories and dizzying surprise flooding through her. "That doesn't matter. The point is my ex-husband loved himself far too much to deprive the world of his existence."

Silence followed the comment. Even a guy in the hall glanced up.

"People don't usually beg us to declare a homicide has occurred then paint themselves as an angry suspect." The detective's voice carried a not-so-subtle warning.

"I didn't do it. Yes, he made me furious, and I might have joked about . . . but I didn't. Never. I couldn't." Gabby took in their unconvinced stares and regretted her nervous laugh and racing mouth. They would not pin this on her. Gabby refused to let that happen. She'd fought all her life and she wouldn't stop now. "What about the other person?"

They stared at her.

"There was someone else was in the room when I walked in," Gabby said, growing more confident in the declaration the longer she talked. The strange sound and odd sensation right before she blacked out. "Someone attacked me."

Chapter Five

THE FOUNDATION

THEY MET ON the second Tuesday of the month. Members only.

A month had passed since they'd last assembled at the massive property tucked behind a high wall and locked gate. Over the years, the owners of the historic home had welcomed presidents, political operatives, and Supreme Court justices. The structure's size still confused many passersby into thinking it was a school. Little did they know the people inside used the spectacular house to carry out spectacular work.

Inclusion in the private group grew out of a carefully curated list and remained limited. No one could wander in or bring a guest. Potential new members—something of a rarity, for obvious reasons—had to pass a rigorous background check and be vetted by more than one existing member.

The rules required that the vote to consider issuing an invitation be unanimous, followed by a probationary period where the potential candidate underwent an assessment then another vote before the formal invitation. All of this occurred without the candidate ever knowing they were being considered for membership. That was the only way for an ongoing enterprise like this to work. Strict compliance. Complete secrecy. Unbending commitment.

No one had passed the intense scrutiny or been considered for membership in more than two years. Until now.

The monthly agenda didn't allow for a lot of socializing, but at the start of each meeting the members talked about families and work as they settled into oversized chairs in what used to be the music room of the three-story white stone mansion in Chevy Chase, Maryland, just outside of Washington, DC. The one with the split staircase in the entry and the second-floor grand ballroom, complete with an orchestra pit.

This brief initial icebreaking time worked as a bridge between their lives *out there* and the work they did in this room. Those precious ten minutes, never longer, allowed for the pressures of the day to ease and a calming breath before handling an ever-growing list of serious business.

They were busy women. Some drank wine after a long, tedious day. Others stuck to water, wanting top mental acuity for the meeting. None took what they did for granted.

"Let's get started." As usual, that was enough to stop the talk and begin the meeting. "A motion has been made to reconsider an individual for membership. The previous two votes were not unanimous. We must begin—"

"Dissecting her life and testing her endurance."

A round of murmurs and seat shifting followed the statement from the back of the room. Most of the women turned to the files in front of them. Some sat almost at attention, as if excited to weigh in.

The leader didn't flinch. "The old system may seem draconian, but we all survived it. As it stands now, it is the best way to assess commitment, drive, and ability to handle our workload."

She waited until the woman who had interrupted nodded. "Good. Then let's open the discussion so we can move for a third vote. If the vote is again 'no,' we will not reconsider this person for membership again."

Chapter Six

JESSA

THEIR SMALL GROUP went out to dinner at least once a month. Jessa prided herself on being practical and thought it was weird to hear grown-ups talk about having best friends, but hers was Faith Rabara. They'd met during freshman orientation at Georgetown almost twenty years ago, and their lives had circled around each other ever since.

Faith, from a big Filipino family that believed in frequent gatherings filled with laughter and unending plates of food. Jessa, raised in relative quiet by her dad in Ohio as he juggled extra shifts at the plant and nonstop requests by her maternal grandparents to see her as a way of staying connected to the daughter they lost when Jessa was born.

The third member of their little group joined in fourteen months ago. Tim Abner. Specifically, Timothy Aloysius Abner, grandson of a former congressman from Connecticut and Jessa's live-in boyfriend. She wasn't great at remembering dates or names, but she knew the exact date she met Tim because it was the day a one-night stand stretched into a weekend-long sex session and eventually a relationship. Jessa couldn't figure out if that was romantic or not, so she pretended it was.

Tim was also an attorney, but almost everyone in DC seemed to be, so that wasn't special. He practiced international business law, and a few sentences about his day were enough to put Jessa to sleep.

Tim arrived late to the bustling restaurant, as usual, taking off his suit jacket as he rounded the table and kissed Jessa. "What did I miss?"

Faith lowered her wineglass long enough to answer over the murmur of conversation in the open dining room. "The details of Jessa's scary day in court."

He slid into the chair next to Jessa. "I'm going to need something stronger than wine if we're going to talk about couples fighting over lawn furniture or whatever it is this time."

The waitress swung by then was off again, but she'd temporarily derailed the conversation, just as Jessa hoped. She'd be happy to talk about any subject except this one case.

Faith missed the silent woman-to-woman signal or something, because she chugged on. "You need to tell your law partners that—"

"I'm not going to make the jump from associate to partner if I whine." There. Done. Ending the conversation there would make her evening less bumpy. The idea of engaging in endless rounds of arguments with Tim on this topic sounded exhausting. Jessa had had enough male wrangling for one day.

"He threatened to kill you," Faith said, not letting the topic go.

"Wait." Tim stopped in the middle of reaching for Jessa's wineglass. "Rewind."

Jessa shot Faith a quick *thanks a lot* glare before diving in. "Darren Bartholomew lost it outside of the courtroom. I bet tomorrow he calls and apologizes and is back to his nerdy self."

Faith saluted them with her glass. "And you'll accept his groveling because the rich always get a pass."

The return of the waitress with more drinks cut off Tim's response, but he had it loaded and ready for the second she left the table again. "Let's not turn this into class warfare."

Faith winked at him. "Says the boarding-school dude with the funky middle name."

"I'll have you know it's a very revered name . . . or so my mom says," he said in a voice loaded with sarcasm. "Hell, I didn't pick it." He laughed as he looked at Jessa. "But let's stay on topic. The Bartholomews?"

Jessa hated talking about *her* work. She hadn't picked family law as her specialty. She fell into it. Right out of law school, she'd worked for a small firm. No one wanted to turn clients away or refer them out, so she'd done a little bit of everything and had gotten into a courtroom, trying cases, long before she likely was ready to handle them.

A few divorce cases got her noticed by her current firm, Covington, Irving and Bach. They specialized in family matters, building up an impressive reputation among the wealthy and connected in the DC area. Being good at something she hated trapped her in a cycle of high salary and low happiness that she couldn't seem to break out of for thirteen years and two firms.

Since that was a pretty nice problem to have, she kept quiet about it.

Tim sighed. "Maybe—and just listen for a second before you get ticked off—maybe you should get out of this case."

Faith froze. "Are you really worried about her safety?"

"He's not," Jessa said. He was worried about his job. His reputation. His partners getting ticked off. He never said any of it out loud, but he clearly weighed and assessed their respective careers and found his far more important and worthy of preservation than hers.

"What I'm hearing . . ." Faith took another sip of her drink. "Is that this is not the first time you two have had this conversation."

Some people sitting in the third-wheel position might feel uncomfortable. Not Faith. She ran a charity called Safe Harbor Limited that helped women and children displaced by domestic violence find alternative living arrangements, so she listened to people's darkest secrets and worst moments all day. Nothing shook her or lessened her sarcasm.

"If you don't think Darren has that power, you at least have to admit his family does," Tim said, clearly ignoring the tension whirling around the table and the *don't do it* side eye from Jessa. "The Bartholomews are related to the vice president."

"Whoa." Faith leaned forward now, fully engaged. "Is that true?"

Tim spoke right over her as he continued his lawyerly pitch. "They have pull. You could lose the support of your partners. There is a huge downside for you here, Jessa."

This was shaping up to be one of *those* get-togethers. Faith and Tim, both extroverted and chatty, shot comments at each other, over and around Jessa, until she wondered if they even needed her here for the conversation.

"Are your fellow partners putting pressure on you?" Jessa asked Tim because that was the only question in her head at that second. The one that sat out there, blinking and begging for attention. "Poor Tim and his big, important firm."

Faith whistled as she sat back hard in her chair. "Oh, shit."

"Fine." Tim's gruff voice sounded the exact opposite of fine. "Yes, your continuing with this case could be . . . problematic for me. For both of us, actually."

Jessa lost interest in her drink, this outing . . . this topic.

He reached out and put his hand over hers. "If this case goes sideways on the Bartholomews, which they don't expect because they always get what they want, they will destroy you. Head-on, behind-the-scenes, through me. It won't matter how."

Jessa tried to block out the sound of his voice. She looked around him, searching for the waitress. "We should order."

His hand dropped away from hers. "I'm not the asshole here."

Faith made a humming sound. "Are you sure?"

Jessa wasn't in the mood to console Tim and protect his ego, but she did it anyway. Her hand slipped to his leg, and she gave his thigh a little squeeze. "Trust me. I can handle Darren."

Tim's expression didn't change. "I hope you're still saying that a month from now."

Chapter Seven

BREAKING NEWS: TECH BILLIONAIRE
FOUND DEAD—Washington, DC

Alexander Carlisle, 49, founder and CEO of The Carlisle Collective, who sold his online gaming company for nearly a billion dollars two years ago and recently announced his intention to start a production company and enter the Hollywood arena, was found dead at his Georgetown home this afternoon. Sources at the scene who asked not to be identified said the death was the result of what is believed to be an accidental, self-inflicted gunshot wound to the pelvic area. Carlisle was alone in the property's guesthouse at the time of the incident.

Carlisle's wife, Ingrid, told witnesses at the scene that her husband did not own a gun and there were no guns on the property. The police have reassured the community that this is not an ongoing dangerous situation.

Carlisle has been in the news for personal matters

lately. He was implicated in the death of an erotic dancer and escort during a party on his yacht, *Undaunted*, over the July 4 weekend. Following the allegation, five other women, all of whom worked as escorts, and some of whom had previous convictions for prostitution, have come forward to accuse Carlisle of assault and other violent acts during the last three years. Carlisle's spokeswoman dismissed the allegations as part of a "vicious harassment campaign" to undermine Mr. Carlisle. The US Attorney's Office for the District of Columbia, citing a lack of credible evidence, has, so far, declined to press charges.

Carlisle is survived by his wife, his son, Maddox, and his parents, Victor and Honey Carlisle of Greenwich, Connecticut. The shooting investigation is ongoing.

Chapter Eight

GABBY

THE NEXT TWO days passed in a whirlwind of grief and funeral arrangements. Gabby filled every minute with a long task list designed to keep the despair from seeping in. She pinged from one obligation to the next. Talking to the detective. Helping Baines's brother, Liam, pick out a casket. Feeling useless while Kennedy wept uncontrollably. Exhausting herself so she didn't have to process the clash of her seething anger at Baines that had grown wild over the last few years and the heartbreak of how his life ended.

Old memories and long-buried emotions rushed in at the oddest times. Baines's silly grin the minute he saw her dress on their wedding day. The relieved tears when Kennedy finally arrived after twenty-three hours of intense labor. The endless work hours. Their exhausted laughter over pizza and cheap beer as they sat at a folding table, the only furniture in their first house for six months other than a bed and a ratty sofa.

The day she found out his secret, only to realize he'd discovered hers.

Divorce intensified every emotion and every slight. Shaded the good memories with a thick layer of disgust. Ratcheted up the tension until every word, every attorney letter, every long-resolved argument got dragged up and relitigated.

"Where's Kennedy?"

Gabby turned from the window and stared out at the trees that blocked her view of the C&O Canal when she heard Liam's deep voice. He'd abandoned his suit jacket and tie and rolled up his shirtsleeves as he sat down on her couch. Fatigue tugged at the corners of his mouth. His usual high level of energy dripped away as she watched.

"Upstairs. Crying, sleeping . . . both." Her daughter loved to sing and dance. She'd inherited her bouncy, don't-need-rest attributes from the Fielding side of the family. But she'd barely said a word since Gabby brought her home. "Nothing will ever be the same."

"Tell me about it. I've buried my parents and a sister. Now my brother." Liam leaned his head back and closed his eyes for a second. "Damn, it's just me now."

Gabby had known the three Fielding kids, Baines, Liam, and Natalie, for decades. They'd lived on the same street growing up. Natalie was the middle child. She used to say she'd drawn the unlucky Fielding straw. She dealt with learning difficulties and devastating anxieties that left her unable to handle open water, most animals, some food, elevators, or crowds. As an adult, she'd rarely left the house and depended on her brothers and an inheritance from her author aunt to survive.

Until the fire.

"I know. I'm . . ." Gabby sat down next to Liam. Their thighs touched, and she reached over to put a reassuring hand on his knee. The closeness immediately wrapped around her, suffocating her. Clearing her throat, trying to think about anything other than Natalie's death and the long history between their families, she shot to her feet to put a bit of distance between them. "I know this isn't the right time to talk about Baines. I'm not sure if there is one. Who knows how—"

"Gabby."

Right. Not the time for babbling. She skipped right to the hard truth. "They've got this all wrong. The police, I mean. Baines didn't kill himself."

Liam blew out a long breath as he settled deeper into the sofa cushions. His gaze was unreadable. It was as if he barely saw her. "The medical examiner said suicide."

"Listen to me." She slid onto the coffee table and sat in front of him. "Someone was in that room with him when I walked in there. I felt this—"

"This story won't change anything, you know. No matter how many details you suddenly remember. I'm not saying that to upset you. It's reality."

They'd always been close. Talked, shared . . . ganged up on Baines when needed. But she wasn't understanding him now. "What are you talking about?"

"His assets."

The words hit her like a hard smack. So cold and out of place. "When did we start talking about money?"

"Do we ever stop?" Liam asked.

"Your family? No." The elder Mr. Fielding had been obsessed

with get-rich-quick schemes and died without a dollar to his name. "I'd also point out that money never mattered to Baines. Not before the business took off."

"First, money always matters." Liam shrugged. "It just does. The difference is back then we didn't have any, so there was nothing to lose. That's not the case now."

"Which is why you should listen to me. What happened had nothing to do with Baines being despondent or suicidal. We both know that's true. He compartmentalized. Kept his emotions separate from the business." He hadn't always been that way. He'd been driven. Determined to give Kennedy the financial stability he'd lacked growing up, but at some point a switch clicked and he changed. "Not sure when he learned that skill, but he'd refined it by the time we divorced."

"I'm talking about you, Gabby." Liam's eyes narrowed as he studied her. "The alimony stops."

The words sat there, heavy and damning. She hadn't read the support or other financial provisions in the divorce agreement in months, but she knew some of them would matter now. She just hadn't had time to figure out how they worked together or what they mean for her now. "You can't think—"

"The insurance policy he bought to protect the alimony in case something happened to him, a provision your attorney insisted on, has a self-injury clause for the first two years." He hesitated before continuing. "The clause was in effect for forty-one more days. His suicide means you don't get ongoing support. No alimony. No insurance that protected the alimony."

Her brain scrambled. The reality of that loss ran right up

against her frustration that he thought she cared about the money right now. "And because of that you think I'm making up the story about the intruder?"

"Honestly? It would be better for you financially if someone had killed Baines."

Chapter Nine

JESSA

JESSA WASN'T SURE why she'd been pulled into an emergency meeting with a few of her bosses. She'd hoped, after being an associate for an embarrassing number of years, and on a hamster wheel of obscene billable hours, that they'd called her in to talk about finally making partner—a position she should have achieved at least five years ago, but switching firms had temporarily derailed her.

Looking around, she saw a group of people, all at the top of their field. None of them smiling. Nothing telegraphed *congratulations*.

Shit.

She mentally ran through her caseload and never-ending to-do list. Exhaustion pulled at her because she'd stayed in the office until almost midnight last night, finishing discovery responses and documents before they were sent to opposing counsel this morning. Messing up and missing an important filing deadline was more than unforgivable. It amounted to malpractice and likely a one-way ticket out of the profession.

She thought about the agreements she needed to write and the draft order a judge wanted to review tomorrow. Every *t* had been crossed, as far as she knew, but just barely. "Is something wrong?"

Eight white men, who her friend Faith insisted looked so much alike she could only identify them by how much hair they still had, sat around the conference room table with her. One woman, the managing partner, hadn't lifted her head from studying whatever file she had in front of her.

The partner directly across from her, Jon Covington, who literally preferred to be called Covington in the office, started them off. "We need to talk about the Bartholomew case."

So, Darren. She'd told the partners about what happened outside of the courtroom last week. Downplayed it. Said it was no big deal. Put it in a damn email rather than calling a meeting or asking for help, because this crowd would never invite her into the partnership club if she showed weakness. Last year a new associate cried when a senior partner screamed at her about forgetting to give him a message and was fired the next morning.

"If this is about the threat, I've decided—"

"No." Covington waved a hand in the air as he cut Jessa off. "Those things happen in divorce cases because tensions are high. You'll get used to it."

Okay, that bit of condescension pissed her off. She was an expert in cases like these. And no one should get comfortable with threats. She knew that, and he should, too.

She tried not to let the *you've got to be kidding* anger seep into her voice. "I know that people aren't at their best during a divorce. I've been doing this work for more than a decade now, but this was different. I thought—"

"Bartholomew's attorney, Stan, is a friend of mine. He mentioned that you might not be the right person for the case. He pointed out you're not married and don't have children, so you might not understand the nuances of the situation." Covington let out a labored breath. "It's nonsense, of course, but we wanted you to know a whisper campaign has started against you."

Jessa guessed she'd have to focus all her energy on not letting her growing distaste for Darren and his knuckle-dragging attorney influence what she told the judge or how she talked with her young client, Curtis, but damn. As far as she was concerned, Ellie Bartholomew couldn't run far enough or fast enough to get away from the man she'd inexplicably married.

But she also wanted to be clear about her position. All of this posturing and good-old-boy crap made her more invested in Curtis. "I can do my job."

Covington reached for his coffee. "No one is suggesting otherwise."

Well, actually . . . "Good, because I have no intention of dropping this case."

"We'll keep an eye on the progress. Have regular check-ins," he continued because he'd clearly been picked as the spokesperson for the meeting. Most of the other partners, especially those who hated anything related to contested custody cases and gravitated toward money-only cases, barely paid attention.

"We just need to know everything is on track and that the firm isn't implicated in any trouble."

"How would it be?"

"The Bartholomews have contacts with our clients. I belong to the same club. Bottom line is they have clout and could impact referrals to our firm." He shook his head. "Let's just say there are mutual issues between us."

She wasn't clear on who the "us" were, but it sounded as if Tim's worries about her staying on the case weren't irrational after all. "You've never micromanaged a GAL appointment before."

"This is a special case."

"You know, it's entirely possible Darren Bartholomew won't get joint custody or what he really wants, which seems to be for his wife to disappear forever." She had their attention now. No one played on a cell phone or looked around. Plenty of eye contact. More than a few frowns. "I just wanted to make sure everyone is prepared for that."

Silence screamed through the room. Covington didn't say anything for a few seconds, then . . . "We'll watch and decide if it makes sense for you to continue."

"I really want—"

"You can go back to your office now."

Chapter Ten

GABBY

MORE THAN A week had passed since Baines's death. Gabby tried to focus on the newspaper but couldn't stand reading another story about the tech guy who'd shot himself in the groin. In this interview, his wife insisted the police got it wrong because her husband could not have died that way.

Gabby knew all too well how that felt.

The more she thought about those terrifying, life-changing minutes in Baines's library, the more convinced she became that someone else had been in the room with her. She'd run into a body. Someone had grabbed her . . . maybe? The end was such a blur, but she hadn't just fainted. She knew there was more to what happened than her passing out from shock.

"Mom?"

Kennedy walked into the kitchen with her long brown hair in a ponytail, wearing a black dress and looking far too pale. She'd been home from school since the day after Baines died. She'd been quiet since she came home, except when she was being grumpy and sensitive. The only thing that could rouse her usual feisty spirit was the suggestion her dad had killed himself. They agreed the idea of him being so despondent or desperate didn't fit with what they knew about him those last days. If anything, according to Kennedy, who sometimes acted as her dad's far-too-young confidante, he'd been upbeat and talking about some big secret deal the company was about to bid on.

"What's wrong with you?" Kennedy asked.

"Huh?" Gabby realized she was standing there, out of it, instead of cutting the watermelon in front of her. She'd meant to make fruit salad, but there had been so many things she'd *meant* to do over the last few days and failed. She spent most of her time dazed, trying to remember why she'd walked into a room and if she'd remembered to brush her hair that morning.

"It's not the first time she didn't hear me knock." Liam stepped into the doorway and put an arm around Kennedy. "Hey, kiddo. How are you feeling?"

She grabbed on to him. "Uncle Liam."

Seeing them together brought a rush of tears to Gabby's eyes. She fought them back because a weepy mother was an annoying mother. Kennedy had been quite clear about that.

"Are you checking on us?" Gabby asked.

Liam winked at her. "Sort of."

Kennedy let go of her uncle just long enough to deliver a withering sigh. "Mom."

Gabby wasn't sure what she'd done this time, but she could play the name game all day. "Kennedy."

Kennedy rolled her eyes. "At least let him come inside before you bombard him with questions."

A dramatic teen. Gabby barely had the bandwidth for that nonsense on a good day, and she hadn't had one of those in a long time. "I didn't—"

"Maybe put the knife down first." Liam glanced at Gabby's hand. "Just a suggestion."

"What?" Gabby looked down at the blade clenched in her fist. She dropped it, earning a second sigh from Kennedy. "Sorry."

"He'll agree with me," Kennedy said without moving from Liam's side.

Gabby knew the context without having it spelled out for her. She chalked that skill up to years of living with a child whose mind raced ahead of her words. But this topic . . . Gabby was not in the mood. "Not now, Kennedy."

Kennedy turned to her uncle. "She insists I go back to boarding school. The same school she supposedly hated and told Dad and the court I should leave."

Because, of course, Baines had filled Kennedy in on the marital arguments. The fact he used his daughter as a divorce sounding board was one of his many questionable life choices.

"Admit it." Kennedy's tone switched from sullen to taunting. "Now that it's not a reason to fight with Dad, you're fine with the school."

At least she wasn't crying. Gabby hoped that was a good sign.

"It's about consistency. You should finish out the semester then make a decision when we've all had a little distance from . . ." Gabby didn't bother to finish the sentence. Dr. Downing, the child psychologist she talked to, had suggested the school might provide stability right now, and that advice boxed Gabby in.

Kennedy snorted. "Whatever."

"I think, maybe, you should give your mom a break," Liam said.

"You always side with her." Then Kennedy was off. She delivered her opinion and left in a huff.

Gabby was ready for this phase, whatever it was, to be over.

She picked up the knife, thinking to give that fruit salad idea a second shot. "Sorry. It's a defense mechanism."

Liam smiled. "What is?"

"I have no idea. I've been reading about grief in this book a counselor gave me about helping teens through losing a parent. Honestly, I want all of this to end. To somehow feel better." Gabby had never felt more useless as a mom. She'd thought the divorce was a low point, but this showed them all a new low.

"Funny you should mention something being over." Liam slid onto the bar stool across from her at the kitchen island. "Detective Melissa Schone came to see me this morning."

That didn't sound great. Gabby gave up trying to cut the fruit and threw the knife in the sink this time. "Lucky you."

"She said she talked to you again yesterday and you're still saying Baines didn't kill himself."

Gabby intended to say it until someone listened to her. "You know he didn't."

He must have seen the confusion in her face because he sighed before continuing, "She said there's no evidence anyone hit you on the head or anything else."

"The guy from the ambulance crew looked me over for two whole minutes. I admit I feel fine, but he could have missed something." But the lack of blood or a bump or some sign of being knocked out was a problem. She'd searched her hair and scalp looking for some verification but couldn't find any.

"While the ambulance crew checked on you, the detective checked Baines's security feed."

His what? She knew about the alarm system and motion sensor lights in the yard but not about anything more extensive. "Okay."

"According to the detective, you're the only one on the video. No one goes in or out of the house all morning, except you. That means if someone killed Baines it was probably you." He said the words, then leaned over and picked up a few grapes. Sat there munching as if he hadn't said something completely obscene.

The words struck her, leaving her a little breathless. "You don't believe that."

"Of course not, but I think you need to stop talking about the cause of his death, no matter what that means for you financially." Some of the tension ran out of him, and his shoulders fell. "Look, I'll help on that score. You know that."

During the divorce, Liam had pushed Baines to agree to a reasonable amount of alimony and child support even though Baines thought she deserved neither. Liam was a good man, but she wasn't his financial responsibility. She didn't want to depend on anyone for money, even him.

"Now and then during the divorce I thought about strangling him. While we were in mediation. In the courthouse, in front of everyone. While he was driving. At his stupid desk . . ."

His library and all that blood. The vision kept looping through her head, haunting her. She tried to push the hollow pain out and concentrate on Liam's concerned face. "I'm guessing most people trapped in a contested divorce have stray homicidal thoughts, or at least some pretty unhealthy ones, but they don't act on them."

"You forget that I've been divorced twice."

Two lovely, smart, amazing women. Gabby liked both and thought in each case Liam had finally found "the one" before the end came. She had enough trouble figuring out her love life without taking on his. "And you're friends with your exes, which is weird. It also says something about the type of man you are. Very different from your brother."

Liam shook his head. "He changed from the guy you married, but the point is you should let this go. If I thought there was any chance someone had done something to Baines, I'd be on the detective's doorstep, questioning her until she gave in and investigated or arrested me."

"How can you be so sure?" She had to admit Liam had seen Baines every day. She no longer had, but suicide still didn't feel right.

"There's no evidence of murder. Anywhere. And he was under a lot of pressure. Self-imposed but still." A pained expression flashed across Liam's face. "He hadn't been great since the separation. I'm not blaming, just stating a fact."

She teared up and fought to clear her throat. "I get it. Go on."

"But the last few weeks something changed. He was out of it. Acting odd. Not talking. I didn't tell you because he's not your responsibility, but now I wonder if he was trying to hide the depression from me. If I missed the clues."

Liam already shouldered so much. She didn't want him to carry this burden, too. "You are not to blame, Liam. If Baines did this . . . then *he* did it, not you."

"He would have seen it as weakness, and we both know he hated to show weakness." Liam sighed. "Just please, for your sake, let this go."

She doubted that would be possible.

Chapter Eleven

JESSA

JESSA WANTED TO be anywhere else. Literally, anywhere. She'd dug the black dress out of the back of her closet. Not the cute little-black-dress one. The serious one. The kind that Covington, her boss and work date to this business-related event, would find appropriate. The same one she wore to the other funerals she'd attended for clients and colleagues.

Four funerals in ten months. She hadn't been to four funerals in her entire life up until then.

The reality of those numbers left her feeling claustrophobic and aching to claw her way out of the room. For someone who made her living talking, convincing, finding the right argument, she had no idea what to say to the grieving people she barely knew or to the one person she did.

She'd walked into the service with Covington. Sat there listening to the eulogy and heartfelt speech from the deceased's brother. As he spoke, Jessa fixated on the women in the first pew. Mother and daughter. Mirror images with wavy brown hair and big blue eyes. Attractive in a way that drew attention, though they'd be the type to pretend not to notice. As if their looks didn't open doors, even though they clearly did.

Jessa could hear the low thrum of painful cries coming from the teenager as tears rolled down her cheeks. Jessa had always been so detached from the idea of a mom. She knew the indifference was nothing more than a protective mechanism subconsciously built up over years to make her loss bearable. Never knowing her mom, and her dad rarely dating anyone seriously, left Jessa both confused by the mother-child connection and deeply envious of it.

Her maternal grandparents waged a relentless campaign for custody. Her father spent hours talking about how terrible they were. Both sides weaponized her until the fight morphed into habit and focused on "winning" her time, not her genuine affection.

Her dad did his best. She didn't know if that was true. Concerned friends and a series of judges told her often enough that she'd internalized the phrase. He worked hard at his manufacturing job until his choices about spending money on household expenses over insulin caught up with him. He died while she was in college. She grieved for a few weeks then never again.

Jessa didn't realize the funeral service had ended until people started standing up and filing out of the room. She wanted to race down the aisle and sit in the car, but Covington didn't move. He stood at the end of the pew, nodding to people he knew as they passed. The sudden choking sensation made her want to shove him out of the way and get to fresh air, but that wasn't an option.

Gabby Fielding watched them as she walked out of the church

with her brother-in-law on one side and her daughter on the other. Jessa could feel the weight of her hatred. Gabby aimed all that loathing at them as she walked away. She'd clearly marked them as the enemy, and the loss of life didn't change that.

A few more minutes of uncomfortable shifting and stifled conversation with the other mourners, and Jessa broke free. She gulped in hot air as she stepped outside and into the sunshine.

"Did Baines leave an unpaid legal bill? If so, you can scurry along because I'm not paying it."

Jessa recognized the sarcastic slap of a voice before she turned around. She skipped the pleasantries and any fake attempts to pretend they didn't know each other. "Gabby, I'm truly sorry for your loss."

"How publicly decent of you."

Jessa had expected a chill. This was more like an ice storm.

"Are we friends again?" Gabby asked.

Were they ever really friends? Law school classmates years ago at George Washington. People who knew some of the same people. Not close, and that distance widened when Jessa's firm took on Gabby's ex, the deceased Baines, as a client in his divorce.

Gabby had fought her then-husband's choice in representation, insisting there was a conflict. At first, she claimed Baines had purposely met with most of the best family lawyers in the metro area to conflict them out and keep Gabby from retaining them. She wasn't wrong. Baines, like many other people in the middle of a contentious divorce proceedings, had deployed that strategy, and the court had let him do it. When Gabby then argued that the law school connection to Jessa conflicted out Covington and the entire firm from representing Baines, she lost. Again.

Jessa tried to find the right words to cut through the mess piled between them and realized there weren't any. "I know the divorce was—"

"Save it." Gabby leaned in. "You've done your duty and played the good soldier. You can leave now."

Before Jessa could respond, Covington popped up by her side. "Ms. Fielding, I'm sorry for your loss."

"Yeah, I got the office memo."

He frowned. "Excuse me?"

The daughter joined them. "Mom?"

Jessa hadn't been an official part of the divorce case team because that was the promise the firm had made to the court to overcome Gabby's objection to the firm remaining on the case for Baines, but Jessa knew this was Kennedy. The divorce of wealthy, powerful people drew attention, and the Fieldings landed in that category.

"There are the lawyers who represented your dad in the divorce," Gabby told her daughter.

Kennedy's sniffling and teary-eyed look disappeared. "Should you be here?"

"They're leaving." Gabby handed Kennedy off to her uncle and watched Covington wander away. Her full attention centered on Jessa. "You can take your bullshit concern and go home."

Jessa didn't want to fight. She didn't want a scene or any sort of confrontation. Her being there amounted to an uncomfortable obligation and nothing more. Even without working on the case, Jessa knew Gabby got screwed by a system run mostly by men who played golf together. The rules applied to her but were loosened for her ex so he could have the attorney he wanted— Covington, a man who treated divorce cases as open warfare without any emotion.

There was no way to repair even the limited relationship she'd had with Gabby before and make things easier for the friends they still shared. So Jessa stood there and took it. Part of her thought she owed that much to Gabby. Jessa had made some serious mistakes in the past . . . and Gabby was one of the people who knew that.

"How do you sleep at night?" Gabby asked.

Jessa got the question a lot. How could you represent that guy or that horrible woman? Don't you care about the kids, the alimony, if I can eat? It was a part of the job she could barely tolerate.

But she did have a limit. Gabby might never have practiced law, but she'd gone to law school. She understood the concept of zealous representation even if she was pretending not to.

"I sleep fine."

Gabby snorted. "Yeah, of course you do."

Chapter Twelve

GABBY

SEEING JESSA PUT Gabby in a terrible mood. The slim redhead had a way of making everything worse.

The grumbling in Gabby's head still lingered an hour later at the gravesite ceremony. The emotions ping-ponging inside her for more than a week stopped bouncing around and settled on hate. Heat had flooded through her as she watched Jessa climb into her boss's fancy sedan and simmered even now.

Maybe she should be grateful to feel something other than confusion. Baines being gone had left a huge gaping hole in her life and in Kennedy's. The end to the marriage had been terrible, but the years before came with a sprinkling of humor and good times. They'd built this life together, and she still couldn't believe how quickly it had crumbled under her.

Her emotions bounced all over the place. None of them rose to the level of true grief, of weeping in pain over his loss, because she wouldn't let herself think of anything but the questions about his death.

That probably explained why she'd become fixated on the man who lingered in the back of the church during the reception before the service. The same man who followed them to the private gravesite ceremony and stood away from the crowd now.

Any other time she would have ignored him. He probably wouldn't have registered at all, but she was on edge. Every noise and movement caught her eye and dragged her mind away from the finality of the day. The stranger wore jeans and a blazer, a bit too casual and not what she'd expect from one of Baines's business associates. His face didn't look familiar at all.

She walked toward him, noting how his eyes grew larger the closer she got. "Are you a friend of Baines?"

Present tense. It would take weeks, maybe months, to think of him in the past tense.

"Uh . . . no. I'm a reporter."

"You've got to be kidding." The tenuous hold on control snapped inside Gabby. She couldn't think of a worse time for some big business angle to a story. "Why are you here?"

"Rob Greene." He held out his hand.

She stared at it. "Answer the question."

The last minutes in Baines's office circled in her head. Not suicide. Maybe this guy had found out and was doing an article. That would be more than Kennedy could handle right now.

"This is the seventh funeral this year," he said.

Not the answer she expected at all. "What are you talking about?"

"Powerful, very wealthy men in the DC metro area. All killed in strange accidents. The most recent being Alexander

Carlisle's supposed accidental shooting. The one before that, a suicide."

Gabby's head started spinning. She could hear Kennedy calling for her from about fifty feet away and caught a brief glimpse of Liam's concerned expression.

The reporter held out a card. "I didn't mean to bother you. Not today. This is the wrong time for this talk."

"No kidding." But she looked at the card. Just a name and a phone number. No organization or any media identifier that she could see.

"There have been too many deaths, Mrs. Fielding. Too many for this to be a coincidence. It's a pattern."

Kennedy called out again. Gabby was torn, fascinated by the nonsense this guy was spewing but desperate to be there for Liam and Kennedy.

She should walk away. Rip up the card and go . . . but she knew Baines didn't kill himself. Something else happened in that room. That was her only excuse for prodding for more information. "What exactly are you saying?"

He nodded at the card in her hand. "Call me when you're ready to hear the truth about how Baines really died."

Chapter Thirteen

THE FOUNDATION

THE FOUNDATION DIDN'T hold many emergency meetings. This week they did.

They couldn't exactly use phones or email to communicate. The Foundation chat group, to anyone outside looking in, read as nothing more than a scheduling tool. But they had a secret code. When someone asked about trying to arrange a book club, they all knew to access their burner phones and prepare to meet.

Little more than a week had passed since their usual session.

After a bit of shuffling, everyone took a seat. Quiet fell over the room as they all looked up, bright-eyed and ready to take on a new challenge. Metaphorically ready for battle while sitting in business suits and sipping coffee.

"I apologize for the emergency session."

The mumbling and shifting didn't break informal protocol or any stated rule, but a pulsing feeling of dread descended on the room, and that wasn't normal.

"We have a problem."

Chapter Fourteen

JESSA

WITH THE FUNERAL over and behind her, Jessa wanted to concentrate on an impromptu ladies' night of pizza and wine at home, but Gabby's outrage still rang in her head. Jessa had attended as part of an obligation. To be nice.

That would teach her.

Jessa didn't want to admit it, but seeing Gabby had been unsettling. That haughty tone of hers, the voice reeking of disappointment. The biting verbal strikes. Jessa didn't need any of it. She worked for condescending assholes and had enough crap unloaded on her every day, thanks.

Gabby's and Jessa's lives had diverged so dramatically after law school. Gabby, already engaged during second year, chose marriage over a legal career. A man instead of using that great big brain of hers. Those choices, shortsighted and lame to Jessa—a waste of ability and promise—filled her with a silent sense of superiority. Those feelings only grew when she found out Gabby's marriage was over. Now what? Would Gabby run back to a career track she'd abandoned or relax into the role of rich, pissed-off *former* wife?

Something about Gabby brought out the worst in Jessa. Neither of them had been graced with an easy upbringing. Both raised without much money or family support. They'd discussed that when they met. Gabby never knew her dad, and her mom died of breast cancer during junior high, leaving her to be raised by a concerned aunt and uncle.

Jessa resented that they were so alike in life history and so different in their goals. She shouldn't care. Gabby's life really wasn't her business, but she did care. It was as if she held up an invisible measuring stick and judged her accomplishments against Gabby's.

Jessa wanted to be a better person. To not get trapped in the same patterns she'd been using for years—deny, demean, and deflect. But seeing Gabby brought the insecurities and doubts back. One word from Gabby made Jessa forget about her promises to herself and about her progress.

She wasn't the same person she'd been in law school. She'd made better choices. Concentrated and worked to the point of straining. She shoved thoughts of Gabby out of her head. The woman didn't know her these days and should just shut up.

Jessa leaned back in the corner of the sectional sofa, letting the cushions and piles of pillows basically swallow her. Wine in hand and her mood starting to lighten, she glanced over at Faith. She sprawled a few feet away, dressed in floral lounge pants and a T-shirt. Totally relaxed, a mood that Jessa never quite accomplished but Faith worked very hard to achieve outside of the office.

"Today sucked," Jessa said.

Faith nodded. "Funerals are seldom fun."

Jessa thought about Tim being in New Jersey for depositions for a few days and tried not to dwell on how relieved his absence made her. She loved spending time with him, but the more entwined their lives became, the more anxious she grew. The excuses about needing to work late or go into the office on a Sunday now just flowed out of her without thinking.

"The Gabby situation made everything so much worse." Okay, so Jessa could admit she hadn't shoved Gabby all the way out of her head yet. "I think if she could have thrown me in the hole in the ground and left me there, she would have done it."

Faith winced. "Well . . ."

Jessa eyed up Faith. "You're siding with her? And as my best friend there is a right answer here, you know."

"Not at all, but you had to expect some anger from her." Faither swirled the wine in her glass. "Can you really blame her? You said the divorce started as a bloodbath. It settled out of the blue but only after a lot of ugly fighting."

"I wasn't on the case." But Gabby had to admit that wasn't totally true.

Baines sudden shift toward a semi-amicable settlement never made sense to anyone at the firm. He went from yelling and vengeance to being conciliatory in the span of a few days. The turnaround ticked off Covington, who had spent a lot of time preparing for war. But that's all Jessa knew about the specifics . . . sort of . . . well, for the most part.

Faith's eyes narrowed. "And it's not as if you hear Gabby's voice in your head sometimes . . . judging you."

What the hell? "No. Really, no."

"Okay."

Sure, she was a bit obsessed about Gabby, but she'd never told anyone that. There was no way Faith could know. "Not at all. No."

"So, no?"

Jessa ignored the laughter in Faith's voice. "Right. If I wasn't clear, I'm going with no."

"And I'm weighing my words carefully here." Faith smiled, but it quickly disappeared again. "Let's just say if your firm represented my girlfriend, wife, partner, or whatever—the pretend one I don't have because I'm exhausted and don't want to fight over who gets the bathroom first in the morning—I'd be pissed."

"That's totally different." Jessa gave up on relaxing. She set the wineglass down when she realized she held it in a death grip. "We're close. I barely know Gabby."

Okay, not really the truth, but Jessa had invested a lot of time in selling that to her office, to Covington, and to the court. She wasn't about to engage in a self-assessment and back down now.

"I love you, but you're in denial or feeling guilty because . . ." Faith held up a hand when Jessa tried to take over the conversation. "Despite all your protests to the contrary, you and Gabby were more than general acquaintances. I'm not judging. Just saying, I was there—not in law school, but as your friend, so I know."

That's not how Jessa saw the relationship with Gabby at all. It was an understated, unspoken thing. Really, it was more of a problem. Her problem, and she didn't even know why she had it. Gabby didn't deserve this much of her time or attention.

"I think you're revising history a bit to make yourself feel better about helping to screw her in the divorce." Faith started counting on her fingers. "You did moot court competitions together. You had that study group. You went to—"

Jessa's cell phone buzzed, but she ignored it. "We weren't . . . I mean, I didn't consider her . . ."

"Uh-huh." Faith nodded at the cell. "Answer the phone while you make up an answer."

Jessa grabbed on to the diversion, hoping her brain would kick into gear and she'd come up with something intelligent to say. Then she saw the name of the caller. "Shit. It's my office."

Faither rolled her eyes. "Of course it is. After ten on a Thursday night. A totally reasonable time for a work call."

"Hello?"

Covington's stern voice broke across the line. "There's been an accident."

Chapter Fifteen

JESSA

POLICE CARS LINED the cul-de-sac in the usually quiet Bethesda, Maryland, neighborhood by the time Jessa arrived. Faith had insisted on tagging along but waited in the car. Jessa barely made it five steps up the long driveway toward the Bartholomews' marital home before Darren stepped in front of her.

He pushed up his glasses. "I told you this would happen."

He shouldn't be here. He'd moved out, but only temporarily and under great protest. The current living arrangement was one of the many disputed items between the couple. His being here at all made the anxiety churning in Jessa's stomach spin even faster. "What's going on?"

"She tried to run. But you knew that." His boyish features curled into a snarl even as his voice remained calm. "You did this."

She was not in the mood to appease him like everyone else clearly did. "Where's Curtis?"

"You mean *my* son?"

"Ms. Hall?" The woman who stepped up next to Darren flashed a badge. She was fortyish and tall, almost as tall as Darren, and he was about six feet, with pronounced cheekbones and a *don't waste my time* attitude that hummed around her. "I'm Detective Melissa Schone."

Police cars. Flashing lights. Neighbors on the sidewalk. Curtis wrapped in a blanket and sitting wide-eyed and visibly shaking in the back of an ambulance. The massive seven-bedroom, three-story French country–style family home was lit up, with the front door standing wide open.

This was quite a show. A big, scary show.

Darren turned on the detective. "Have you arrested my wife yet?"

The detective glared at him. "For backing out of her driveaway? No."

"That's not what happened, and you know it." Darren looked past Jessa then started to walk away. "My attorney just got here. Now we'll settle this."

Jessa waited until he left to get the details. "What did happen?"

"His wife and son were in the car and he purposely ran into them from behind, blocking them in." The detective pointed to the broken glass and banged-up SUV. "The crash isn't in question because he admits he did it but claims he had no choice."

The damage to the expensive vehicles suggested the hit wasn't a little tap either. He'd aimed and crashed. Jessa couldn't think of a single logical reason why he'd do that and further endanger his case. "Were his wife and son hurt?"

"Shaken up, but fine."

"Why is he still walking around?" Jessa meant *free*, because it sounded like he should be in jail for this dangerous, unhinged stunt.

"He says she was trying to kidnap the kid and leave the jurisdiction."

Something about the dismissive way the detective said *kid*, like the same way she might say *pool table* or *sneakers*, annoyed Jessa. "Ellie Bartholomew has temporary custody of Curtis, not Darren."

"We're waiting for clarification of that. Unfortunately, Mrs. Bartholomew doesn't have a copy of the order."

"Consider me the verification. I represent Curtis—the *kid*—so I know what's in the order. She has temporary custody."

The detective nodded. "So, any truth to the idea that the mother could be taking off with the kid?"

"Good question." Darren's attorney walked up to them dressed in a suit and carrying a briefcase, as if he'd just stepped out of the office at eleven at night. "Maybe your friend can answer that."

Jessa glanced at Faith. She'd gotten out of the car but still stood over there, behind the police tape, leaning against the door. She had nothing to do with this case, and Jessa didn't want her dragged into the middle of Darren's terrible decision-making.

"Who are you?" the detective asked.

"Mr. Bartholomew's attorney." He gestured over his shoulder in Faith's general direction. "It's interesting Ms. Hall here showed up to the scene with an individual who runs a so-called charity that's been accused of helping women sneak out of the area with children in violation of court orders."

Sneak? Jessa wondered how long he'd been waiting to fire that allegation, but she wasn't about to let him derail or downplay his client's behavior. "None of this is true or relevant. You know your client's wife has custody."

"She doesn't have the right to abscond with the child."

Jessa decided he was as annoying outside of the courtroom as he was in it. "What is wrong with you?"

"He's performing for his client." The detective made her comment and eyed up the attorney, as if waiting for him to object. "Is Ms. Hall correct about the custody order?"

The attorney blustered on. "That isn't the point. Explain why Ms. Bartholomew is creeping around late at night with luggage in the car."

"I have a better idea." Jessa refused to give any ground. "Explain why your client is stalking her. Why is he here? How did he know she was in her car?"

"He simply took precautions to prevent the worst from happening, and it's good he did." The attorney's shout rose over the din of activity. The ambulance workers stopped talking to Ellie and Curtis to follow the voice behind the yelling.

Detective Schone let out a long exhale. "Mrs. Bartholomew says she was going to her father's house outside of Annapolis for the long weekend. She doesn't feel safe in the family home even though her husband was ordered to leave it."

Jessa couldn't help but snort. "Gee, I wonder why she feels that way."

"This is not a fight you want, Jessa," the attorney said, the warning clear in his booming voice.

She refused to be scolded like an inexperienced little girl who'd gotten caught doing something wrong. "Are you threatening me in front of the detective, *Stan*?"

He shook his head. "Expect an emergency motion tomorrow."

"Good. I'm excited to tell the judge about this stunt." Jessa watched him go over to Darren and try to calm him down. She could feel the detective staring at her, assessing. "What?"

"I'm wondering if you'd really be dumb enough to risk your reputation by telling Mrs. Bartholomew to flee the jurisdiction."

Sounded like no one thought she could do her job. Jessa didn't love that. "Come on. Really?"

"I'm familiar with your friend and those old allegations." The detective's expression didn't give anything away. "It was years ago, but there isn't a judge, police officer, or politician in the metro area who doesn't know about that one. Hell, it made the national news."

The case that nearly broke Faith. Jessa remembered. There was no way to forget, but she didn't want to talk about it, or Faith, or anything but Darren's outrageous behavior . . . the same behavior everyone seemed to be downplaying. "Your focus should be on putting Darren in a cell until we're sure his family is safe."

The detective walked away without responding.

Faith passed Detective Schone in the driveway without exchanging a word.

"Are you okay?" Faith asked Jessa.

Shaky and furious, nerve endings half on fire from adrenaline and worry about what would happen when this case *really* got started. With a beginning marked with police intervention and crashing cars, Jessa assumed nothing good. "Apparently, your charity is a front for some sort of underground network that smuggles abused women to safety."

"I can barely afford a desk." Then Faith winced. "But I'm sorry. The Young case, right? It gets brought up a lot. The press back then was pretty intense."

Four years ago. Jessa knew the details. A guy killed his wife and child, hid the bodies, and then manufactured a story about Faith helping them run away. "Not your fault. It's fake outrage. Darren's attorney is trying to get the police to focus on something other than his client's hideous and dangerous behavior."

Jessa thought about Tim's dire warnings about the Bartholomews burning the world down to win and wondered if she'd just gotten a taste of what that meant.

Faith looked around. "This is going to get nasty for you."

Too late. "It already is."

Chapter Sixteen

GABBY

RETURNING KENNEDY TO school had been the longest drive of Gabby's life. A flurry of yelling, crying, and blaming until Kennedy finally declared she was done talking. Gabby had never been so relieved to drive in silence.

Since getting back home, nothing had gone smoothly. Not breathing, getting out of bed, or arguing with the insurance company. No longer being married to Baines and living in a world without him in it both sucked.

She'd been on the phone with more professionals—school counselors, lawyers, and people in Baines's office—in the week since the funeral than she had during her entire divorce. She sat at her kitchen island now with the laptop in front of her, but not turned on yet, and that reporter's card *right there*.

Curiosity gnawed at her until the card all but whistled for attention. He'd said something about unexplained deaths, and that's how she viewed Baines's death, and . . . yeah, she did not need one more problem.

"Are you asleep?"

She jumped at the sound of Liam's voice. He always knocked before he came inside, so she assumed he had this time, too, and she'd missed it. "Just daydreaming."

"I brought coffee." Liam set down the travel cup and sat next to her. He glanced at the laptop, but mostly in the way anyone would and not in the being-overly-nosy way.

But none of that explained why he was here.

"It's Tuesday," she said, meaning he should be in the office.

"Wednesday, but you were close." He smiled as he took a sip from his cup.

She refused to be derailed by his usual easy charm. "How bad is it?"

His eyes narrowed. "What?"

"The news you're about to drop. You're here, with your tie loosened and your hair kind of standing up on the side."

His hand went to the wrong side of his head. "Is it?"

She fought the urge to smooth the stray strands down for him. "And you forgot a belt this morning."

He glanced down. "Oh, shit."

He was a business guy, born to juggling deadlines and handling messes. Life had thrown barrier after barrier in front of him, and he'd stayed calm. The only time she'd seen him break down was at his sister's funeral. Even then, he'd cried silent tears, which were gone by the time the service ended.

His strength fueled her. She'd spent most of her life leaning on him. He was *that* guy. The dependable one. Handsome, protective, understanding. Having more money didn't change who he was or how he saw the world. Except to make him more empathetic. In other words, the exact opposite of Baines.

She vowed not to be Liam's responsibility now. Not when his employees and the business already sucked up so much of his time.

Not when they had such a confusing history.

She tried not to mother him, but . . . "Have you slept?"

"Did Baines leave any business documents here?" he asked at the same time.

"Wait . . ." She stopped in the middle of reaching for the coffee cup. "What?"

"Nothing." He shook his head. "There's just some . . . Never mind. Forget I said anything."

She thought that might have been the lamest *no big deal* shrug she'd ever seen. "What is it?"

He fidgeted on the stool. Shifted until he looked ready to squirm out of his skin. "Would you believe me if I said nothing?"

"Not even a little."

It took him a few minutes to spit out the words. "There's a money issue."

"Oh, that." She picked up her cup and took a long sip, trying to fortify herself with caffeine. "I have this house. Baines referred to it as the 'tiny bungalow in Glen Echo,' but it was a good investment. The location right outside DC makes it worth more than it should be. I can sell and move farther out, discover the Maryland countryside, if I need to."

"Gabby—"

"I also invested some of the money I got in the divorce, and

I still get the quarterly payout from the business, which I trust you to run. All of that will keep me going until I can find a job. It's been years, but I'd like to think . . . That's not what you're talking about." She could tell by the way the tension pulled around his mouth. "Tell me."

"There are some discrepancies in the business accounting."

She recognized the empty words as having a big meaning. "Are you saying money is missing from the office accounts?"

Liam got off the stool and started pacing. After a few steps, he stopped and stared at her. "Did you know?"

"How would I know? I'm still not even sure what you're saying."

"Right." Liam shook his head. "Of course . . . it's just . . . I don't understand what Baines was doing."

Dizziness overtook her. She had to breathe in through her nose to keep from getting sick. "Back up. You're saying Baines, my millionaire, account-for-every-penny ex, was taking money from the family business? As in stealing money?"

"I . . . maybe? I don't know yet. I just hired an outside firm to perform an audit." Liam's shoulders fell as he let out a long breath. "Did he say anything to you about money being tight?"

He blamed her for everything, but he'd never mentioned this issue—though it wouldn't reflect well on him, so he would have hidden it. "We hadn't had a civil conversation since I left him."

Liam started to talk then stopped.

Silence drummed through the room. She could hear it thumping in her head. "What?"

"It looks bad, Gab."

That didn't make sense. Baines had plenty of money. He and Liam had used the small inheritance left to them by their aunt to build a business where they bought and leased a network of warehouses up and down the East Coast. Big companies leased them. They had been growing, looking to expand deeper into transportation and distribution, when Baines died. Now all of that work would fall on Liam.

Baines bragged about having funding and access to money. They had trucks and contracts. Ongoing connections and significant money coming in. A "big deal" on the horizon. She knew some details about the company because she'd helped set up the business years ago and then insisted on seeing every document during the divorce despite Baines's claims that she wasn't entitled to look at or touch anything.

"How do you know Rob Greene?" Liam asked out of nowhere.

"What?" She blinked out of her mental wandering and saw Liam staring at the odd business card. "That guy? He was at the funeral, but about Baines and the—"

"Did he ask about Baines or the business?"

She didn't know how to explain what they talked about. Coincidence, pattern—the words swirled in her mind, so she ignored the question. "How do you know who Rob Greene is?"

"His name is all over the news this morning. He was fired from the *Washington Post* yesterday, and the paper posted this big splashy statement about how Greene's articles would all be investigated for accuracy."

"The *Post*? His business card doesn't mention the newspaper."

Liam frowned. "I doubt it's a different Rob Greene."

The weird way her life bumped along recently, it was possible. "How did I miss what sounds like a major scandal?"

"You were out of town with Kennedy, and this sounded like a sudden thing. The downfall of an award-winning journalist." Liam put his empty coffee cup in the trash under the sink.

The twisty answer about the reporter's convoluted life should have made her write him off and move on, but the urgency in Greene's voice that horrible day had tugged at her. He'd seemed so sure Baines's death matched nameless others.

"The general sense was that he's a big conspiracy guy and may have lost it." Liam nodded at the card. "I'd throw that away and forget you ever met him."

She handed the card to Liam, who ripped it up and stuffed it in his pocket. A second later, she wondered if she'd made a mistake.

Chapter Seventeen

JESSA

NO ONE IGNORED a call from Loretta Swain. If they did, they only did it once. She was not the type to offer second chances. Jessa knew because the Honorable Loretta Swain, senior judge of the Maryland Court of Appeals, the state's highest court, happened to be her informal mentor.

They met back when she taught a seminar during Jessa's third year of law school. Retta—the name Jessa was only recently given permission to call her—must have seen potential, because Jessa had been blessed with her wisdom, guidance, and no-nonsense opinions ever since.

Tonight, she'd been called to Retta's house. Jessa wore that as a badge of honor. Not many people got invited into the private sanctuary Retta shared with her husband, Earl. Jessa usually met with Retta for a meal or coffee, or at the office. Jessa had only been in the Chevy Chase mansion one time before, and that was for a charity event. She couldn't imagine living in a house with a ballroom on the second floor, but that was Retta's life.

Jessa waited in the marble entryway as the person who opened the door—maybe a housekeeper—suggested. Fresh flowers in an intricate arrangement you might find at an expensive hotel sat in a vase that likely cost more than her car. She was about to touch the inlaid tiles on the entry table in front of her when a door to her left opened.

Retta smiled. "The call took longer than expected. I apologize. Come in, Jessa."

Jessa followed Retta inside the library . . . or an office. Jessa wasn't sure what the official name might be for a room filled with bookshelves with a desk at one end and a plush seating area at the other. A conservatory. A den. One of a rich person's many spare rooms. Who knew?

"You've had a few difficult weeks," Retta said as she sat in an oversized chair, wearing a bold red-and-black geometric-print dress, along with full jewelry and makeup.

She was not an informal, dressed-down kind of woman. Jessa couldn't remember a time when Retta didn't look perfect. She preached *dress for success* and lived it.

In her midfifties with twin boys away at prestigious Ivy League universities, Retta showed no signs of winding down. Everything about Retta screamed power and determination. She was outspoken in her belief that women could have it all and rolled her eyes whenever anyone mentioned a glass ceiling. She fought for what she had, and she held on to it with an unrelenting grip.

Jessa didn't pretend to be confused by Retta's comment. "You somehow know about my week even though the Bartholomews' PR team kept the car crash out of the news."

Jessa had waited for a scandal to break or word of Darren's being arrested to leak out, but neither happened. In a phone call this morning, his attorney insisted the driveway *incident* was a *misunderstanding*. Ellie's attorney wasn't saying much of anything. Jessa still waited on a return call from Detective Schone with an actual explanation.

Retta reached for the water pitcher and a glass on the tray on the table between them. "Covington called me. He's worried about you."

Jessa never understood the ongoing Retta-Covington friendship. Their personalities didn't match except that both excelled in their fields. Jessa assumed being law partners before Retta's appointment to the bench forged some sort of bond.

"He's upset about the case." Jessa took a sip of water, impressed with her ability to tiptoe through the truth.

"True."

"He's actually worried about the firm's reputation and potential fallout as the Bartholomew family grows more frustrated by this custody case."

Retta laughed. "Very astute. I'm happy you see his concern for what it is."

"That doesn't make it any easier to stay on the case." But withdrawing meant letting Darren win, having Tim be right . . . suggesting to Covington and the rest of the partners that she couldn't hack the pressure. Jessa hated all of those options.

"Sometimes you need to hold your ground, Jessa. No matter how difficult that may be. That's what you're paid to do. You were appointed by the judge to protect that little boy." Retta's words echoed through the long room. "You put your body in front of his. You take the heat. You give him the best chance possible. And if you can't handle those objectives, then you find another job."

Retta never minced words. She didn't pretty her thoughts up and make them easier to swallow by delivering them with a spoonful of tact. Not ever.

Retta sighed. "Why do you think we bought this house?"

Jessa's gaze shot to the desk then to the French doors lining one wall and the lighted patio outside. She knew a fountain, stone walkways, and a dazzling pool all sat just out of sight. "Because you like to entertain or—"

"We bought it because we could. Not that many decades ago we wouldn't have been allowed to own it." Her words rang out as if she were lecturing a lawyer from the bench. "This house has a rich history. Powerful people have paraded through here. The structure and its lineage demand respect."

All true, but Jessa wasn't sure how any of that related to the Bartholomew topic. "It's beautiful."

"It's obscene, but it's better than the gaudy mess it was when we first moved in." Retta swore under her breath. "Everything was gold, white, and over-the-top. Not a clean line in sight." She topped the description off with an eye roll. "But the point is my husband wanted to own a house some people didn't believe we'd earned or deserved. He wanted to send the message that strong, successful Black couples exist and deserve to be in every space. To dare anyone to contradict him."

"I can't imagine." Jessa guessed some neighbors and a few

people at the country club Retta and Earl belonged to likely questioned their *right* to be there. Jessa didn't have any personal experience with that sort of biased, unfair scrutiny. Back at Georgetown, some students had sniffed out how she only owned four shirts and a ripped, too-small winter jacket and made snide comments, but this was a completely different thing.

"The angry whispers flew when we won the bidding war for the estate, but we're still here," Retta continued. "People couldn't question *if* we had money. Earl's transportation company had grown. He bought land other people undervalued and didn't want and built there. He made his services enticing and created the infrastructure to support his plans. He had the power to smother the stray grumbling."

Jessa thought about Earl and his gray beard. That big smile. His watchful eyes didn't miss much. "He's never been anything but kind to me."

"He's very giving to the people he cares about. Loyal and fierce. But he's ruthless in the way he walks through this world. He's had to be." Retta lifted an eyebrow. "You should take a lesson."

Jessa envied the confidence of a self-made millionaire. "I don't have that kind of . . . what, voice? Presence? Seniority?"

Retta made a strained noise before she spoke. "Demand it."

"Okay." Jessa didn't know what else to say, so she went with that.

"I have a suggestion."

Thank God. "I'm open to any advice."

"I belong to an exclusive group of talented, professional women." Retta settled back farther into her chair.

"Are you talking about the Sophie Foundation?" Jessa knew *of* it. She wasn't a hundred percent sure what it did or who worked there except that it sponsored events and clothing drives.

"That's the official charity. I'm referring to a group behind the Foundation. Some members are officially affiliated with the Foundation. Some aren't." She hesitated for a second, as if expecting a question. "We meet in private and don't advertise the work we do. The membership is confidential. We don't seek out press."

Jessa tried to wade through her growing excitement at being considered for a private group and all the words to figure out exactly what Retta was talking about. "What kind of work?"

"We help other women find their footing. Give support. Sometimes more."

"That sounds perfect." A little light on details, but Jessa hungered for a support group. For people who understood her position and the pressures of having everyone throwing self-focused advice at her.

Retta rubbed her hand up and down the armrest. "Your membership isn't guaranteed, but the two of us could start meeting more regularly. Run through scenarios. Get you ready to take on the whole group."

Jessa couldn't remember engaging in a more cryptic conversation. "You mean research?"

"Not really." Retta shook her head. "You see, sometimes we need to work outside of the justice system. Away from the courts and the web of therapists and groups designed to help. We brainstorm the most effective ways to do that."

"What role would I play? Or is it about donating?" Jessa hated this part and fought not to be plowed under by the disappointment she saw coming. She made good money, but she had student loans to pay. Piles of them. She could offer sweaty equity in the limited time a day she wasn't getting pummeled by billable hour requirements.

"It's about assessing your boundaries and problem-solving, though I have a good idea of your abilities as to the latter," Retta continued before Jessa could ask for more clarification. "I'll slowly introduce you to the others and the work we do."

Jessa still didn't understand exactly what this group did, but this was Retta. A legal superstar. A legend. This was the type of opportunity a smart, upwardly mobile person jumped on, so Jessa jumped. "I appreciate the opportunity, and I won't disappoint you."

Retta's smile widened. "Let's hope not."

Chapter Eighteen

GABBY

GABBY VENTURED OUT to the grocery store. She wanted to hide in the house, play the last few weeks over and over in her head until she found clarity, maybe force Liam to cough up more details about the Baines money issue, but she needed boring items like coffee and toilet paper. She checked out and made it back to her car before she heard the familiar voice.

"We need to talk."

Rob Greene. She'd spent hours online searching about him, reading articles about the reporter's steep decline. Now she knew way too much about this guy, and none of it good. He'd broken the rules, lied, made up sources. Liam was right to warn her away from this mess. She had enough of her own.

She balanced two bags in one hand and reached for her key fob. The alarm chirped. "I knew I should have stayed in the house."

"Please don't ignore me." He sounded more desperate than angry. "I'm trying to help you."

She glanced around the parking lot. People rushed in and out of the store. Parents unloaded groceries and kids from carts. If she hit the right combination of buttons on the key fob, an alarm would screech, grabbing everyone's attention away from their hurried tasks. For some reason, all those factors gave her the confidence to stay calm and keep moving.

"You'll notice I didn't call you." She shoved the bags in the back seat and quickly closed the door. "Take a hint. I have no interest in your nonsense."

His expression changed. Every muscle seemed to crumble, as if he couldn't take one more thing. "You've seen the news."

She understood feeling defeated, but this was not a guy who deserved her empathy. His behavior snarled him in the very public disaster now unfolding around him. "You're a fraud. You faked your sources for stories. You lied to your bosses. Worse, you're a conspiracy clown who believes school shootings are fake and—"

"No, listen." He took a step closer and only stopped when she held up her key chain. "None of what you've heard about me is true. I'm being set up."

"There's probably a better argument to convince me you're not dangerous or delusional." She angled her body so she could get to the front door and keep him on the outside of it. "Excuse me."

"They'll find out, you know."

She stopped moving and fidgeting and trying to race away and faced him. "I have no idea what you're talking about."

Nothing about him suggested he was out of it or invested in wild stories. He looked like every other guy in the neighborhood. He wore jeans and a blazer and running shoes, completely what she'd expect in the Bethesda area . . . but maybe that was the scary thing about conspiracy theorists. They were far too easy to take seriously, at least at first.

"The group," he said.

"What group? Do you hear yourself?" She tried to reason with him, even though she knew that was useless. He wasn't rational, no matter what he looked like. "I know you were some big-time reporter, and then . . . I don't know. Something happened, I guess?" She kept her voice calm. Aimed at being supportive but in a *we don't even know each other* kind of way. "You should talk to someone. Get help."

He rested his hand on the roof of her car. "You need me."

Too close. Adrenaline pumped through her. "I really don't."

"I have information about your ex-husband's death," he said in an almost manic rush.

"Right." But Gabby hated the way her heartbeat ticked up. He'd hit on the one subject that refused to leave her mind, but she couldn't let him know about her interest. He was too much of a wild card. "Did you tell the police?"

"They won't believe me."

She could feel her body deflate. "I can't say I blame them. That seems to be a problem you created."

"Not me. The group." He shook his head, looking as lost as he sounded. "If you dig too much or get close, they close in."

She saw a man watching them a few cars away. She wanted everyone's attention now, because this had crossed a line into batshit territory. "You have ten seconds to leave, or I'm going to scream and keep screaming until you leave me alone."

But he was lost in the story playing in his head. Words rushed out of him. "They'll have to keep you quiet. You pointing out the truth about your ex threatens their plans."

"Uh-huh." She slid her hand under the door handle and heard the door unlock again.

"I know this sounds unbelievable."

"That's one word for it."

"They can't have you questioning the suicide. Their plans only work if no one looks too closely and so long as their inside people work fast enough to bury the truth."

She fumbled for her cell phone and started punching buttons. "This is me calling the police."

"Stop." He reached for her phone. "God, please just listen to what I'm saying."

The man who had been watching them—tall, from the haircut probably military or retired military—started toward them. Lethal-looking. Good. That's exactly what she needed right now.

"Ma'am, are you okay?" the man asked as he stepped in close. His presence had the reporter pulling back.

Relief whooshed through her. That fast, she could feel the tension easing from her as she forced her fingers to unclench around her keys. "Thank you. He's leaving."

The man nodded, but he didn't go far. He hovered right behind the reporter as if ready to lunge, if needed.

"They'll find out your secret," Rob said in a near whisper this time. "If I could find out, so can they. They know, and they'll release the secret in the way calculated to hurt you the most, to discredit you. To keep you quiet."

What? There was no way . . . right? She'd been careful. He had to be throwing out words, hoping he picked the right ones to scare her. Well, it worked. She opened the car door and slipped inside. She had it closed and locked a second later. But she could still hear him through the window.

"We're running out of time, and I have to keep moving because I'm a target," he said as he tucked another one of his cards under her windshield wiper blade. "Don't wait."

Chapter Nineteen

JESSA

COVINGTON WALKED INTO her office without any greeting and shut the door behind him. "We need to remove you from the Bartholomew matter. It's time."

The bold statement made Jessa cough up her sip of coffee. "The judge is taking me off the case?"

He handed her a sheet of paper. "I had my secretary draft a motion to withdraw as guardian ad litem for Curtis. You need to review it and sign."

She refused to touch the document. "No."

"This isn't a request, Jessa."

"Why?" She'd been on the phone all morning with various players in the case, trying to figure out if Curtis was safe after Darren's willingness to smash cars to get his way. *He* was the problem, not her.

"Darren's attorney intends to file an ethics complaint with the bar then file a motion in the case—a public document—regarding your competency."

Destroy her. That was the obvious goal here. Make it so that her testimony would be discounted. Never mind that she didn't have enough information to actually have a legal opinion yet.

She decided to point out the obvious. "I'm not the one who slammed into my spouse's car in a driveway."

"They're accusing you of conspiring with a woman who is known to assist allegedly abused women. Your friend, Faith. The belief is you are predisposed, thanks to your relationship with Faith or otherwise, to side with the wife in the Bartholomew case."

"The wife's name is Ellie."

He threw the document on her desk. "Are you listening to me?"

"Of course." Jessa searched for the right words, any words, to convince him. Like it or not, he was the boss, and she couldn't yell at him unless she wanted to be unemployed and flailing without a safety net. "You know Faith. You've used her as an expert witness in more than one case, despite all the old rumors. And, for the record, those rumors were started by Mr. Young back then to hide the fact he'd killed his family. He muddied the waters enough to get away with it."

"What did or did not happen in an unrelated case is not the issue today."

She didn't bother to point out that he was the one relating the cases, not her. "Darren Bartholomew is angry because he can't control me or charm me, or whatever he's trying to do."

"You've been talking with the wife's attorney and to Dr. Downing, the child psychologist assigned to do the custody evaluation."

"That's my job," she pointed out.

His exasperated exhale filled the room. "I know this is a bullshit claim against you, Jessa."

"That's good to hear." At least they agreed on something.

"But we can't ignore the allegations that you're pushing an agenda here." He held up his hand when she started to respond. "No one in the firm is saying it, but it's being said. We still believe in you, but Stan, Darren's attorney, is following the orders of his client and making this situation very difficult."

"This is asinine." Jessa tried to lower her coffee mug without slamming it down. When she heard the crack, she knew she'd been unsuccessful.

"If you withdraw, Darren and his attorney will stand down. They will work with his wife's counsel to pick a new GAL."

"You mean someone with the Darren seal of approval." Energy pinged through Jessa. It was all she could do to stay in her chair. To pretend to be calm while tiny explosions destroyed her from the inside.

"The firm has decided these court appointments take up too much billable time. We will no longer be accepting them," he said.

"That's fine for *next* time, but not this case." She could hear her voice getting tighter and louder, matching his. After a few deep breaths, she tried again. "We need to send a message to people like the Bartholomews that we do not fold. Then, in the future, when their friends want tough and determined lawyers, they'll come to us."

He grabbed the draft motion and crumpled it in his fist. "That is wildly naïve."

But she sensed she'd gotten through, if only a little. "I've been called worse."

"You better have a very clean house. Like it or not, this custody case may turn on your believability."

"I shouldn't be in the spotlight. This is about Curtis's best interests."

He shoved the wadded-up paper in his pocket. "Talk like that makes me doubt your ability to make it in this profession."

Chapter Twenty

GABBY

GABBY SAT AT Liam's dining room table and looked through financial documents. These belonged to Fielding Enterprises, the family business. She pretended to be interested, but the work wasn't exactly sexy. Lucrative, yes, and that's what Baines had focused on. Building an empire. Guaranteeing financial security for the family for generations to come. He used to talk about those dreams, but none of them hinted at stealing money.

"Here." Liam set down a fresh pot of coffee on the table between them.

"This will be my fourth cup."

He winked. "My third pot, so I have you beat."

This wasn't how she intended to spend her Saturday, but when she came over to ask Liam a few questions about the bombshell he'd dropped, she found him plowing through paperwork. Boxes and boxes of it.

He said he'd grabbed copies of everything he gave to the auditors and brought it all home for a personal look. She dove in with him. Between them they had a law degree and a business degree and years of street savvy. Hers had dulled with age, but she hoped it still lingered somewhere in the background.

She looked at the list of vendors and saw debits to the accounts. Some of the checks didn't line up with Fielding Enterprises' actual bills. The deducted money went somewhere, and she feared the answer was *into Baines's pocket.*

Tension swirled around the quiet room. Liam's shoulders stiffened as he traced payments. Today, he stayed casual, jeans and a T-shirt. Every now and then he would wince or swear under his breath.

She tried to lighten the weight pressing down on the room. "Some of these are the documents Baines insisted didn't exist during the divorce."

Liam glanced up. It took another few seconds for his eyes to clear and for him to focus on her. "I compiled everything when the business got the subpoena. I wasn't going to hold anything back, no matter how much Baines begged."

Now she'd made him defensive. The exact opposite of what she wanted. But . . . "Did he?"

"Of course." Liam poured another cup of coffee for both of them as some of the tension drained from him. "He had this very elaborate, very convoluted argument about how financially screwing you would ultimately help Kennedy."

"That sounds like your brother." He'd been determined to make her pay, either through the bank balance or through Kennedy.

"He was named after our grandfather. They shared the same

'do whatever works' attitude." Liam saluted with his cup as some of his general lightness returned. "Word is my grandmother hit him with a shovel."

She thought she'd heard every family story, but she'd missed this one. "I thought your grandfather died when he fell into a well."

"Wouldn't you fall if someone hit you with a shovel?" Liam smiled at her over the rim of his mug. "But the document subpoena became moot because Baines suddenly agreed to a divorce settlement."

"You gave him a brotherly 'get your head out of your ass' speech, and I thank you for that." She returned the mug salute.

"His attitude changed right before the settlement." Liam's expression morphed from open and friendly to unreadable. "I stayed out of his way because I thought he was pissed about my constant 'she's your daughter's mom' lectures. But then he announced a surprise settlement offer, and I wondered if you had leverage."

"Like what?" She had a hard time keeping up with Liam's changing mood. He shifted from joking to serious to somewhere in between over the span of ten minutes. She depended on him to be solid. Not being able to trust his mood left her feeling unmoored. And she hated this topic.

"It must have been something you did or said." He sounded so sure. "Want to fess up?"

He wasn't wrong. She knew why. Of course she knew. "It was nothing. You know how marriage is. People collect slights. They remember harsh words and bad behavior. You end up compiling these secrets without even realizing you're doing it, then an unexpected divorce gives you a way to weaponize and unload them."

"I was married and never did any of that."

Because he didn't suck like his brother. "Right, well, you had two nice marriages with two nice women, followed by two very civil divorces. No fighting or yelling. You handed over cash and property without balking or unleashing war." The ease with which he exited a committed relationship always fascinated her. He should give classes to other men. "Your lack of anger was . . . unusual."

"It was a lack of *passion*." He slid his hand toward her. "You know why."

She pulled back, putting as much room between them as the chairs and table would allow. "Don't."

He stared at her for a few charged seconds of silence before nodding. "Then tell me what you had on him. If it wasn't whatever he was doing with the business accounts, what was it?"

Terrible secrets that would result in mutually assured destruction and epic collateral damage. In other words, nothing she could say out loud or divulge even to Liam. "I honestly didn't know about the money."

His mood shifted again. "He's dead, Jessa."

"I'm aware." Just hearing the word started that hollow sensation in her stomach again. Money problems. Asshole. Bad divorce. It all mattered, but it didn't change the fact she'd married him, hoping for, and dreaming about, a very different ending.

"I won't judge," Liam said.

She really looked at him then. Searched his face. Watched his hands. Did he know? But he couldn't know. There was no way. No matter what that annoying reporter said.

The secrets she harbored needed to stay buried with Baines.

She forced a smile. "Maybe someday."

Chapter Twenty-One

GABBY

SPENDING ALL DAY looking at financial documents on Saturday made Gabby obsess the next day about what she *didn't* know. By the time she got to Monday, she needed to investigate. The word sounded silly even in her head. What she really wanted to do was snoop around Baines's house in search of answers. What he'd done with the money, why and how he'd really died . . . and who was in that room with her when she lived her worst moment.

That all sounded good in theory, but she'd forgotten about the crime scene tape at his front door. Getting in was easy enough since she had a key and could go around the back of the house, out of sight of nosy neighbors and without having to disturb the yellow tape. Walking inside—crossing the threshold—proved almost impossible.

She forced her legs to move and stepped into the kitchen. She could smell him even in here. The peppery scent of his soap. Weeks had passed, and Liam had paid a special crew to come in and clean up, but none of that had killed Baines's looming presence. She saw him reflected in the crisp white quartz countertops, a choice he'd made during some minor remodeling after she'd moved out.

Walking through the house led her to the great room with its vaulted ceiling and wooden beams. Past the fireplace with the photograph of all three of them above it. To the photographs of them on various vacations throughout the years. This room gave the impression of family, of still being together, of moments of happiness before the divorce.

The fake happiness suffocated her. She raced from the room into the hallway that led to the office. Memories of Baines's last day bombarded her as she slowed to small, halting steps.

She stood in the doorway and peered inside. In a small mercy, all signs of the bloodbath had been erased. It looked normal, as if a life hadn't ended there in a flash of horror.

She forced her mind to concentrate. She breathed through the shudder running through her. Closed her eyes and tried to think like Baines. Where would he hide damning evidence? The police and forensic professionals had been all over the house, and they weren't talking.

The safe in the bedroom seemed too obvious. She doubted the file cabinet held anything of any real interest. The police would have dumped those drawers into boxes and taken them out of the house along with all the computers anyway.

So . . . in books? In drawers? "Baines, give me a hint."

She laughed at how ridiculous she sounded. He would love that he had her spinning in circles, questioning her sanity, and racing around after him. Any act that gave him power or shifted attention to him counted as a win.

"Asshole." The word slipped out, but maybe that was a good sign. She'd spent years calling him that in her head or with her friends. This was the first time since finding his body she'd let her mind go there. "I will not grant you sainthood in death, my dear ex-husband."

She looked at the framed photo of Kennedy on the table behind his desk. Photos and family . . . and in the next second her mind wandered back to that misplaced family photograph over the fireplace. He hadn't asked for that in the divorce. She'd lost track of it, forgot about it, really, until five minutes ago.

Who kept a near-life-sized photo with their ex-spouse right there—boom—where it couldn't be avoided?

She turned and walked back into the great room and stared the damn thing down. It looked . . . different. She studied the photo and, no, that was the same. The frame. It was bigger, maybe bulkier.

She slipped her fingers under the bottom edge. Nothing but smooth paper backing until . . . a bump. She peeked under but couldn't see anything.

"Damn it, Baines. This is so needlessly dramatic."

Keys. That's all she had on her. She yanked them out of her pants pocket and poked through the brown paper. Trying to angle for some light while she balanced the heavy frame on her shoulder, she reached under and poked through the paper. Made a hole big enough to squeeze a finger in and heard the tear rip through the quiet room.

She thought she felt an envelope. She wriggled it out, ripping a bigger hole in the paper backing. "You've got to be kidding me."

She heard the footsteps behind her, but it was too late.

"What are you doing here?"

Chapter Twenty-Two

GABBY

"I'LL ASK AGAIN," Detective Schone said. "What are you doing in here?"

Gabby folded the envelope and shoved it in her pocket as she turned around to face the detective. "I needed to get something for Kennedy."

The detective didn't break eye contact. "This is a crime scene."

How convenient. "You said Baines's death was a suicide."

"And you insisted it wasn't, so now we're looking a little deeper."

"Good." But anxiety welled up inside Gabby. Accountability, an investigation. Exactly what Gabby had wanted, but for some reason hearing the words made her fidgety. Worried.

The detective's gaze bounced to Gabby's pocket. "Is it?"

"Of course. I think—"

The detective kept staring. "What are you hiding?"

"Nothing." Gabby held up her hands, hoping the envelope was thin enough not to show a bulge in the side of her pants.

"I could physically search you."

Gabby slowly lowered her arms. "You forget I actually went to law school. Graduated and took the bar and everything, so no, you can't."

"Trespassing."

That was technically true, but Gabby didn't give in. "Try again."

"You're not helping your case," Detective Schone said, speaking in her now-familiar clipped way that created uncomfortable silences and awkward fumbling.

Gabby fought not to react. "Am I a suspect in something?"

"Who else would want your ex-husband dead?"

Ten years ago, Gabby would have laughed and said, *No one.* Now? That list might be pretty damn long. "That's your job to figure out."

"Give me your best guess."

Gabby hated this game. Her frazzled nerves kicked to life. She had to concentrate to keep her words slow and clear. No babbling. "I don't know. A business associate? Disgruntled employee? Someone he ticked off?"

"His brother."

A warning signal blared in her head. Not Liam. She refused to entertain even a fleeting thought about Liam killing Baines. Liam wasn't that guy. "Liam is grieving."

"He voluntarily turned over business documents that potentially confirm criminal activity by his own brother. Had the boxes packed and ready for pickup by the time we arrived at the office with a search warrant."

That sounded like typical Liam behavior to her. He wouldn't want to risk the business by being accused of hiding information. "So?"

The detective made a strange humming sound. "Convenient, don't you think?"

"Liam was as stunned as I was to find out about missing money."

"Yeah, you seem devastated as you crawl around your dead husband's mansion. Oh, sorry. *Ex*-husband."

Gabby could only tolerate so much sarcasm before she exploded. Detective Melissa Schone inched close to that line. "Goodbye, Detective."

Gabby tried to edge around the other woman. The detective was tall with a slight build but managed to take up a lot of space. Maybe it was the gun, but there was something challenging about her, as if she wanted to dare you to *try it*.

"You should probably also know we found accounts, including two your ex hid from you during the divorce," the detective said.

The asshole. "I'm not surprised."

"Fights over lawyers, the house, your daughter. That kind of back-and-forth can generate a lot of hate. The killing kind," the detective said in a singsongy voice.

Gabby hated every part of this conversation. She was not in the mood to be assessed or tested or whatever the hell this was. "If every person going through a divorce killed their spouse, you'd never have a minute off."

"My focus is this case, so I'm telling you to stay out of this house and the investigation. Otherwise, I might decide you're racing to find and hide damaging evidence before I see it." The detective hesitated for a second before continuing. "You don't want to be in my spotlight."

"We agree on that last part."

"One more thing." The detective pointed at the air-conditioning vent on the ceiling. "You never know where a security camera might be hidden, so be smarter."

Chapter Twenty-Three

JESSA

"**SLOW DOWN.**" **RETTA** poured the tea then placed the delicate cup and saucer on the table in front of Jessa. "I know you're upset, but you've been talking nonstop for five minutes and have yet to match a subject to a verb."

Jessa inhaled nice and deep. She'd called for reinforcements. She'd asked for advice. That meant she had to push through her usual discomfort and risk looking unsure and incompetent. She faked her way through a lot. It was her advanced coping mechanism, but she couldn't do that here.

The stupid Bartholomew custody matter sucked up all her energy until she had very little bandwidth left for anything else. "You'd never know I have other clients."

"Jessa, stay on topic."

"Right." Jessa took a big gulp of scalding hot tea and nearly spit it back out again. Her mouth was on fire. She cleared her throat then coughed. "Once that damning motion to remove me from the case is in the court file, other attorneys, my clients—anyone—can look it up and read it. It will be used against me."

"Just because a motion is filed doesn't make it true." Retta held her teacup in front of her, not drinking but not putting it down either. "Once you prove you don't have a bias, you can ask that the motion be removed. Depending on what good old Stan chooses to say in the document, you might be able to ask for sanctions."

All after the fact and too late. Jessa wanted to be proactive. She really wanted to go to Darren's house and set fire to his car, but even she recognized that was over the top. "How do I prove a negative?"

Retta made a humming sound as she balanced the saucer on her legs. "Are you biased?"

"Of course not."

"'Bias' is a loaded word. Try another one—'decided.' With all the game-playing, you haven't made a decision about Darren and what custody arrangement you'd recommend to the court?" Retta looked skeptical.

"No."

"Jessa, come on." Retta snorted and managed to sound regal doing it. Probably had something to do with her royal-blue pantsuit and wearing the exact right amount of gold jewelry. "It's just the two of us in this room."

"I haven't heard the evidence or spoken with enough witnesses yet." That was the right answer. Not really the truth, but the commonsense, good-lawyer answer. "I'm waiting on Dr. Downing's report, and I don't think she's anywhere near ready to make a custody recommendation."

"Do you think you will ever collect enough evidence to convince Darren he caused this mess?"

Jessa knew the right answer to that one. "Not that guy. No."

"Do you think Darren Bartholomew's actions put Curtis in danger?"

"Yes, I—"

"Are you worried about his wife Ellie's behavior negatively impacting Curtis?"

"Not really."

"Be more specific."

Jessa got swept up in the informal cross-examination and didn't dare fail to answer. "I wish she were . . . stronger so she could fight back against Darren and his connected family. I worry about them running over her, but—"

"Which would endanger Curtis, her son, correct?"

When she put it that way . . . "Well, yes."

"And he is your only concern here. He is your responsibility, not his parents' precious feelings."

Despite what Covington might think, yes. "Right."

"Then you've decided." Retta's tone had a bit of a *gotcha* tone to it.

Jessa wasn't ready to admit she'd made up her mind this early because it sounded like failure. She should plow through. Remain even and keep listening as the case progressed. "Things could change. The evidence could show—"

Retta frowned. "People rarely change for the better as a contested divorce drags on."

"Your take is a little surprising." From anyone else, the

interrupting would be too much. Jessa lashed out at people for less. Retta could do and say whatever the hell she wanted.

"What we talk about here, between us, or possibly at some point in the future with the group, is separate from the outside world and my job as a judge."

"Can you really compartmentalize like that?" Jessa could barely maintain a private life, let alone nurture it and separate it and give it room to grow.

"The unique view of the court system that comes from sitting in my chair only intensifies what I learned as a family law attorney. The court is ill-equipped to handle these cases. Emotional issues, domestic violence, privacy concerns, who is the best parent outside of a contentious divorce. These aren't subjects that can be assessed during the brief snapshot in time of a trial." Retta moved her untouched teacup to the table. "There's a reason the judges assigned to these cases insist they'd rather review a mediocre agreement than sit through a fantastic trial."

"Mediation isn't appropriate here. Darren would try to intimidate Ellie like he did during the marriage. Though, to her credit, Ellie is willing to fight when it comes to Curtis." Jessa feared this would be one of those cases that kicked around the courthouse for years. Motions filed. Allegations of this and that. Attempts to change the custody arrangements and tens of thousands of dollars, or more, spent fighting rather than raising Curtis.

"So, you wouldn't advise Ellie to run." Retta didn't ask it as a question.

Jessa decided to answer it as a hypothetical. "No."

"What would you suggest she do?"

"I'm not her attorney," Jessa said, parroting back Retta's earlier point.

Retta frowned again. "You wouldn't suggest to her that fighting fair might not be enough? That she might need to take drastic steps to protect her son?"

"She needs to let the process work." Silence followed Jessa's bold statement, highlighting how juvenile and unrealistic it sounded.

Retta stared at Jessa for a few seconds before speaking again. "Interesting."

Jessa knew that was bad.

"Do you know why Earl and I called our charitable organization the Sophie Foundation?" Retta asked.

Jessa still wasn't clear on much about the organization or the group behind it. "No."

"It's named in honor of Sophie Kline. Sophie and I went to law school together. Lived together before I got married." Retta's voice shook through the first few words but quickly eased back to its usual steady cadence. "She was fun and vibrant. Smart. My closest friend. She had an incredible daughter, my goddaughter, Claire."

Past tense. Jessa didn't say a word. She had heard rumors about a tragedy in Retta's past and watched now as a broad smile stretched across Retta's face at the mention of Claire then vanished as a bleak chill blew through the room.

Part of Jessa didn't want the conversation to end. The private, between-friends loosening of the formality made her ache for more. But she sensed pain coming and knew it would blanket and smother every other emotion in the room.

"Sophie married one of our classmates, Adam. There was no stopping her. She was in love, and that love was infectious. She wanted kids. Adam was ambivalent. Still, they tried for years to have Claire, and that pressure drove Sophie to dark and sad places." Retta let out a soft sigh. "Claire finally arrived, but the marriage never bounced back. The love flatlined, leaving too much room for anger to seep in. The last two years were filled with shouting matches and allegations of bad parenting. Open warfare that took a flamethrower to every good memory."

"That's the worst." Jessa was too familiar with that type of case. She'd had her share of ones that settled, or at least calmed down, but the burn-it-down ones stole every ounce of energy and left her raw and reeling.

"One day, Adam asked Sophie if he could come to the house to talk things out. Settle their disagreements amicably." Retta visibly swallowed. "He walked into the living room, shot and killed Claire and Sophie, then killed himself."

Jessa should have seen that turn coming but didn't. "Oh my God. Retta . . ."

"Just one more story about a horrible family tragedy, followed by public calls for greater protection for women, followed by society's practiced forgetfulness until the next tragedy strikes." Retta sat there, unblinking and monotone, as if lost in the horror of those moments.

She sounded like Faith, cataloging the swath of destruction that cut through families and communities. A festering hatred of women that wiped out every ounce of common sense.

"I watch cases now where the media praises the strength and courage of family members and friends for forgiving the killers of their loved ones." Retta shrugged. "I do not forgive."

Jessa tried to process the information. Tried not to think about the magnitude of that kind of loss. She'd had her dad for years and an empty hole where her mom should have been. She had a frame with a photo of a woman she never knew but no memories, bittersweet or otherwise.

"The pain never dulls. The loss doesn't ease with more time and distance. The hole remains, and with every year, each missed moment and lost celebration, it grows deeper and darker as you throw more loss in it. I've been unrelentingly rageful since that day. Lost kicking and screaming in a thick, black sea of it." Retta let out a harsh breath "I would trade anything to bring Adam back to life just so I could relish beating him to death. That's where I am years later."

Jessa wasn't sure what to say to that, but she didn't have to say anything. Retta continued to talk. Despair and fury wrapped around her, pushing through the claustrophobic pressure choking the room. She seemed frozen in memories that held her hostage.

"People talk tough about fairness and due process until the day they're the ones begging for help; then they realize the formal justice process is bullshit," Retta said.

That, from a judge. Jessa sat there, afraid to speak, because she had no idea what the *right* thing to say could be.

Retta let out a harsh chuckle. "You don't have to say what you're thinking. I only want to be clear that the robe doesn't insulate a person from human feelings, including hate."

Jessa rushed to clean up whatever thought her expression telegraphed. "No, I—"

"I thought becoming a judge would change things. I'd be able to see justice through to the end. The parade of abusers and human garbage standing in front of me would finally understand that enough was enough." Retta sighed. "But that's not how it works. There are technical errors, surprise jury verdicts, and cases that never see the inside of a courtroom."

"The system is imperfect," Jessa said, repeating back a phrase Retta often said as a professor.

Retta's focus sharpened. "If I offered you a way to cut through the Bartholomew case, to get to the very heart of it without the power and posturing, would you do it?"

Was she saying . . . No, it couldn't be. Jessa stalled as she mentally scrambled to find the *right* answer. She did not want to fail this test. "I don't know what that means."

"I think you do," Retta said in a firm voice. "Let's say there was a different system, one outside of the courts. A system that answered to the victims. Would you agree to do anything to preserve that sort of alternative system?"

Jessa started her legal career by taking the easy road. She never let her mind go there, to how willing and eager she'd been for a shortcut that made her light shine brighter, but it raced there now. The bright line that should be there in her mind, the one that balked at trampling all over the parameters of what should be possible, got lost in a cloud of confusion.

"Yes or no." Retta snapped her fingers. "Go with your gut."

"We have a system that works."

Retta made a face. "Does it?"

Jessa didn't understand this test . . . or if it was one. "Are you saying this alternative exists?"

"If it did, would you use it?"

"I'm not—"

"Even if it meant breaking the rules?"

Jessa waded through all the twisting and confusion and rapid-fire questions and still wasn't sure what the conversation was about, but the answer should be *no*. Everything she'd learned in law school, including from this woman, pointed to *no*. "I should be able to handle Darren and his attorney within the current system, regardless of their lies."

Retta frowned. "That wasn't the question."

"No, I'm fine." If Retta needed a specific response for the rest of the club, some sort of ethics check or something, that should do it. "I can do this the right way. Without special help."

Retta's expression didn't change. "I guess we'll see."

Chapter Twenty-Four

GABBY

GABBY SAT AT the breakfast bar in her kitchen and read through the paperwork again. She'd grabbed the envelope out of Baines's house yesterday and had not been able to think of anything since.

Bids. That was the deep dark secret worth hiding. Bids on a job. A big job, sure. The kind that changes lives and expands companies, but boring, basic, job-related bids. Nothing special. Talk about an anticlimactic conclusion.

She didn't understand the top secret behavior here. Baines was not an innocent actor. He'd done appalling things to secure the life he wanted, and knowing that scared her enough to leave. But this?

The alarm chirped when the front door opened. Before Gabby could get off the stool, she heard the beeps from the code sequence being entered. Liam. Must be. Maybe he could help her understand the bid issue.

"Mom."

Gabby jerked at the unexpected sound of her daughter's voice. "Kennedy?"

She spun around in time to see Kennedy blow in, long hair escaping her ponytail and a bag slung over her shoulder. She stopped right before entering the kitchen. Tension pulled around her mouth, and her mood bounced around in that scary slip of space between screaming and crying.

"What are you doing here?" Gabby's mind refused to focus. "How did you get home?"

"That doesn't matter." Kennedy's voice sounded strained.

"It does to me." She attended school in New York, more than five hours away. She couldn't drive. "Answer me. Are you okay?"

"Bus and train."

"*What?*" The enormity of the situation stole Gabby's breath. She grabbed onto the chair she just abandoned to keep from being knocked down by the mental images flashing in her brain. Kennedy traveling alone. Somebody grabbing her. Being vulnerable. Lost and desperate. It took all of Gabby's control not to yell, but a rabid scream rumbled in her throat, ready to release. "You are supposed to be in school, young lady. You can't just leave and—"

"You lied to me."

That stopped Gabby cold. "What are you talking about?"

"Did he know?"

"Who? Are you hurt?" The conversation fragments and accusatory tone punched through Gabby's confusion. This wasn't a random teen tantrum. The staccato beat to Kennedy's voice. The hint of pain as her voice grew louder. No, this attack came from a different place, meaning something terrible careened right for her.

"Is this why you really wanted me gone? Away, so I can't see what's happening?" Kennedy shook her hand and whatever she held in it. "I begged to come home but instead, I got shipped off so you can sleep around—"

"Hey!" *What the hell?* "Be very careful of what you say next. I know you're grieving over your father, but I am your mother. You will not disrespect me."

"Explain this." Kennedy made the demand then held out a crumpled envelope. She'd obviously opened it and held it and spent time studying it.

"What is it?" Gabby took out the wrinkled piece of paper inside.

"It was delivered to my room. Where everyone could see." Kennedy choked on a sob. "How could you?"

Gabby glanced down at the blur of words. They moved and danced because her hands shook. A second later the horrible sentences came into focus.

Baines Fielding is not your father. Ask your mother how she really feels about Uncle Liam.

The blood left Gabby's head. Secrets littered their family's history, but this one threatened to drain the life out of all of them.

She reached out to Kennedy, needing the small connection between them. "Honey, listen—"

"No." Kennedy pulled back before Gabby could comfort her. "Tell me the truth. No lectures or lies. Tell me."

"This is . . ." Gabby stared at the typewritten words again. What the hell did she say now, after spending a lifetime running from this conversation? She needed to avoid this fallout just a bit longer, but—

"Gabby?"

No, no, no. Not now. He couldn't be here.

Kennedy nodded, looking determined and superior, as if she'd won some silent battle by dragging Liam into this without warning. "I texted him and asked him to come over. He deserves to know . . . unless you guys have been in on this, fooling around, for years."

"Hey." Liam stopped beside Kennedy. "What are you doing here? What's going on?"

Kennedy's chin lifted. "Ask Mom."

Them. Together. Demanding answers. Gabby could barely give them eye contact.

This was her nightmare.

Chapter Twenty-Five

JESSA

JESSA WAS STILL reeling a half hour later, when she walked out the front gate at Retta's house. The conversation was . . . *What the hell was that?*

She wanted to run the comments by Faith, but could she? Retta drove home the point about the group being confidential and the topics they discussed being off-limits outside of the room. But the odd talk wasn't with the group, so Jessa wasn't clear on the rules. She just needed to go somewhere and think.

She took out her phone to call for a car service to get home and ran right into some guy. Smacked her arm right into his shoulder. "I'm sorry!"

"It's fine."

She could hear the laughter in the man's voice and for a second thought they might know each other. He did look familiar, but that might be because he looked like a lot of forty-something men in the metro area. Put him in a navy suit and slap a striped tie on him, and he could work in her office.

"Excuse me." She tried to maneuver around him and get to the street corner and a spot with better cell service.

"Jessa?"

She turned around to face him again. Something in the way he said her name made her twitch. A cool breeze blew over her. She shifted until she stood closer to the street and all the cars idling while waiting for the light a few blocks up to change.

"Do we know each other?" Maybe from law school or a case. His face ticked off a memory that she couldn't quite grab.

"Baines Fielding."

Okay, so from *that* case. One she wanted to forget. Better yet, pretend never happened. "What about him?"

"Did you know him?"

She swiped her finger to unlock her phone. She didn't have to memorize the man's face if she took his photo. Snap and hit the emergency SOS button. That was the plan.

"I'm Rob Greene." He held out his hand. "I'm doing a story on a series of unexplained deaths in the area."

Oh, hell no.

"I'm leaving." She hated to put her back to him, but running into traffic struck her as an equally bad idea. She slipped her hand into her bag and pulled out her keys. Let them jangle. Let him realize she would punch, kick, and stab her way to safety, if needed.

She got a few steps before he spoke again. "This issue is not going away."

Neither was he, apparently. New strategy. She shifted and

went back to the gate to Retta's house and pressed the button on the security pad.

"Good. I'd like to talk to the judge, too," Greene said, moving closer.

The intercom barely made a sound before Earl, Retta's husband, stepped out of the gate and onto the sidewalk. He made quite the impression in his expensive suit and equally expensive gold watch . . . holding a baseball bat.

A few passing cars honked their horns. Earl ignored the noise and looked at Jessa, as if to satisfy himself she wasn't hurt. Then he turned to Rob Greene. "Is there a problem here?"

"He says he's a reporter." Wait, is that what he said? Something about a story. The anxiety pumping through Jessa made it hard for her to concentrate.

"Get lost," Earl said and didn't sound like he was joking.

"I've been trying to talk with you and your wife for weeks." Greene didn't move, but his calm assurance had vanished. He scanned the area, as if looking for reinforcements, but his gaze kept coming back to the bat in Earl's hand. "Just a few questions. Some background."

"You want me to beat the shit out of you out here, where everyone can see?" The menace in Earl's voice was impossible to miss.

Jessa couldn't help but shift until she stood closer to Earl and the weapon. Age didn't matter; he looked ready to swing and was fit enough to connect with bone and make it hurt. At least Jessa hoped so.

"This is a serious matter. Right now, I'm not at the office, so I'm hard to reach. Here's the best way to contact me." Greene held out what looked like a business card. "Your wife knows people who—"

Earl knocked the card out of Greene's hand, sending it to the sidewalk.

Jessa took that as a sign his patience had expired. "I'll call the police."

A car slowed down and parked next to them by the sidewalk. The vehicles lined up behind it blew their horns as they tried to maneuver around. Someone shouted, and a couple across the street stopped and watched.

Fear revved up and spilled over inside Jessa. No one got out of the stopped car, but having it nearby kept her from shouting for help.

Earl didn't seem to notice any of the movement on the street. All of his attention centered on Greene. "Do you want more trouble?"

Greene lifted his hands in what looked like surrender. "Listen—"

"You have enough problems right now. You don't want to add me to your list. Don't let the clothes and the fancy house fool you. I came from a place where I learned to protect what's mine and to fight dirty to do it. You understand me?"

The door of the parked car opened. A man stood up and called out to Earl, "Do you need some help, sir?"

Earl shook his head. "Mr. Greene is leaving and never coming back. Isn't that right, Mr. Greene?"

Greene hesitated but not for long. He looked at Jessa. "I'll be in touch."

"My warning extends to her. You stay away from her." Earl pointed the bat down the street. "Go."

The man from the car stepped onto the sidewalk. He was tall with a military haircut. Wore nondescript clothing but looked like he punched people for a living. Security. Had to be. He escorted Greene away then came back and hovered nearby.

Jessa didn't know much about Earl's business, but the house suggested it was damn lucrative. She assumed a guy that powerful would have a detail of people ready to help him if he picked up a bat.

Earl's icy demeanor softened the second they were alone. "Are you okay, Jessa?"

Shaking. Queasy and really confused. "What was that about?"

She bent down to get the business card, thinking that might explain. But Earl beat her to it.

"It's nonsense." He tucked the card into his pants pocket. "He's unhinged. You don't want any part of that."

"He was talking about deaths and—"

"He's a disgraced reporter who sees conspiracies wherever he looks. It's pathetic and annoying." Earl smiled, but the fury reflected in his eyes didn't diminish. From his grip on the bat to the stiffness in his body, anger clearly ran through him, and he'd barely banked it.

He motioned for the man from the car to step closer. "Trent will take you home."

"It's okay." A mix of adrenaline and panic clashed inside of her. She wasn't convinced she could walk to the car without falling down. Standing there for a few minutes struck her as the right decision. "That's not necessary."

"We want you to be safe," Earl said.

Despite living in the city and having been schooled in every precaution a woman needed to take to survive, Jessa rarely felt unsafe in the DC area . . . until now.

Chapter Twenty-Six

GABBY

DENY. DENY. DENY.

Gabby didn't want to tell them like this. She didn't want to tell them at all. She tried to find the right words, but there weren't any. The train rolled right for her, bearing down and speeding up. She couldn't jump or shift. She had to stand there and let it slam into her then hope enough pieces remained for her to rebuild from the chaos.

Liam and Kennedy were the two people Gabby loved most in the world, and she was about to lose them.

Liam's eyes narrowed. "Gabby, tell me what's going on."

He acted like this was easy, but Gabby faced a wall of furious indignation. Kennedy, wound up and wrung out both emotionally and physically, looked ready to drop. Except for her expression. That fierce determination to push the issue and condemn her mother bubbled to the surface.

Gabby thought about trying to pivot, about falling back on Liam's need to get work done, especially now, and Kennedy's need to rest. Push off. Deflect. Ignore. That had been the strategy both in her mind and in reality for years, and Gabby watched it all crumble in front of her.

Kennedy glared at Jessa. "Show him the note."

"What's happening?" Poor Liam rushed to catch up but kept falling behind. Most of his focus seemed to be on Kennedy and her reason for being unexpectedly home. "Are you okay?"

"No."

Gabby's world upended and kept spinning. She tried to stay on her feet and ended up leaning into the kitchen stool. "Liam, we need—"

"Tell him!" Kennedy's scream echoed off the kitchen walls.

Mother. She still had a role, and she needed to play it. "Kennedy, that's enough. I know you're upset, but this isn't easy for any of us."

Wrong words. Gabby heard her mistake as soon as the sentence slipped out.

"*Us?* Like, this is about you?" Kennedy didn't hold back. "You can't be serious."

In any other situation, on any other topic, Gabby would step in and hold the line. There were limits to Kennedy's behavior. She'd grown up with commonsense discipline and had slammed more than one door over the years, but this intensity, the hate rolling off her, stunned Gabby. She wanted to stop it, but she knew she deserved every spite-filled word.

But Liam didn't know this wasn't the average teen meltdown. "Hey, that's enough. Since when do you talk to your mother like that?" He sounded shocked and appalled.

Kennedy turned on him. "Did you know?"

No, Gabby couldn't let Kennedy blame Liam. Not for this. Only one person deserved to shoulder the blame here. "He doesn't."

"I hate you." Kennedy put all her energy into the horrible yell. Her voice shook, and she nearly doubled over before she ran out of the room and stomped down the hall.

Liam's eyes widened. "What the hell? Why is she even home?"

"You should sit."

"Is that about her dad?"

Oh, Liam. "There are reasons for what I did. You're not going to want to hear them at first. You'll be too lost. Too pissed off. But I hope you'll let me explain. Later."

He sat down, putting them almost at eye level. "Gab, I have no idea what's going on."

Of course he didn't. He trusted and believed and was about to learn what a huge mistake it had been to invest anything in her. Their having grown up together didn't forgive this. Her having given in to an attraction she'd fought for as long as she could remember didn't absolve either of them, but most of the blame fell on her.

But who knew? Who would do this?

She inhaled, trying to center her body for what was to come, and handed over the envelope. "Someone gave this to Kennedy at school."

"Did she do something wrong, because right now that shouldn't be held . . ." He kept staring at the paper, likely reading it over and over, until his head finally snapped up. "Gabby?"

She didn't have to explain the meaning behind the sentences. She and Baines had separated years ago, for the first time, after only a few months of marriage. He'd immediately settled in and started focusing every minute on the business while she wrestled with bar exam preparations and nagging doubts about them as a couple. And Liam was there. He was always there, and for so long she'd pretended not to know how he felt about her . . . or that she fought an unexpected tug in the same direction.

Two months. That's how long the separation back then lasted, how long she secretly spent every moment she could with Liam instead of her husband.

"No one knows. I don't know how . . . or why. The fact they— whoever *they* are—went after Kennedy is terrifying. It shows they don't have any boundaries." She kept talking, letting the words tumble out. Anything to get a hint of relief before her entire world collapsed on top of her. "They had to . . . I don't know. Invade my privacy? Find my medical records, somehow. I'd been so careful. So—"

The stool screeched against the hardwood floor as Liam pushed back and stood up. "You promised me."

He cut through all her nonsense babbling and dove straight to the point she ached to avoid. She never realized how much she'd tamped down and pushed away to keep this secret, how much energy this lie sucked up, until that moment. But his face. That pained expression. She'd done that to him.

"I know," she said in a whisper.

"When you found out you were pregnant, I came to you. We sat down, and you promised me—"

"I lied." She'd invented a complicated story about birth control and timing, and Liam had bought it. He'd depended on her to be honest, and she'd used the trust built up over a lifetime against him.

"Kennedy is . . ."

"Your daughter." God, she'd never said it out loud before. Not those words. She waited for relief to rush in, but there was no room right now.

"My . . ." He stumbled back before regaining his balance. "Jesus, Gabby. Why would you keep that from me?"

"My choice wasn't about you."

"Bullshit."

She rushed to explain, even though she knew the words wouldn't be enough. "You and Baines jointly shared responsibility for your sister. She'd stopped leaving the house, and her health spiraled. She needed both of you and . . . and . . . I knew if I told you that the battle would be devastating and you two wouldn't have worked together to help her or the business."

She'd convinced herself she was protecting the family unit. All of them. A disastrous choice that made her silently resent Baines. Seeing him after being with Liam cracked the sheen and uncovered who her husband really was and what he was willing to do to get what he wanted.

Yet she stayed. For years, she stayed with Baines. She would have continued as his wife, with her secret about Kennedy deeply buried, until she hit a breaking point where even she could no longer swallow the shame.

"You didn't give me a choice in any of this. I never would

have walked away from you or from a baby if I'd known," Liam said.

"I'm so sorry." Empty words. Not nearly enough, and she knew that.

"You picked Baines and asked me to support you, but I did it based on false information. I thought the baby was his."

She closed her eyes, trying to block out the thump of anger in his voice and the horrible realization that she'd picked the wrong side more than fourteen years ago and had been paying for that ever since. "What we had was only a short fling."

"Not for me."

The words broke her. She fell into the stool next to her. She couldn't even muster the energy to fight back.

Kennedy walked into the room without any fanfare. She might have been hovering outside and listening in or just storming back and forth. Gabby didn't know, and the last thing she could worry about now was someone hearing too much. They'd blown past that point when Kennedy received the note.

"I can't stay here," Kennedy declared in the dramatic way teens said ridiculous things and believed them.

"Kennedy, this is—"

"*Not the time. Not the place. Not the right answer.*" Kennedy mimicked Gabby's voice. "But that's just it. You don't get to tell me that anymore, *Mom*."

Gabby couldn't take much more. "Kennedy, stop. You're fourteen."

"She lied to us. To Dad." Kennedy half pleaded and half argued with Liam as if she wasn't sure how much blame to spread and how far to extend it. "And you. He was your brother."

Gabby tried to deflect the anger back to her. "It's not that simple, honey."

"Explain it to me, then." Kennedy stopped as soon as she started. She held up a hand. "Actually, don't. I can't trust a thing you say. You are a stupid liar."

Every word bore right into Gabby's heart and ripped a piece out. She was the mom, so she'd played the bad-guy role before, but this was so much bigger. This might not be fixable. "That's not true."

"Okay. Let's do this." Liam let out a loud exhale. "Kennedy, come to my house."

"I don't want to be with either of you," she shot back.

"I get that, and I'm as pissed and confused as you are, but we need to know you're safe." He winced as if he knew he'd waded out into dangerous waters but had no choice. "I've been doing some work from home since the funeral. We can coexist there."

Without her. That's what Gabby heard. "Liam, please."

"You don't really get a vote tonight, Gabby." He shot Kennedy a struggling half-smile. "Go wait for me in the car. We'll figure out the school part tomorrow."

Gabby waited until Kennedy headed for the front door to drop her voice and try one more time with Liam. "We need to talk about this and where we go next."

"You had fourteen years to talk." Liam started to leave but stopped. "Did Baines know the truth?"

"Eventually, yes." There was so much more to it, but this secret was enough. Unloading the rest might be too much even for Liam's strong shoulders.

Liam shook his head. "And you think Baines was the asshole in your relationship? Sounds to me like you were perfect for each other."

Chapter Twenty-Seven

JESSA

NO TIME FOR lunch out. No time for a talk. No time to figure out what Retta was trying to say the other night. That's exactly how Jessa thought of her day: as one big rush of nothing. But she needed contact with a nonlawyer to preserve her sanity. Someone rational, who didn't think in terms of wins and losses all the time. So she begged Faith to come to the office and share a sandwich.

"I looked up Rob Greene after you told me about him stopping you." Faith sat on the opposite side of Jessa's desk, stabbing her fork into the container of potato salad. "Stay away from him."

Jessa had seen the same articles and warnings, and she got it. "That's the plan."

"I'm serious. In addition to the dangerous and unstable part, which you should not ignore because *damn*, you don't want to be seen with him and have his putrid reputation spill over and splash onto you."

"What a lovely visual image."

The door opened as someone knocked. Jessa's assistant stuck her head in the room. "Excuse me."

"I'm at lunch." A fact Jessa thought should have been obvious.

The door opened wider, and Detective Melissa Schone walked in. "She's warning you I'm here."

Jessa dropped her sandwich. "And that kills my appetite."

"I've heard worse." The detective stared at the assistant until she backed out of the room and closed the door behind her. "Good afternoon."

"Detective." Jessa wiped her hands on her napkin. "This is my friend Faith, but you know that."

"Yes, I'm aware," the detective said.

Faith frowned. "Okay. That's scary."

"I have a call into your office to speak with you after I meet with Jessa."

That sounded like a threat, and Jessa wasn't in the mood, so she skipped over the introductory blather and went right to the main question. "What's going on?"

"We need to find somewhere private to—"

"No." Jessa wasn't in the mood for closed-door meetings in conference rooms and the explanations she'd have to dole out after to appease the partners. "You can say whatever it is in front of Faith, because I will fill her in five seconds from now anyway."

"Ellie Bartholomew came in today and gave us more background on the driveway incident," the detective said, sounding very serious and in charge.

Jessa had been waiting for this news. "Good. It's about time."

"The information implicates you," the detective said.

Faith made an odd sound before she started whispering, "Oh, shit."

"Implicates me in what?" Jessa refused to panic. She hadn't done anything wrong. Hell, the case only started a few weeks ago, and it already took up too much time, but it was only at the beginning stages.

The detective leaned against the closed door. "Mrs. Bartholomew says you advised her to ignore the judge's order and leave the jurisdiction with Curtis. That you provided her with information about setting up new identities for her and her son."

Why would Ellie do that? Why lie and hand Darren that sort of ammunition? "You can't believe that. It's not true."

The detective looked at Faith. "You're familiar with this case, aren't you? Assisting women in trouble is your specialty. Some say making them disappear is your expertise."

Faith being Faith, she didn't ruffle. She continued chewing. "I'm just sitting here eating a sandwich."

The idea of this case spilling out on the people she loved—in a real way, not in the way where Tim worried his boss would get ticked off—was not okay. Jessa rushed to put the attention back on her. "Faith is not involved in the Bartholomew case. At all."

The detective shrugged. "Mr. and Mrs. Bartholomew believe otherwise. They're contemplating their options."

And Mrs.? "What the hell does that mean?"

The detective smiled now, clearly pleased with her verbal bombshell. "Civil charges. Possibly criminal."

"No . . . no." The panic hit Jessa in waves now. In a blink, she saw all her hard work, all the sacrifices she'd made, the good and bad choices, wither into nothingness. "This can't be happening."

Faith threw the half-eaten sandwich on the desk and gestured toward the desk phone. "Jessa, I think you should get another lawyer in your office to hear this."

Right. Counsel. The pros and cons, mostly cons, swirled in Jessa's head. She should have enough experience and presence to handle this without bringing in the big guns, but the assurance in the detective's voice had Jessa shaking from the inside out.

The detective nodded in Faith's direction. "What about you?"

"Again, trying to eat my lunch." But Faith's usual joking tone had disappeared.

"Do you have a lawyer?" the detective asked.

Faith didn't break eye contact. "The shelter and charity have lawyers."

The detective's smile deepened. "Good."

"Wait a second." Jessa struggled to make sense of the conversation and to keep Faith firmly out of it. "You're saying Ellie and Darren came into the police station together?"

The detective nodded. "Yes."

"They couldn't stand in the same courthouse together." When the detective didn't say anything, Jessa tried again. "He's pressuring her to make up these lies. He has to be."

Nothing else made sense. Darren had crashed into Ellie's car. Maybe that was a message that he would do anything to win. A warning, and Ellie had heeded it. She was too worried about Curtis not to listen to it.

Jessa tried to make the detective understand. "Faith can explain this better than I can, but this is how these cases go. It's about control. Ellie is doing what Darren wants because he's convinced her he has power over her. He might be threatening her behind the scenes."

The detective stood there, not saying anything for a few minutes. "This is a courtesy call. I wanted you to know the case is moving, but not in the direction you expected."

The pressure ratcheted up. Jessa could feel the walls caving in around her. If the professionals who saw cases like this couldn't stop Darren's games, no one could. "Please tell me you see through this bullshit."

"If either of you would like to make a statement, sooner would be good. You're already on the defensive." The detective handed Faith a card and dropped a second one on the corner of Jessa's desk.

Jessa couldn't take much more. "Please leave."

"In these situations, the first to talk wins." The detective opened the door. "Enjoy your lunch."

Chapter Twenty-Eight

GABBY

GABBY ENTERED THE near-empty coffeehouse a few blocks from the National Portrait Gallery and went straight to the table at the back. She didn't stop for a drink or say hello. Today was about one thing—making Rob Greene back down.

Rob moved a stack of folders off the table and shoved them into his bag as she got closer. He waited until she'd almost gotten to the table to stand up. "Thanks for agreeing to meet with me."

"I'm here to warn you." She didn't bother to lower her voice. Only a few people lingered thanks to the off-morning hour, but she knew more would pile in the closer they got to lunchtime. She planned to be gone by then. "Don't go near my daughter again."

"They got to her." He shook his head. "This is what I feared."

"No *they*. You." She ignored the comment. "And do you hear me? Stop your games. Never again."

"They came after you. Just as I predicted. Do you see it now?"

"Stop talking in circles."

Since yesterday's big family reveal, and after hours of not being able to get any response from Kennedy except a terse "she's fine" text from Liam, Gabby was out of patience. She didn't have much in the way of understanding or mercy either. The man in front of her had screwed with her family, she was certain about that, and he was going to stop, or she was going to cause a scene that would make everyone forget about his invented news sources.

"Whatever happened is a message for you. Subtle but firm. They want you to know they can find out about the secrets you thought you had buried. That they can get to you and the people you care about." Rob took out a lined yellow legal pad, as if he was going to take notes on this mess.

They, they, they. She wasn't buying the idea of some secret cabal turning her life upside down. "You did this."

Some of the feral excitement that had flowed around him at the mention of a possible conspiracy faded. Now he looked concerned. "What exactly happened?"

He dared to sound confused, which cleared the haze off her growing rage. "Pretend ignorance doesn't suit you. I'm talking about the note you sent to my daughter."

"Please sit down." He used his foot to push out the chair across from him.

The few people in the place, including the innocent barista, started looking a little twitchy about her hovering over the table, so she sat. "Fine."

"I didn't send anything to your daughter. I don't even know your daughter." He leaned in. "Think about it. There's no reason for me to sneak around and threaten your kid. I came straight to you, just as I've gone to others, trying to warn you before it was too late."

"Other what?" Every word he said dragged her in deeper, but she had to know the endgame here. That was the only way to stop him.

"We shouldn't discuss this out in the open."

As if she'd never taken a self-protection class and would just invite some disgraced guy to join her in private. "This is your only choice. Say what you have to say to me here, or I'm leaving."

"You don't understand what—"

"You have exactly one shot to convince me what everyone is saying about you is wrong. Choose your conversation topic with care." That was a lie, which she'd apparently gotten very good at over the years. She needed fodder, evidence to discredit him and protect Kennedy. She needed him to talk and keep talking.

"So that we're clear, I've never faked a story or made up a source. Every piece I've written was fact-checked for accuracy. I don't follow or support wild conspiracy theories." His whisper grew raspier, more insistent, as he talked. "What's happening to me now, to my reputation, it's part of a disinformation campaign about me and my beliefs."

She wondered if this was what she sounded like when she rambled. "You're blowing your one shot."

He grabbed a notebook and held it in front of him. "Several very well-connected, influential people in the metro area, so far only men, have died under questionable circumstances. In all those cases, negative information leaked either before or right after the deaths. Anyone who questioned the manner of death had some part of their lives blow up."

"That sounds like you're guessing." Rambling, actually, but she didn't want to upset him. Not when she sat this close and didn't know what he would do.

"If it only happened once, maybe," he said. "Look at the most recent case. Alex Carlisle. Do you really think he shot himself in the dick then bled out?"

That case seemed to have a new twist every day. But he was connecting dots that didn't exist. Using generalities and possibilities to invent a case for nothing. "I agree his death sounds—"

"Ridiculous and planned to look that way. Like he was being made to answer in the most obvious way for messing with women he'd paid to have sex with him. Hell, he should have been punished, but by a jury. Not a vigilante group."

She thought about Alex Carlisle and the very strange way he'd died. His wife insisted he didn't own a gun, and now this morning's news talked about her being brought in for questioning, the implication being that the wife had believed the allegations against him and killed him. Almost as if she'd balked at the official story and now she was in trouble.

Damn, now Rob had her connecting phantom dots.

He sat back in his chair. "Look, I get that this sounds impossible. But it's real, and following this, unraveling the puzzle, is personal."

"How?" She wanted to write him off. Get up, walk away . . . but so little of her life made sense right now. Someone had sent that letter to Kennedy. The longer Gabby sat here, the less convinced she was that Rob had done it. Then who?

"I didn't figure this conspiracy out on my own. Like you, I had to be convinced, and I fought it. Thought it sounded too twisted, too fantastical, to be real," he said.

"Okay. Let me talk to this other person who convinced you."

"She's dead."

Gabby knew she should have seen that coming. So many dead bodies. Gabby felt like she was swimming in a sea of them. She hated to ask—tried not to, but . . . "How did she die?"

"They killed her."

Chapter Twenty-Nine

GABBY

GABBY BALANCED HER elbows on the table. No way was she walking away now, not after that line. "Okay, let's start again."

"Tami Zimmer." Rob tapped a few buttons on his phone then turned the screen around for her to read the headline.

Award-Winning Reporter Killed on Capitol Hill

The photo showed a smiling brunette, young, probably in her thirties, more ponytail-wearing than DC chic. Someone you'd want to sit down with and chat over coffee.

He flipped through a few more photos. These were personal. They showed him with Tami. Her smiling. Hiking. Out to dinner. Laughing on a couch with a cat stretched out on her lap. Images so intimate and personal that Gabby felt like she was intruding on private moments between lovers.

He took the phone back, not bothering to shut it off as he cradled it in his hands. "More than six months ago. I lost her in a supposed purse grab gone wrong."

The screen faded to black, but Rob's pain lingered. Gabby fought to breathe as it swallowed the air around them.

"They say the attacker slammed her to the pavement. She had a head injury that put her in a coma. She never woke up again."

"I'm so sorry." Gabby was all too familiar with the debilitating grief of a sudden, unexpected death. She'd been stuck in the mire of it, unable to reason or push the horror of it out of her mind. "You were close."

"She was my fiancée." He visibly swallowed. "And the story was flawed. The angle about stealing her purse? Impossible. She didn't carry one. She used a small wallet. The kind she could loop around her wrist. It was in her backpack when the police returned her personal items to me."

Gabby had to admit that sounded odd, but then she didn't know how great Rob was at reciting facts. He could be comingling the truth with an alternate one he invented to survive Tami's death. That sort of anguish twisted and gutted a person. Him not being okay made sense.

"We met in college," Rob continued. "After graduation, I became the typical skeptical newspaper journalist, following stories about corrupt politicians and misspent government funds. She wrote for magazines, taking weeks, months, or however long she needed, to draw out the story behind the story. She wrote beautifully lyrical prose with heart and nuance."

Not the talk of a man wrapped up in conspiracy theories. The pain poured out of him, spilling out and covering every word and movement with a thick layer of loss.

"A friend of hers was the daughter of one of the men killed two years ago, Ken Turner." Rob reached into his bag and slapped a file down on the table between them. "After a years-long whisper campaign about inappropriate behavior with the women in his office—touching them, demanding sex, demoting them if they turned him down, tying moving up in the company to sucking him off—he was killed. In a single-car accident just days after an internal investigation cleared him to a great deal of public outcry."

"Did the daughter think he was innocent?"

"She wanted to, but no. She knew who he was and how little regard he had for women. But she didn't buy the single-car accident explanation for his death. After years of not talking, she had texted her father. She said he was apologetic and begged to see her. He was supposed to be on his way to visit her but never arrived. His car was found a day later, nowhere near where they were supposed to meet. In a lake. He was wrapped up in the seat belt as if he'd tried to escape but couldn't."

Poetic, maybe, but Gabby wasn't convinced that proved anything. "He could have changed his mind about the meeting. Felt guilty . . ."

"This guy's daughter was pretty vocal about the story of his death not making sense, and asked Tami to investigate it. Then the daughter, a respected teacher, became the target of suggestions that she did something with a student." Rob finished his coffee. "The daughter abruptly agreed with the police findings, and the nasty rumors stopped. An unnamed jealous coworker was blamed but never outed or disciplined."

"Unnamed?" Gabby would have sued the pants off that liar.

"Strange, right? The daughter stopped talking to Tami.

Blocked her calls. So Tami dug deeper. She found more cases. Similar circumstances."

Gabby remembered the story about this Ken Turner guy and how relieved the women who knew him sounded when he died. But that still didn't prove anything. "Coincidence."

A second file went on top of the first. "Damon Scott. A politician and slum landlord who evaded criminal prosecution even after two of his tenants died when a poorly maintained balcony collapsed. One month after that he died in a fall off the rooftop deck of his Georgetown home. His wife insisted an accidental fall was impossible due to the railing. As soon as she spoke up, criminal charges were filed against her. Those were later dropped when she agreed to the medical examiner's findings about her husband's death."

She read about that strange fall. "Okay."

"Need more?" He stacked a third file on the pile. "Richard Kellerman, pediatrician accused of molesting his patients. Children. He drowned in the Potomac even though he hated water and didn't have a boat." Rob reached into his bag and brought out the files he previously shoved away. "Amos Prince, another doctor accused of molestation, but this one by his daughters."

The facts made Gabby sick. "I can't—"

"Leonard Waters. Kane Long. Bart Thomas. Are you seeing the pattern?"

The long list of names sounded compelling. Again, not evidence of a conspiracy, but she was tempted to sort through those files and see what he and Tami had compiled.

Still, one of them had to be rational and it looked like she'd won that prize. "People die, Rob. Accidents are horrible, but they happen."

"Do you think I want to believe this? I have lost *everything*. Don't you get that?" His voice rose until a few people in the coffee shop glanced his way. He ignored the stares but lowered his voice. "I sat with her, watched her while machines pumped air into her broken body. Argued with the doctors for more time, but I wasn't officially family. Not yet. I didn't get to make the decision to give up on her."

Gabby ached for him. For Tami. But she tried to separate out that empathy and heartache from reality. "Is it possible . . . Could you be too close to this?"

"Maybe. Probably." He exhaled. "But what choice do I have? This was Tami's legacy. If I'm right, she literally gave her life to find out the truth. I owe it to her to follow this to the end."

The haunting sound of his voice pulled at Gabby. "Even though you lost your job and your reputation?"

"Tami was worth more than all of that."

They sat in silence for a few minutes. Gabby skimmed her fingertips over the file in front of her, wanting both to open it and to walk away. Not knowing gave her an odd sort of power. It shielded her, let her wallow in possible ignorance and not take a stand. She could pretend to be noble without ever risking a failed test.

Rob's voice cut across the quiet stretching between them. "These men, by paying hush money or falling back on their positions, got away with the unthinkable. They weren't held accountable by the legal system. In the age of supposed cancel culture, they didn't lose anything in the way of reputation or serious cash. Then they died."

After a quick glance around to make sure no one was watching this little scene, she tried to reason with him. "Say you're right. Say someone is taking the law into their own hands and deciding judgment, why assume it's a group?"

"Wouldn't it have to be? This type of concerted effort would take serious planning as well as access to forensics, weapons. They would need the connections. People who would look the other way. Brains and money. Even more important, they'd need the will and ability to tamper with evidence and make it disappear. Mess with cars and drugs. Create or destroy forensics."

"That's daunting." Impossible, really. She tried to think of even bigger words to describe the unlikelihood of that sort of massive covert undertaking.

"But a certain type of crowd does have access to all those things." He tapped one final file: a thick one that he placed on top of the others. "Here are copies of all of Tami's notes. It shows how she put the pieces together and why she discounted some deaths as actual accidents or suicides and not others."

Okay, that didn't sound completely irrational, which scared her a bit. "But why was Baines on this covert group's hit list?"

He shrugged. "I think you'd know the answer to that better than I would."

Secrets. The word flashed in her mind, and she concentrated on blinking it away. "Who would do this? The risk is huge, both in getting caught and in having someone else from the group talk. There are too many variables, and people have too little discipline for this to actually work."

She talked herself into a *maybe* then right back out again. In her experience, secrets like this leaked out. People couldn't sit on volatile information . . . except maybe her. But the idea that a group of people, all working in tandem, would be able to keep the ruse up, keep killing, and no one would talk or mess up? Nope. Humans didn't work like that.

"I thought that, too." Rob leaned forward. "Then I started digging. There are names that show up more than once in these cases. Prosecutors. Police. Judges. Lawyers."

"Yeah, now I know you're wrong. I went to law school. I know lawyers. You're talking about a competitive crowd that craves the spotlight. They'd never pull off secretive and trusting, even in a small group. They'd be too busy fighting to take credit." Which was one of the reasons she got the degree then never used it. A legal career wasn't for her, not after she saw what some of her classmates were willing to do to succeed.

"Do you know who Judge Loretta Swain is?" he asked.

Everybody did. The woman was a legend. The first Black woman on the state's highest court. A millionaire who chose public service. She'd taught at Gabby's law school. Students fought to be in her class then tripped over one another trying to impress her.

"You're saying she's involved?" Gabby used her best *you've lost it* tone.

Rob didn't seem to notice. "I'm not. The file does, or it suggests she could be, which is why I've been trying to talk with the judge. To study the people closest to her. Someone inside must feel . . . I don't know, sickened by all of this?" His voice grew more distant. "I can't believe killing Tami was part of the original plan. She stumbled in and . . ."

His words crashed together as he spoke. He drifted from one idea to another as if he needed to race to get all his theories out. She wondered if his grief had manifested into something almost delusional.

"I think the group is expanding, which means even more people will die," he said.

That sounded like a leap. "How do you know that?"

"Her. She's been visiting Retta." He grabbed his phone and flipped through the stored photos until he got to what looked like a woman standing outside of a gate. "Jessa Hall."

Oh, come on. Speaking of fellow law school students who would trample over anyone who got in the way of her capturing the spotlight. Jessa rose to the top of the sludge pile. "Why does messed-up garbage always come back to Jessa?"

"If I'm right, you'll soon see bad press about her."

"Not surprising." The way Jessa lived, the corners she cut, a bad end was all but guaranteed. Gabby had predicted that years ago.

"If that public attention immediately shifts from negative to positive, you know she's in the group. It means she gave in and joined up," he said, reinforcing his own theory.

Gabby regretted not ordering coffee. She needed caffeine to get through this. "I'm happy to jump on the anti-Jessa bandwagon. Honestly, I've been on that ride for a long time, but you don't have any evidence. All you have is theories. And loss, and for that part I'm really sorry."

He shoved the stack of files closer to her. "These are for you. Review them."

There had to be twenty files, maybe more. "I don't have time for this."

Rob's manic arguing and attempting to convince slowed long enough for him to lean back in his chair. "If they came for you through your daughter, do you really have a choice?"

Chapter Thirty

JESSA

THE OFFICE VISIT Jessa dreaded happened an hour after Faith left. Covington walked in and shut the door behind him. He held a file and didn't give her eye contact. That could only mean more bad news.

She tried to launch an offensive strike. "I'm guessing you've heard. But you should know—"

"Detective Schone had some questions for me about your work activities."

Not what Jessa expected. She almost hated to ask for more information but did anyway. "What did you say to her?"

Covington finally looked at Jessa. "Tell me how concerned I should be about your behavior."

Uh . . . "Not at all."

"People are going to dig around and find the worst, Jessa. They'll look at your law school performance. Your friends. Your activities. The meetings you attend. The groups you join. Your previous casework here and at your other firm."

Okay, that last part could be problematic. No one had a shiny, perfect record. There were issues and bad calls, totally unrelated to her legal prowess, that could be embellished and taken the wrong way. "I've done good work for this firm."

Covington sighed. "That's a classic lawyer nonanswer."

Fine. She jumped right to the point. "I didn't tell Ellie Bartholomew to run."

"She says you did."

"Her husband threatened her. Clearly, that's the only explanation."

Covington's stiff stance unclenched a bit. "Do you have proof of that?"

She'd thought about it from the minute the detective left the office. "Not yet, but I'm going to ask the judge for a hearing. Let Darren come into court and try to defend his actions. I don't think Ellie will be able to hold his lie together under oath or during cross-examination."

"No."

Jessa had other ideas, but the curt *no* stopped her. "To which part?"

"As of right now, you're suspended. You are not authorized to work on behalf of this firm, including as the GAL for Curtis Bartholomew. Any work you do from now forward will be at your own peril. The law firm's liability insurance will not cover you." He put a sealed envelope on her desk.

She assumed the letter contained notice of the law firm action. She refused to let him drop it and run. He needed to say whatever he had to say right to her face. "Why aren't you supporting me?"

"This will be an administrative suspension with pay while the firm conducts an independent review of—"

"Answer me." This was ass-covering bullshit. They both knew it, but only she had the guts to admit it. "You can't believe these allegations are true."

He glanced at his notes. Flipped the first page, letting her see the lines of scribble from a blue pen. "Did anything happen at your previous firm that might show a tendency for recklessness?"

As if she would let all her secrets come tumbling out. She knew not to volunteer any more information. "Let me prove I didn't do this. This is my reputation."

He glanced up, giving her full eye contact. "It's actually your career. If we find you failed to do your duty or acted in contravention of the ethics rules—"

He sounded like a textbook, which sent her anxiety spinning. "Covington, please."

"—we will join in the request that you be disciplined, including being disbarred."

"If you're so sure, or really not sure about me, why not just fire me?"

"That would reflect poorly on the firm. This way you get a fair review and still get paid." He cleared his throat. "For now."

One sharp knock and the office door opened. Two building security guards stepped inside. The same men who smiled at her and wished her a good morning every day.

"I need you to stand up and hand me your key card. These gentlemen will look in your bag to make sure you don't have any firm property. After that, they will escort you out of the building."

Her muscles refused to move. She tried to concentrate over loud buzzing in her head. "Don't do this. I'm begging you."

"Your access to the computer, including the sign-in feature from home, will be terminated, pending the investigation," he continued as if he was reading from a list.

One of the security guards stepped around Covington and headed for Jessa. Not wanting to be dragged and not knowing how to stop the inevitable, she put her hands up in surrender. "I'll go willingly. This . . . this isn't necessary."

Covington nodded for the guards to continue. "It's firm policy."

This would destroy her. Stomp down and shatter her world into a million pieces.

She switched to begging, pleading, trying to appeal to a tiny spot of affection he might have for her. "My reputation won't recover from this."

"I did everything I could, Jessa. You should have withdrawn from the case when I told you to."

Chapter Thirty-One

GABBY

THE LINES ON the papers blurred together. Gabby stared at her empty coffee mug as she stretched. The pinch in her lower back made her groan. "It sucks getting older."

She blamed Rob Greene. His files littered her dining room table. She'd read and reread and assessed since their meeting. At one point she had to rush and retrieve the computer charger because she'd burned through the battery doing her own research on the various jackasses who abused, battered, and killed the women unlucky enough to veer into their paths.

Alex Carlisle was the most recent peculiar death, and his seemed fitting because of what he did to the women around him—treating women as disposable, only existing for his pleasure—but he certainly was not the only aggressor. Not even the worst, though she wasn't sure how to weigh one horror inflicted on a woman against another. Every act demanded that a woman left behind somehow overcome and take on the role of survivor . . . but only if the man didn't kill her first.

Carlisle's wife went from shuffling on the sidelines to a starring role when she claimed the accusations weren't true. Fingers pointed at her. Police sources—anonymous, of course—talked about her killing her husband out of revenge. But over the last two days the conversation had shifted again. Unnamed third parties stepped up and offered new stories that cast her as damaged by a decades-long marriage filled with terror due to abuse.

The up-and-down, the rolling in and out of responsibility, reminded Gabby of Rob's claims and his relentless need to convince her that something bigger was at play here. If his grief and passion were pieces of a delusion . . . she couldn't see it.

After hours knee-deep in what she'd expected to be nonsense, she had to admit it wasn't nonsense at all. Damn it. She teetered back and forth, getting sucked into his arguments. To battle that, she supplemented his files with her own online searches into the deaths. The circumstances stacked up until it all looked . . . odd. Each death sounded reasonable when you looked at it individually. But an isolated incident morphed into something else when you looked at them as a group. It was all too coincidental. Too close to a potential pattern.

She hated that the pieces fit together. She'd read a book on confirmation bias. Part of her thought she was watching the idea in action. Rob talked and talked about his theories and planted them in her head, and now she could only see the fragments that supported his theory. She wanted this to amount to an irrational mess promoted by an unhealthy guy fueled by scary paranoia. All the talk still could be that, but she doubted the answer was that easy.

She looked at his cached articles. Nothing raised any alarms. He didn't spew or rant about secret societies. He and his writing partner had won awards. They'd appeared on television and come off fine. Then the partner had died, and the tone of Rob's reporting had changed.

She knew from experience grief was a nasty bastard. It wiggled its way in and shrouded every moment in darkness. It leaked and spread until it kidnapped the good memories and created minefields of pain. All of this—the desperate researching and clinging to things he couldn't see—could be a reaction to loss. She just didn't know.

She got up from the chair, happy her legs supported her after hours of not moving very much. She opened the utensil drawer and felt around underneath. The envelope. The one Baines had hidden. A voice told her to hide it, and she did, even though the move reflected a paranoia level that made her uncomfortable.

None of the files Rob had given her contained a single comment or stray thought about Baines. If Rob held negative information on her ex, he wasn't sharing it . . . yet. She didn't know if this hidden bid related to any of Rob's files, but she felt compelled to look.

What she really needed was a second set of eyes. Only one person might know why Baines thought this document was important enough to hide, but that person hated her right now. Might always hate her, but she had to ask.

She took out her phone and texted Liam, but not before scanning in the three-page document and forwarding that.

Her: Do you know what this is?

Liam: A bid proposal

Yeah, no shit. She'd helped Baines and Liam set up the company. She knew how the bidding process worked.

She debated not going into details but decided that wasn't an option. She'd kept enough secrets from Liam. He deserved to know about this.

Her: Could you skim it? I found it hidden behind a photo in Baines's house.

Liam: When?

Her: After he died.

The three dots sat there on the phone screen, taunting her. Either Liam was typing out a long explanation or thinking or . . . who knew? The longer the wait, the more her stomach rolled and churned. She was about to tell him to forget it when his return text appeared.

Liam: He shouldn't have this

That sounded dire. Now they were getting somewhere.

Her: Why?

Liam: It's from the company we're bidding against for a big job

Her: So . . . ?

Liam: It's confidential and now that I know the outline of the other bid, I can adjust ours to be a better, winning bid

Baines, what did you do?

Her: How did he get the top-secret document?

Liam: Excellent question

Her: Who's the other bidder? Who are you going up against for this big job?

The wait for a reply chipped away at her patience. The sun

had gone down, and she sat in a mostly dark house with only the light from the laptop and her phone for guidance. She didn't get creeped out very easily, but her nerves sparked to life, and a cold shiver had her rubbing the back of her neck to ease it.

Liam: You know them from law school

Her: ??

Liam: Wilcad, the note at the bottom. That's the name of the company. It's a combination of Will and Cade—the names of Earl and Loretta Swain's sons. She was one of your professors, right? Her husband Earl's company, Wilcad, is the other bidder. This is his confidential bid proposal.

Chapter Thirty-Two

JESSA

NUMB. JESSA COULDN'T feel anything. She sat in her dark condo and listened to the thump of her heartbeat as it echoed in her ears. She'd rolled through two crying jags, screaming in the silent room about how unfair all of this was, and now she waited.

She'd texted Tim and asked him to come home. After days of working outrageous hours, she needed him here. They had to talk this through. He insisted he'd gotten behind from his business trip, but she suspected the truth pointed more to him hiding from her than billable hours.

Now was his chance to say *I told you so*. She'd give him one shot, then she needed his focus. A stifling mix of frustration and disappointment kept her from seeing a way to emerge out of this unscathed.

She heard him at the door and thought about standing up. Running to him was way too "damsel in distress" for her liking. She didn't need a rescue. She needed common sense, and her supply had drained away, leaving her vulnerable.

He stepped inside and threw his keys on the small table next to the door. "Hey."

The deep, rumbling sound of his voice should have comforted her. Instead, she heard judgment.

She closed her eyes as the reality that he already knew her terrible news hit her. "How did you find out?"

"Despite having the most lawyers per square inch, the metro area legal community is pretty small. Covington and a few of the senior partners in my firm are friends, and . . ." Tim shrugged. "Well, you get it."

"Apparently, my private information is fair game." Divulging unfounded allegations against her could get Covington and the entire firm in trouble. More than likely, if she complained he'd deny ever telling anyone and his cronies would back him up.

Tim sat on the armrest of the chair. Not coming one inch closer, keeping the emotional and physical divide between them intact.

He stared at his hands while he talked. "I think the call was meant as a friendly warning to prepare me."

Him. The patriarchy never took a break. Her shitty day was about him.

He lifted his head and met her gaze straight on. "I told you to drop that case."

He sounded exhausted. Resigned. Completely out of energy. He thrived on pressure. He lived for deadlines and meetings and all the things that drove her into a paralyzing panic. He memorized every detail of a case. Every discussion. In many ways, he was the lawyer she pretended to be. Competent and assured.

She worried about missing deadlines and failing to find that one piece of evidence in discovery guaranteed to break a case open in her client's favor. Retta once told her that type of debilitating worry showed a lack of self-confidence.

"You were right." It didn't kill her to say it, which was the only positive thing she could find about today. Being dragged out of her law firm while everyone watched gave her a new perspective on shame and embarrassment. Admitting he'd called this one right didn't come close to that bottom.

He didn't have his briefcase. He hadn't taken off his suit jacket. It was as if he'd swung by for a brief check-in and planned to blow out again. "Do you have to go back to work tonight?"

"No." He rubbed his eyes as he often did when he was about to say something he knew she wouldn't like. "But . . . I can't do this."

That comment pushed away the hollow feeling threatening to swallow her. He had her full attention now. She shifted on the couch, sitting up straighter and putting down the wineglass. "What are you talking about?"

"I've tried to ride this out. Be supportive."

Them. Their relationship. He didn't name the "this," but she knew. "When? This whole thing just happened."

He shook his head as he exhaled. "I mean before."

She didn't realize the exhaustion could press down even harder, but it did. "Really? You mean when you were warning me? For the record, that's not my idea of support."

"You know that's not fair."

"This is my worst day, Tim." She didn't add *ever* because he'd accused her of overreacting before, of jumping in instead of listening, and she refused to have that accusation leveled at her tonight.

"You were so busy trying to get ahead and competing that you missed the obvious signs of trouble. This isn't a new thing, Jessa. It's how you live your life, as if chaos and hope will get you where you want to be."

That hit a little too close. She forced her body up. Somehow, she stood. She kept the coffee table between them, but she closed the yawning emotional gap.

"I begged you. I knew the Bartholomew family would dismantle your career," he said.

Because he knew everything. *Got it.* "I told you that you were right. You win. Can we move forward now?"

His shoulders slumped, and he still didn't move from that perch on the edge of the chair. "Not everything is a battle."

"It sure feels like it."

"I'm sorry, but I need a break." His voice cut out a little before he started again. "From you. Some time away."

With every other aspect of her life in disarray, she needed him to be specific, to spell it out. "How much time?"

"I don't know."

But he did. She could hear the faint *goodbye* in every sentence. "You can't . . . not now. This is . . ." Then the truth hit her. Anger swelled inside her, trying to claw its way out. She'd broken the unspoken rule about not messing up her job, and he wanted out. "Oh my God. This is about your career. You're worried my reputation is going to bring you down."

He stood up. "I don't want to do this with you."

"You piece of shit."

"Don't make this harder than it has to be."

She stalked over to him. Got right in his face. Didn't give him the choice of ignoring her. "You're not even man enough to say you're pushing me away to save your precious job. Things get tough, there goes Tim." The words poured out of her now. She wanted to sharpen each comment and aim them right at him. Tear him apart as he was doing to her. "You have such a perfect life. It's all been so easy. Mommy and Daddy paved the way, gave you the money and the splashy education."

The mention of money and his privileged background seemed to snap his control. "Jessa, that's enough."

"One thing gets a little difficult, and you run away like a coward. When it's not all about looking pretty on your arm at charity events or being able to schmooze your partners, I'm out. I'm a liability." She forced him to look at her. Followed his gaze and stuck her face in front of him. "How could you?"

"I tried. I really . . . I didn't want this."

She thought she saw a tiny sliver, room for her pain to get through to him. She held on to his jacket and tugged him closer to her. "No . . . no. Please. Today is just . . . We can't let the Bartholomews win."

"This is about you and your choices. Your priorities." He peeled her hands off him and shifted until he broke out of the trap between her and the chair. "The condo is in my name."

Her house. The one thing she had left. "You can't."

"I'll be back tomorrow night, but you need to leave. You can stay with Faith while we figure this out."

She tried to step back and look at her life, and the picture made her heave. No job. No house. All stability gone, taking her reputation along with it. "This is my house."

"It's actually *my* house. You moved in with me."

She shoved him. Both hands on his chest, and still he barely moved. "I will burn it down first."

"Listen to me." He grabbed her hands and held her still, keeping her from punching him. "If you destroy one thing or take even one glass that's not yours, I will come after you and ruin whatever you haven't already destroyed. Have some dignity and self-respect."

She yanked her hands out of his hold. "So, the real Tim finally showed up."

"You don't want to mess with me, Jessa."

He was weak and pathetic. Lacked staying power. Things got a little rocky, and he bolted. She saw that now.

She forced her trembling insides to calm and let the rage running through her pull her out of the emotional drowning. She would show him. Show Covington and the other partners. Show Darren Bartholomew.

She did not lose. "You know what, Tim? You aren't worth it."

Chapter Thirty-Three

GABBY

GABBY STEPPED INTO her foyer, arms loaded down with bags of groceries, and kicked the front door shut behind her. She bought food, thinking she could take meals over to Liam and Kennedy, maybe lure them into talking to her, or at least sitting at a table with her. She'd be happy for any contact right now, even the yelling kind.

She walked into the kitchen and set the bags down, ignoring the apple that rolled across the counter. She had much bigger problems than runaway fruit. The two days of silence ate at her, chipped away at her hope and intensified every worry.

She turned to the refrigerator, about to open it, when she saw a flash of movement reflected in the stainless steel. She spun around and stared into the quiet dining room. Stayed completely still, thinking she might be able to pick up on a stray sound.

Nothing.

She groaned, frustrated by her wild imagination. "Nerves."

Rob's theories had her spun up. Her mind raced with conspiracies. Trying to figure out how and if the hidden bid letter fit in, she'd looked up Loretta and Earl Swain and fallen down a rabbit hole of charity dinners and magazine features. One article included photos of her house, and Gabby doubted she'd ever look at her own backyard with love again. The Swains had a *yard*, with a pool and fountains and . . .

Her laptop was closed.

She stared at where it sat on the kitchen table. She'd packed up all the files and papers from Rob before stepping out, but she'd left the laptop open because she was doing a full-system backup and didn't know if closing the laptop would accidentally end it. It was one of those tech questions she usually asked Kennedy, who then rolled her eyes and treated her old mother as if she were born before the invention of electricity. Kennedy would have lectured her for hours if she'd realized Gabby hadn't done a backup in almost eight months.

But the laptop was closed. Habit, maybe? Even though she specifically remembered the internal debate about closing or not, she did tend to shut down everything when she stepped away, so maybe Rob's dire warnings didn't have her daydreaming nonsense.

"Kennedy?" A fourteen-year-old's anger either burned out fast once boredom or hunger set in, or the need for money called . . . or the anger lasted for a lifetime. Gabby hoped for the shorter version.

She was about to walk back to the bedrooms and call out in one last, desperate hope that Kennedy had returned home. She passed the knife block and cursed her silliness as she pulled out the biggest one. She'd seen enough horror movies to know how this ended, but she had an alarm . . . Wait, had she put it on? Now she tried to remember if it had chirped when she'd walked in.

She stepped into the hall and listened for footsteps. She couldn't hear anything over her own panicked breathing. Reinforcements sounded good. She pulled her cell out of her pocket and debated calling Liam. He was her emergency contact. If she hit the SOS, he'd get a call and so would the police. Then she'd probably be fined for wasting law enforcement time on her paranoia.

"This is ridiculous." She blew out a long breath, hoping to leave some room for common sense to seep into her head.

The hit came from her left side. A blow to her back sent her flying into the wall. She pawed and slapped, trying to grab on to something, but there was nothing to hold. She blinked, desperate to keep her bearings and stay on her feet. With a primal scream, she turned around and slashed out with the knife. She heard a grunt then a flash of dark clothing passed in front of her.

A hand clamped down on her wrist and started twisting. A burning sensation raced up her arm.

"No, no, no," she pleaded.

With a squeal, she dropped the knife and heard it clank against the hardwood floor. She tried to see the attacker's face, but the room blurred around her. Fingers wrapped around her arm and yanked. Off-balance, she crashed into the small hall table. A bang rang out, and she fell, hitting the floor and covering her head as a lamp toppled over on her.

This cannot happen. I will not die this way.

Adrenaline pumped through her. She kicked out and yelled. Screamed for help and shouted, "No," over and over. The knife. She needed to find it. Reaching out, she searched, frantic and wild, and felt a shoe. A man's shoe. Her attacker.

She punched his ankle as hard as she could. When he swore under his breath, she hit him a second time. Before she could grab on to his leg and try to trip him, he kicked her in the stomach then in the chest. Pain burst behind her eyes as she doubled over. She could feel the air leave her body while she curled into the fetal position without any signal from her brain.

More stunned than hurt, she tried to keep her eyes open. Be ready for the next shot. She scooted back, trying to evade the slicing of the blade.

Her attacker stepped closer. One second, then two . . . He stabbed the knife into the floor next to her face.

A hiccup of air escaped her. She scrambled to sit up through the thumping mass of aches and the tightness clamping down on her chest. When she finally stopped shifting and crawling and doing all she could to make her body smaller, less of a target, she heard the quiet. Only her heavy breathing and silence.

Her gaze shot to the front door. Closed. Then to the back of the house. The French doors to the deck stood open.

Oh my God. Oh my God. She didn't know if she said the words or just thought them. Tiny shards of glass from the shattered lamp covered her pants. She saw the ripped shade and a black mark along her white wall. She shoved the table off her as she fought to breathe through the pounding in her chest.

She realized she still had her phone. Her hand ached from her crushing hold around it. Blood ran down her arm, but she had no idea why.

Her body shook as she hit the SOS button.

Chapter Thirty-Four

JESSA

JESSA WATCHED HER life implode in real time. She mentally jumped back and forth between crying and throwing things. She'd slammed her laptop against the kitchen counter, welcoming the satisfying crack. Now it didn't turn on.

On the second full day of hiding, she lost it. She'd spent every hour of every day secluded in Faith's small apartment, obsessively reading news about the Bartholomews that framed her as an out-of-control, man-hating, incompetent fraud. She hadn't answered her phone, but she did listen to messages, which consisted of misogynist screeds, seething with hate and talking about how she deserved to be raped and killed, and of reporters asking for quotes. Two people specifically asked about rumors of a "problem" in law school.

She deleted her social media accounts.

Reporters digging into her background blew through the last of her control. She grabbed her bag and a baseball cap and jumped on the bus. She needed to hoard all the money she had, so a taxi was out of the question. She picked the bus, thinking it might be easier to hide there than on the Metro.

She curled into her seat and stared at the floor. A change and fifteen minutes that felt like hours later, she stood outside the gate in front of Retta's house. She leaned on the buzzer, but no one answered. She did it a second time, and a man appeared on the other side of the ornate metal bars. Broad shoulders and a familiar military buzz cut. The same man from the last time she was here.

"Judge Swain isn't home. I'll tell her you were here." He turned back toward the house.

"No, please." She reached out, but the gate stopped her from getting far. "I need to come in."

"You can't."

"Trent, it's fine. I'll handle this." Earl, Retta's husband, patted the other man on the shoulder and stepped in front of Jessa. "What are you doing here?"

His voice sounded soft and soothing. No accusations or anger, but not exactly welcoming either. Jessa didn't know why he was home in the middle of the day or what the magic words were to get him to open his home, but she tried anyway.

"I need to speak with Retta . . . I mean, the judge." The pleading in her voice sounded thick and near tears. "Please."

Earl stared at her for a few seconds without saying anything. When he finally spoke, he sounded firm and in control, every inch of the self-made millionaire he was. "I will not allow my family to be dragged down. Retta isn't your shield or your punching bag, and I will do whatever it takes to make sure you understand that."

"I just want to talk with her."

His eyes narrowed. "Be very sure which side you're on before you come inside."

The words didn't make a lot of sense. Jessa blamed the emotional whirlwind of the last few days. "I don't understand."

"You're poison right now. Being seen with you could be a problem for her."

Jessa's body caved in on itself. Everything inside her shrank, and the few dribbles of self-esteem she'd managed to gather up and hold on to dropped away. "I get that, but—"

"Unless you're ready to make a change."

His words broke through her weepy desperation. She clung to the bars of the gate as reality set in. "You know about—"

He nodded. "I support Retta fully in all things."

Jessa didn't know what that entailed, but she got that he was offering her a chance not only to come into the house but to pick a different way forward, and she grabbed it. "I'm ready."

Earl smiled. "Then come in."

Chapter Thirty-Five

GABBY

HOURS LATER, GABBY sat on the edge of the emergency room bed at Sibley Memorial Hospital. She'd delivered Kennedy here. Breathed through terror and confusion, both of which she experienced now but in a different way. Still wild and out of control but now trembling and gasping at the thought of someone trying to hurt her. Having to deal with Detective Schone didn't help. The woman showed up everywhere, including here.

Before the detective could get off another question, Liam shoved the curtain aside, rattling the hooks on the rod and pushing his way into the small area. "What the hell happened?"

Through all the emotional upheaval and dragging pain, seeing him still comforted her. She wanted to reach out but was convinced she'd lost that right.

"She says she was attacked at home."

It was the way the detective said things that made Gabby so defensive. She was pretty sure the digs were a law enforcement tool. Understanding that and liking it were two different things. "'Says'?"

The detective shrugged. "I believe you this time."

Gabby didn't have the energy for this. Dealing with Detective Melissa Schone meant being in top form, and Gabby had nothing left. No energy and very few working brain cells. "Is there another detective I can talk with?"

"You're stuck with me."

Liam came closer to the side of the bed but didn't touch Gabby. "Are you okay?"

"Small cut on my arm. Bruised ribs." She still didn't know how or when the cut had happened. It wasn't deep, but the second she saw it, it started burning. "Completely confused."

Liam lifted his hand as if to touch the side of her face but then dropped it again without making contact. "I bet."

The detective made a humming sound. "Interesting."

An awkward silence followed the comment. The usual easy back-and-forth Gabby enjoyed with Liam had vanished. She had no idea how to get it back, but she yearned for a return to normal . . . or what they had long accepted as normal between them.

"So . . ." He cleared his throat. "Someone broke in?"

Tense, stifled conversation. Gabby hated it but joined in. "It looks that way."

"She didn't set the alarm," the detective said.

The woman liked to start trouble. Gabby really didn't need more.

Liam frowned. "Gab, why?"

"It's been a hectic few weeks with Baines and the stuff after and . . ." *Good Lord.* What did she say next?

Liam nodded and took a step back from the bed. "Right."

She ached for closeness. For forgiveness she didn't deserve. "I . . . just . . ."

He patted her knee then let his hand drop again. "The important thing is you're okay."

No one said anything.

Gabby tried to think of a word bigger than *awkward*. That's what this was. Messy and broken, filled with half sentences and the kind of made-up affection she usually aimed at the unlikeable mothers of some of Kennedy's friends. *Fake, fake, fake.*

The detective let out a sound that came close to a laugh. "Don't let me stop you two from having a deep conversation."

"Shouldn't you be at her house or investigating?" Liam asked.

Some of the amused nosiness left the detective's face. "Other than the attack in the hallway, the rest of the house is intact. Mrs. Fielding will need to have a look around and tell us if anything is missing, but jewelry, money, laptop, televisions look to be all there."

"Maybe you caught them right as they broke in," Liam said to Gabby, as if trying to make sense of what happened.

"Attacker. Singular, as far as we can tell, and she can remember." The detective shook her head. "And no sign of a break-in."

"I locked the door." Gabby knew she did.

Liam winced. "Are you sure?"

"Yes . . . maybe?" During the divorce she had trouble concentrating and would check and recheck stuff like that. Did she lock the door? Did she leave the stove on? Did she close the refrigerator door? She lost all trust in her ability to do mundane things. Her therapist back then had suggested specific routines for her to use every time she did those tasks and eventually those let her break free from the obsessive cycle of doubt. At least as to that issue.

More awkward silences. "Liam, I'm . . ."

"You should stay at my house until we're sure your place is safe," he said at the same time.

She wanted to say yes, to not be alone, but they had too many issues to work through, and Kennedy didn't deserve endless rounds of yelling and disappointment.

"I don't think that's . . ." Any other time, she'd fall into uncomfortable babbling. Now she could barely form a sentence. "Maybe . . . we could . . ."

He shrugged. "Kennedy is there, and—"

"Your daughter is at his house?" the detective asked.

Liam nodded. "Yes."

"Temporarily," Gabby rushed to add.

"What's going on with you two?"

Before Gabby could make up a reasonable answer, Liam stepped in. "Is there a right way to act when you lose your brother, and your sister-in-law is attacked?"

"Former. She's your *former* sister-in-law." Detective Schone turned her attention back to Gabby. "You claim your husband was killed. You were attacked. Your ex's business is in financial trouble. You see where I might be concerned about the cumulative impact of all those circumstances?"

Liam made a strangled sound. "There are financial irregu-larities at the business, and I reported them."

"You mean you implicated your brother," the detective shot back.

The conversation had shifted to a new place. One with a ma-licious edge, and Gabby didn't know why. "What exactly are you trying to say?"

"Just making conversation." The detective moved the curtain and stepped outside of the protected area. "We'll talk again."

Chapter Thirty-Six

JESSA

JESSA HELD HER second cup of tea in front of her like a precious crystal. She downed the first as soon as she took a seat in Retta and Earl's impressive dining room. From the built-ins to the chandelier, the room screamed elegance and sophistication, in contrast to Jessa's dirty jeans and fraying T-shirt.

A few minutes later, the door opened and Retta stepped inside. Every woman Jessa knew came home from work, sloughed off the dress clothes, and found something old and soft to slip into. Comfy clothes. If Retta owned those, she hid them. Today's outfit consisted of a sleek black pantsuit and green silk blouse. Perfect hair, with just the right number of thin bracelets and a brooch on her lapel.

"You're here." Relaxed or not, Jessa enjoyed a rush of relief. She stood up as if the queen had entered the room.

"I live here," Retta said in an amused voice.

"Yes, of course." Even with the degree and the career, Jessa's self-assurance shrank in Retta's presence. She fell back into the role of overeager mentee, desperate for advice and acceptance. "Over the last few days, everything—"

"Jessa." Retta held up a hand. "There's no rush. Sit down and drink your tea."

Right. Calm and dignity. She could pretend to possess those. "Earl let me in."

"I'm aware," Retta said as she sat at the end of the table, off to Jessa's left.

"He knows . . ." Jessa struggled to find the composure she needed to get through the next few minutes. The string of shaky days dumped her in a dark place that she dug and clawed at but couldn't climb out of. "I mean, of course you talk, so . . ."

Retta poured a cup of tea and sat back in her chair. "Knows about what?"

"About the group." Was she allowed to mention the group? Jessa had no idea what the rules were or if it was okay to bring the topic up again. "What you do . . ." This conversation could not go worse. "I don't really even understand what I'm talking about."

Retta smiled. "Jessa, please calm down."

"I can't." The energy revving up inside her had her shifting in the antique chair. Jessa tried to hold in the pulsing ball of exasperation, anger, and terror, but it spilled out. "Tim told me to leave the condo. I've lost my job. I might be disbarred. I have nowhere to go, no extra money, and now I might not be able to earn any." She gulped in a deep breath and kept going. "Reporters are snooping around my past, and . . . We all have stuff we don't want people to know, right?"

"Well. That's quite a day."

"Too much." Jessa reached her breaking point then went soaring past it. "I can't—"

"Jessa." Retta set her cup down on the table. "Tell me you want help."

"I don't . . ."

"Say the words."

Is this a test? Jessa dropped into the chair. "I want help."

"There."

Uh . . . "There?"

"Do you understand that accepting help means accepting the ties that come with the assistance?" Retta asked. "It's about holding up your end of the bargain. Responsibility."

Jessa wanted to scream, *Yes*, to all of it . . . no matter what it was. "Please just tell me what you want me to do. I'll do anything, but I can't deal in riddles right now."

"First, you're not special." Retta stopped there, as if to let the harsh reality of her words seep in. "You're experiencing the same thing that many people without power, money, or resources in the legal system deal with every single day."

"Justice shouldn't depend on not having a rich person attack you."

"You're on the defensive. People will lie and hurt you. Belittle and disregard you." Retta didn't sugarcoat. If anything, she ramped up the tension by shoveling on the painful truth. "You've lost control of the conversation, to the extent you were invited in the conversation in the first place."

That defensiveness she mentioned kicked up and demanded Jessa's attention. "I didn't do anything wrong."

"You don't need to lie." Retta picked a piece of lint only she could see off her pants. "Perfection is not the price of admission to the group. Your drive comes from being imperfect, and that drive is what the group needs."

Jessa repeated those words in her head, letting them soothe her frazzled nerves. She couldn't claim anything close to perfection. "But . . . I . . ."

"You do need to own your mess. And, let's be honest, that is not one of your strengths." Retta shot Jessa a look that dared her to disagree. When she wisely didn't, Retta continued. "First, Tim is the wrong man for you. He sucks up all the air in your relationship. He wants someone to support him, not a partner."

"True."

"I'm not judging him. That's fine. There's nothing wrong with wanting to be the only member of a household in the spotlight, but it's not what you need. Accept that, because, while your heart feels dented, it will heal."

Tim's face popped into Jessa's mind. That smile. The assured way he moved through the world. She'd been attracted to all of it. All the characteristics she wished she possessed. "I thought he was the one."

"Would 'the one' walk out so quickly or feel threatened by your career?" Retta snorted. "You need to be in sync with your partner, share the same goals. Agree on what's important—I think of these as your absolutes—and agree on what you'll do to protect those absolutes, what you're not willing to compromise on, and how far you'll go to hold that line."

"Like you and Earl." Jessa could see it. The way they looked and acted. Every step matched.

"Exactly." Retta smiled. "It's about understanding the values that bind you as a couple and nurturing them."

"I can't imagine being that close to someone."

"Which is how you should have known Tim was not the one." Retta waved a hand in the air. "And you were wrong before. You still have your job. It's on hold, waiting to see what you do, how you react to the circumstances you've landed in."

Jessa tried to take the cryptic remark apart and make sense of it, but she couldn't. But she was very in touch with how pissed she was. She didn't have a single good thought for Covington or any of the other partners. "I should leave the firm. There's no support there."

"Then demand support."

That's not the first time Jessa had heard that advice. Retta gave it often but never filled in the blanks about how to make it happen. "You make it sound easy, but it's not. I'm not you."

Retta leaned forward, resting her elbows on the table. "I can help you, Jessa. I can make a lot of this go away, but you have to want it. Deep down in your bones."

"I do."

"Then step up and let the fear go."

Yes. Do it now. Go. "How?"

Retta shrugged. "There's a solution, an imperfect one, that levels the field. It makes us proactive instead of reactive."

Some of the haze started to clear. Jessa no longer wanted to crawl out of her skin. Retta had her full attention now. "The alternative system you talked about the other day?"

"Yes, then I was talking about a hypothetical, but the system is very real."

"And it's run by the Sophie Foundation . . . or the group of women behind the Foundation." Not a question, because Jessa knew she was on the right track.

"Our current traditional justice system doesn't work, so we created one of our own, complete with strict rules. It deals with people who abuse the community. We review and we decide, using the same unemotional certainty as a surgeon removing a malignancy."

The harsh words, delivered with such smooth efficiency, stopped Jessa. "Decide what?"

"Punishment."

That couldn't be . . . could it? "Like a judge?"

"I am a judge."

"What if you, as a group, make a mistake?" Because it would happen. People misread cues, acted on emotion, didn't wait for all the evidence. Jessa had been a lawyer long enough to experience all of it.

"We move on."

This sounded like the anti–law school, like the opposite of everything she'd spent years trying to perfect. "It's that simple? Mess up and forget about it?"

"If I help you, you will need to rethink concepts like the law, justice, and revenge to see them in a new way, as pieces of a system defined only by us." Retta's ringing voice didn't leave room for compromise. "We shift the conversation and take the power back for the victims."

The unspoken part lured Jessa: she would be in charge. She could have a group of women to guide her, support her. She'd no longer be out there, flailing and alone. Failing and scrambling not to get kicked out of the legal club.

Jessa didn't weigh the pros and cons, didn't think about downsides or the costs. She did what she'd been doing her whole life—ignored the consequences, convinced she could outmaneuver them later. "I'll do whatever it takes to become a member."

Retta leaned back in her chair again and smiled. "Yes, Jessa. I think you will."

Chapter Thirty-Seven

GABBY

EXHAUSTED. GABBY SEARCHED her mind for another word, but that one fit. By the time Liam pulled into the private garage of his duplex in the swanky Kalorama area of DC, filled with ambassadorial residences and private security details, Gabby didn't want to think about knives or attackers, blood, or Detective Schone. Gabby would barter and beg for a bed and a few hours of quiet, but she had to walk a gauntlet of teenage angst first.

Liam didn't say anything as Gabby put her bag of medicine and gauze on his kitchen counter and walked up the stairs to the second floor. She stood in the doorway to the bedroom he'd let Kennedy decorate last year and claim as her own. The bright blue walls stood out in the sea of light gray and beige Liam preferred.

Kennedy sat in the middle of the bed, watching something on her tablet. She glanced up, and her hold on the device tightened. "You look terrible."

Ah, teenagers. "I went a few rounds with an intruder."

Liam said he'd filled Kennedy in on what happened at the house. He insisted she'd been upset and wanted to come to the hospital, but he made her wait at home until he saw the extent of the injuries. If true, Kennedy hid her concern well. She looked ready for battle despite the rainbow pajamas.

"Did you see the guy who did it?" Kennedy asked.

"No." Gabby hugged her sore ribs. She didn't want to talk about the attack or think about how useless and weak she felt when he grabbed her wrist and took the knife. She could hear the clang of the blade hitting the floor every time she closed her eyes. "We'll both be staying here until we're sure the house is safe."

"You invited yourself to stay with Uncle Liam." Kennedy snorted. "How convenient."

Gabby couldn't think of a less convenient circumstance. The one time she didn't want to see Liam or deal with his pain and disappointment, they were trapped in a condo together. "That's big talk. Are you ready to have a grown-up conversation, or do you just want to take shots at me?"

"A talk about you having an affair with Uncle Liam?"

"So, no to the adult talk."

"Wait . . ." Kennedy set her tablet down on the mattress and tucked her legs up under her. "Okay. Yes. I don't get it, but yes."

The timing sucked. Gabby needed meds and rest. She had no idea who'd come after her or why. Rob's warnings rang in her ears, threatening to drown out everything else. But, like it or not, the gaping emotional wound with Kennedy wouldn't heal until they at least started this conversation.

She sat on the farthest edge of the bed, careful not to infringe on Kennedy's space. "I wouldn't expect you to understand what happened and why. It's still murky for me."

Kennedy shrugged. "That sounds like an excuse."

Well, damn. "You're right." No one could see through you like your own kid. Gabby should have known that from her own upbringing, but she was getting a crash-course reminder right now.

"You lied to everyone," Kennedy said, diving right in. "It's really shitty."

Gabby's instinct was to come out swinging, but she shoved down all the excuses and explanations and gave her daughter the truth. "I did. I had my reasons and convinced myself they were valid. Maybe at the time they were, but that doesn't make things easier now."

"You blamed Aunt Natalie."

Gabby owed Liam for one more thing. He'd been the one stuck there, fielding the anger and the first round of uncomfortable questions.

"Liam said you were trying to protect her. That you thought the truth would rip the family apart and leave Aunt Natalie in danger." Kennedy let out a dramatic exhale. "But you expect us to believe you lied just to save Aunt Natalie from having a bad day?"

Gabby remembered how the family had talked about Natalie back then, carefully and in hushed tones. No one had wanted to upset her or say the one thing that would touch off a depressive spin. It had felt necessary, but it was insulting. They had treated her as if she couldn't hear their whispers . . . as if she didn't get a say in her own life. Gabby saw that now.

Even worse, hiding the truth and covering for Natalie's absences with lame excuses like *she has a migraine and can't leave the house* or *she got behind because she was sick and couldn't come this time* meant Kennedy didn't understand the extent of her aunt's debilitation. "It was more than that. She needed her brothers' support—both of them—to survive."

"Okay, but what about after the fire?" Kennedy asked.

The fire that killed her. The one that changed everything for Gabby by giving her the push she needed to end a marriage that had never worked. "Your aunt died right before the divorce started. Telling the truth about Uncle Liam would have weaponized you, potentially driven a deep division between Liam and your dad."

It wasn't the whole truth, but it was as much of the truth as Gabby could tell.

"Liam *is* my dad." Kennedy's sarcasm disappeared as quickly as it appeared, taking some of the hot wind behind her words with it. "Apparently."

Gabby had expected swearing and hundreds of *I hate you* diatribes, but Kennedy was giving her a more nuanced discussion. One that suggested she might be ready to hear part of the truth. "Fatherhood isn't just biology, Kennedy. Your father figured out the truth about your conception. He secretly took items and did a DNA test then confronted me with the results."

"He suspected?"

"When I said I wanted a divorce, he threatened to turn you against me. I lashed out and said something like, 'You don't have the leverage you think you do in a custody fight,' but, really, I think there was a part of him that always suspected something had happened between me and Liam. My anger just tipped him into action." Gabby didn't believe that's how the timing worked, but the explanation provided a clear line she could give Kennedy in the absence of more information.

"Then he found out the truth." Kennedy made a face. "He must have hated you."

"But he loved you. Biology didn't matter to him. He worked all the time, but always came to your events and told everyone in the audience you were his girl. He talked about you, showed off your picture, to anyone who would listen from the time you were little until the very end." Gabby couldn't think of stronger words to make this point and hoped these were enough. "Nothing changed about that. Through knowing the truth, through the divorce, you were his daughter, and he died protecting your relationship."

Kennedy picked at the comforter, tracing her finger over the subtle pattern on it. "Okay."

Gabby knew that typical teen "okay" packed a punch. That being reassured of Baines's love and devotion meant everything. "Liam also loves you, regardless of what he thought his relationship with you was. He didn't have to be your dad to want to protect you and make you happy."

Kennedy's shoulders slumped, and her hand fell limp. "This is so embarrassing. I don't get how you could do that to the family. They were brothers, which is just gross. Did you two always have sex, even now?"

"No." Gabby needed Kennedy to understand that truth and how the entire mess started. "We all grew up together. Everyone always thought your dad and I would end up together. We hung out. We talked and had fun. Falling into a romance was inevitable—then one day I realized I was more invested and in love with the *idea* of marriage than with your dad."

"That's weird."

"I wouldn't expect you to understand." She'd made sure Kennedy grew up feeling loved and not looking for affection in other places. "Don't get angry. I'm not saying you're too young. I'm pointing out that we were raised differently. Dad and Liam didn't have any stability growing up. Your grandfather gambled away the family car. They got evicted. Lost everything. Your grandfather, who you never knew, was always chasing a new scheme and would take his sons along. Endanger them. Then there was my family. I was with my mom, who was . . ."

"Dad used to call her a bitch."

Baines wasn't wrong about that. Her mother had been selfish and viewed motherhood as a burden. At times she tried to hide it, but the sicker she got as the lung cancer took hold, the angrier and more open about life's disappointments she became.

"She made terrible decisions when it came to men and didn't really love having a kid. She made sure I knew that." Gabby took a deep breath and plunged ahead. "My biological father was married and picked his wife and family over us, and my mom banged that betrayal into my head every single day. She threatened to ruin him, to expose him, all while refusing to let him meet me."

Kennedy followed every word. "That sucks."

"It did, and it made me more reliant on your dad and Liam. None of us had great role models or a lot of parental affection. As a result, I craved security and this vision I had of a healthy, happy family in a nice house. No yelling. Enough food."

Kennedy snorted. "Everybody yells. Especially you."

"You usually deserve it." Some days Gabby wished she'd been blessed with a fraction of her daughter's confidence. "But yeah, my vision of family wasn't very realistic, but in it I had a room instead of the sofa and a corner of the coat closet in the hall for the few things I owned."

"So you married Dad," Kennedy said with more than a hint of confusion in her voice.

"I did, and I loved him. Please know that. I still do, despite a divorce where I wanted to strangle him half the time." When Kennedy started to talk, Gabby rushed to finish her thought. "But I wasn't *in love* with him. We wanted certain things. Being together was convenient."

Kennedy sat there for a few seconds, not saying anything.

The bar had been so low. Gabby saw that now. "I realized early that I'd messed up and wanted out. We separated and—"

"You slept with Uncle Liam."

"We spent time together, and I saw that life could be different. I could feel something. The rest just sort of happened. Neither of us wanted to hurt your dad, and all three of us loved you." There was so much more to the explanation, but Gabby tried to pare it down, keep it on a level a teenager who hadn't experienced life or disappointment or heartache could understand.

"So, why not divorce? Marry Uncle Liam? You didn't have to lie."

They'd hit the tricky part. Gabby attempted to maneuver through it with a bit of dignity. "That sounds right now, but back then ripping Liam and your dad apart, upending everything, risking the family I had created and was desperate to have, seemed impossible."

Kennedy winced. "Mom . . ."

"I wanted better for you than I had. Getting a divorce took every ounce of energy and will I possessed. I cried and doubted. The guilt . . ." Gabby wondered if the guilt would ever subside. Just when she thought she'd conquered it and moved on, it knocked her over again. "You wanted to know about the grown-up decisions and grown-up mess, and I'm telling you."

Kennedy sighed. "Now what? What about Uncle Liam? Do I tell people? Do I call him 'uncle' . . . or 'dad'?"

So many questions and not a single good answer. Gabby thought that described parenthood well. "I really did screw this up for you, didn't I?"

"Uh, yeah." Kennedy folded her arms in front of her and relaxed back into the stack of pillows behind her. "Are you still in love with Uncle Liam?"

Gabby wasn't touching that. Time to pivot. "I love him. Always have. But the real point is that the two of you need to figure out what you are to each other and what to call your relationship. I won't get in the way of that."

"You're okay if everyone knows you slept with both brothers?"

Oh, damn. Not even a little. Fellow mothers could be brutal even without that fodder. She hated to think what they'd do with that bit of juicy gossip.

But she didn't have any choice here. Kennedy came first. "No, but I'll survive."

Chapter Thirty-Eight

JESSA

JESSA SAT ON the middle of the couch in Faith's living room and waited for something to happen. Something big. She had no idea what or how, but Retta had left her with the impression the downward spiral her life had taken was about to change.

That was three days ago. Seventy-two hours of nothing.

The ethics complaint against her had been filed. Darren and his attorney requested her formal removal from the case. The only message from Covington came yesterday and related to the firm's cell phone. She needed to return it within two days. Tim . . . well, she didn't really care about Tim. The second he dumped her, all those big feelings she had for him shifted from sadness to seething anger in record time.

Jessa took another sip of wine. At this rate, she'd demolish the bottle before lunch.

Her office cell buzzed. She thought about throwing it through the window but guessed Faith would not appreciate the replacement cost on top of having a nonpaying unwanted roommate.

The cell buzzed a second time.

"What?" she screamed into the empty condo.

When she looked at the screen, she regretted she hadn't started drinking even earlier. Covington reminding her about office property. Come in tomorrow at ten. Now he didn't just want the phone back, he wanted it in the morning.

Fine. Whatever.

She may have dozed off or gone into some sort of *my life is a tragic mess* trance. She'd put the wine down without spilling, which was a triumph, but now . . . knocking. The thudding banged around inside her head. It took her a full minute to realize it came from the outside hallway.

She scrambled off the couch and got to the door, sliding across the last two steps in her thick cotton socks. She looked through the peephole and . . . *Hell no.* She was not in the mood for Detective Melissa Schone now—or ever, really.

"Ms. Hall?"

Jessa jumped away from the door at the sound of the detective's voice. Every time the woman showed up, she dragged a rattling train of bad luck behind her.

Thump. Thump.

She wasn't going away. Jessa was not that lucky.

Jessa opened the door. "What?"

The detective almost smiled but seemed to catch the amusement in time and bury it. "May I come in?"

"It's not my house."

The detective sighed. "I have news."

She didn't say *warrant* or *arrest*, so this was going better than Jessa feared. She stepped back and gestured for the other woman to come inside.

"What are you going to accuse me of today?" Jessa heard the snideness of her voice and didn't care. Hiding the pettiness flowing through her would take too much energy, so she didn't try.

The detective's gaze narrowed. "You've been drinking?"

"Is that illegal now?"

"It's ten in the morning."

"It's been a shitty week." Jessa resumed her seat on the couch and picked up the glass to let the detective know her judgment wasn't welcome.

"Ellie Bartholomew recanted this morning."

Jessa sat up straighter. She didn't want to mess this up or confuse the point. "Recanted again . . . or are you—"

"She admitted Darren threatened her. He told her that he would kill her and their son if she didn't implicate you and lie about you convincing her to run away. She really was on her way to visit her father when Darren caused the car accident."

Jessa tried to name the reason for the churning inside her. It felt a lot like excitement, maybe mixed with a bit of *gotcha*. "You mean I was right. I told you the allegations were bullshit."

"Darren Bartholomew put significant pressure on his wife, but if you wish to file charges against her, then I can—"

"Oh, please. Stop." Jessa refused to play the bad-guy role in this scenario. "I'm not angry at Ellie Bartholomew. I'm pissed at you. You believed Darren's crap even though you knew better."

"Are you gloating?"

Jessa didn't need a minute to think about it. "Actually, yes."

The detective leaned against the back of the chair across from Jessa. "I'm sure you understand that it takes time to investigate allegations."

"Not the ones against me, apparently. You ran with those. Right to the press, I assume?"

"I didn't arrest you."

"My name is all over the news. I've been sidelined at work." But now Covington's call made sense. The jackass. She could hardly wait to hear the verbal gymnastics he'd use to cover his butt and blame everyone else. "Darren turned my life upside down and you assisted him."

"He's in jail."

"What?" The wineglass tipped but Jessa righted it before spilling red wine all over the beige couch.

"When he blocked his wife's car in the driveaway, he violated the protective order she obtained when they first separated. Then, when he hit her car, he invited other charges—assault, attempted kidnapping."

Jessa really wanted to call Stan and ask how Darren was doing in prison. Hearing that blowhard lawyer stammer would be worth it. "I thought Darren's daddy would make the bad stuff go away. He hates negative press."

"There's something out there stronger than the Bartholomew family." The detective smiled. "Justice."

That sounded ridiculous. The good detective's reasoning was also wrong. Jessa knew the real answer. The one thing that could beat the powerful Bartholomews didn't have anything to do with a courtroom or a jail. It was Retta Swain and the Sophie Foundation.

Chapter Thirty-Nine

GABBY

GABBY STARED AT the headline. In less than a week, Jessa had gone from an incompetent, ethical black hole—a pariah—to a hero. A guardian ad litem fighting for children everywhere, regardless of the wounds to her ego and reputation.

Total nonsense. The Jessa she knew would have sacrificed a child for a better class rank in law school. The hero bullshit . . . well, it made Gabby think about Rob and his fiancée Tami and all they'd lost. They tracked down the impossible—a group that didn't exist.

Rob had predicted Jessa might go from being nearly ruined to overly praised. Gabby wondered what else he'd gotten right. If she'd quickly agreed Baines's death was a suicide, would that have stopped her from being attacked?

"You're glaring at the laptop screen."

Gabby jumped at the sound of Liam's voice. She hid a wince of pain from her still-healing ribs. He'd barely said a word to her in days, so she welcomed even this small greeting. "Sorry. Just reading about a woman I once knew."

"That sounds mysterious." He filled his coffee mug then walked over to the kitchen table where she sat.

She appreciated his effort at normalcy, at mindless conversation, but the strain between them destroyed her. She'd stayed up most of the last two nights, staring wide-eyed at the ceiling of his guest bedroom as she tried to think of a way to bridge the divide she'd accidentally slammed down between them.

"I talked with the school. Convinced them Kennedy was struggling due to her dad . . . Baines's death. She's attending classes via video." He took a long sip of coffee before continuing, "I guess that's the benefit of a shockingly expensive boarding school."

He'd handled a responsibility she'd missed. Through all the unburdening and anger, secret sharing, and careful conversations, she'd failed to do simple mother things. "Thank you for taking care of it."

"Kennedy was under the mistaken impression she could come home, be pissed at you, pout, and watch videos and movies all day." Liam sounded very much like a father in that moment.

"Like any smart teen would." Gabby couldn't fault her daughter for having kid priorities. "In my guilt-ridden state, I might have let her."

Liam stood there, frozen. He stared into his mug and didn't say anything. A few seconds passed before he made a sound that came out like "well" and started walking out of the kitchen again.

She needed him to stay. Wanted him to. "Liam . . ."

He shook his head. "Not yet, Gabby. The only words I have are profane and terrible. I fear if I say them, I'll never be able to call them back."

Old habits like completing each other's thoughts and diving into a conversation midthought remained. She hadn't had to explain the hesitance in her voice because he knew. "I want you to be a part of her life."

"I already am, and I intend to continue to be." The firmness of his voice suggested he'd made some decisions even though he hadn't filled her in yet. "With or without your approval."

"Right."

"Shit." He blew out a long breath. "I'm not trying to be a—"

"You're not being anything but honest, and I appreciate it. I just want us to get to a point where we can talk about what happened and why I did it." She hadn't strayed into babbling, but she was right on the edge. A little push and words and worries would come rushing out. "I mean, in more depth."

"If you're looking for forgiveness . . ."

"Well, yeah. I admit it. I want that, but I get that it might not happen." Before he could say *no way in hell* or whatever he planned to shoot back to her, she switched topics. "This is for you."

"The bid you found." He flipped through the pages.

"Does it help explain the financial issues you're worried about?" When he glanced up, she saw a question in his expression. "What? You can tell me. Unless you think I was in on whatever Baines was doing."

"From the initial investigation, it looks like he took money from the company, using fake invoices, and moved it through a series of shell companies registered in the Cayman Islands."

"To hide assets from me in the divorce?"

"No, this all happened after the divorce settlement, so I don't think this is about you . . . or even about hiding assets from me." He shook his head. "I'm still connecting the dots with the help of an expensive team of lawyers and forensic accountants, but it looks like Baines's assets were secure. He wasn't in financial trouble."

She debated telling Liam her biggest secret, a piece of the puzzle he didn't have. Already under fire and dealing with waves of debilitating vulnerability and unwanted self-doubt, she couldn't bring herself to plunge into one more horrible bout of truth-telling.

She tried to dodge around what she really should say. "Baines was a bit like your dad, in that once he started stockpiling money, he craved an even bigger pile."

"I get that, but there's this." He shook the papers in his hand. "This suggests a different issue. Corporate espionage."

She wondered if he was messing with her. "That sounds like a bad movie plot."

"It's very real." His expression said he was looking for the right words to explain. "We are a small-to-medium-sized company. I'm not being humble. We make a lot of money, but in the distribution and warehousing game, the players are very big. We're talking serious money. Baines was obsessed with growing, with knocking out the competition."

Always wanting more. That described her ex perfectly. "Not a surprise."

"He was obsessed with Earl Swain's company. We'd started winning smaller contracts, contracts Swain used to pick up to pad his portfolio, but Baines wanted more. He was determined to match him, be Earl's equal. Now I wonder if that drive made him take terrible, even illegal, risks." He pointed at the bid documents. "Those confidential papers should be locked in a safe and not in Baines's possession. They give our company an advantage when bidding on a thirty-million-dollar job."

"Damn." She knew Liam and Baines had taken the company into new territory, but not those numbers.

"Exactly. So spending half a million to steal our opponent's business trade secrets so that we can bid lower and be in a better position to win the overall contract wouldn't be a terrible investment."

"But you wouldn't have agreed, so he hid it from you." Just as Baines did with so many things.

"Baines didn't exactly leave a road map, but I think that's what we're dealing with here. He had this thing about Earl and his company. We go up against each other a lot." Liam refilled his coffee mug. "Look, I'm not going to find a check notation that says 'corporate espionage,' so this is all guessing."

Earl Swain and Loretta Swain. Gabby hadn't thought about her professor for years, but her name kept popping up these days. Every time it did, Gabby felt a new piece of Rob's puzzle come into sharper focus.

"I don't know what to say next except I'm sorry you're stuck figuring out Baines's mess," she said.

"Honestly, you have enough to feel bad about. Don't take on blame that rightly belongs to Baines." Liam looked like he wanted to add something else but shrugged instead. "I have to get back to work."

"I need to check on Kennedy. She might be shopping or in an *I Hate My Mom* chat room instead of in class." Gabby got off the stool at the same time and smashed into him. He mumbled as she jumped back. "Sorry."

Awkward. Every minute together bounced between uncomfortable and stumbling these days.

"I'll do it," he said as he cleared his throat. "You continue scowling at your laptop."

She waited until he left to look at the computer again. She exhaled as some of her discomfort of being alone with Liam started to ease.

As she stared at the blinking cursor a new sensation crept in. A different kind of twinge. She didn't ask the question she wanted to ask. Would it make sense for someone—someone like Earl or Retta—to kill Baines if they found out what he was doing?

Jessa Hall. Loretta Swain. Rob Greene. Baines's death. All those deaths, including Tami's. The pieces that shouldn't be related, but Gabby couldn't help but think they were.

She took out her cell and did the one thing she'd vowed not to do. She sent the text and immediately regretted it.

We need to meet.

Chapter Forty

JESSA

AN ARTISANAL COFFEE place a few blocks from Union Station was not where Jessa wanted to be on Friday morning. She'd almost ignored the frantic text. But Gabby never asked to meet before, and Jessa didn't want this to become a habit, so she agreed. This one time.

After battling typical DC traffic and a delay due to the presidential motorcade, Jessa sat in the café, watching Gabby get her coffee order. She walked toward the table Jessa had picked. One away from the window and other patrons.

Jessa waited until Gabby joined her to give some sort of greeting. "Your text was a surprise."

Gabby shrugged. "To me, too. I never thought our paths would cross after law school, but lately they intersect too often."

They didn't agree on much, but on that point they did.

"Why now? Why the rush?" Jessa took a second to look at her acquaintance-turned-enemy. The jerky movements and rushed breath suggested a problem. "You sounded pretty desperate."

"What do you know about Rob Greene?" Gabby asked.

Not the topic Jessa had expected, but one she could quickly discount. "The reporter guy in the news? Nothing."

Gabby sighed. "Jessa, look. I get that you have this instinctive need to cover your ass, even if it means lying about stupid, everyday stuff, but I need you to tell me the truth here."

First shot fired. Didn't take long, not that the rapid speed surprised Jessa. "You're still a sweet talker, I see."

"Oh, I'm sorry. Are we pretending you're not a liar?"

Jessa schooled her reaction, sending fake signals that the word didn't bother her, that Gabby's perception meant nothing. Jessa used most of her energy to give off a cool and unconcerned vibe. "Gee, why wouldn't I want to help you?"

"Fine. You're right. Maybe you've changed."

After getting out from under the Darren mess, Jessa wasn't looking for a new problem. She didn't want to go backward. She'd made some bad choices. Relied on learned survival skills that she hid even from Faith for fear of scaring her off. "You don't know me, Gabby. You didn't back then, and you don't now."

"Just because you wrote that in an affidavit during my divorce doesn't make it true."

Jessa grabbed her bag and started to stand up. "Goodbye, Gabby."

Even with the uncharacteristic jumpiness, Gabby didn't ruffle. "I know things about you. Things you don't want others to know. Corners you cut so tight I'm surprised you aren't still bleeding."

Jessa hated that Gabby could *see* her. "Are you threatening me?"

"Whatever it takes."

"What do you want?" Jessa sat back down as a familiar pounding started deep inside her. A whirling need to run and deny, to lash out . . . to get out from under a pile of lies by adding one more to the heap.

Gabby balanced her elbows on the table and leaned in as her voice dipped to a whisper. "Baines didn't kill himself."

Okay. Another curveball. "That's not what I've heard."

"What if I told you there's a group of people—looking at their targets, probably powerful, professional women—who believe they are the law and have handed down sentences?"

Oh, shit. Retta hadn't warned her about how to handle this sort of thing. "I'd say you should get a job and stop watching so much television."

"Loretta Swain."

Shit, shit, shit. "What about her?" *Laugh it off.* The thought floated into Jessa's head, and she went with it. "Wait, you think she's an assassin? I would love to see her swing a sword like some sort of avenging angel."

No amount of sarcasm or amusement seemed to throw Gabby off. She didn't break eye contact as she pushed on. "Do you know anyone who would want to kill Baines?"

Jessa gave in to an eye roll. "Yeah, you. Isn't the former spouse always the presumed guilty party?"

Gabby shook her head, clearly annoyed that Jessa wasn't spilling whatever she knew. "Did anything come up during the divorce? Something he said, maybe a piece of information you found, to suggest Baines was in danger?"

Jessa's fingers tightened around her coffee cup. "Gabby, really. Hear me when I tell you I didn't work on the case."

A sharp snap of silence traveled between them.

Gabby slumped back in her chair. The frenetic energy bouncing off her slowed. She seemed to regain control of whatever had her in a mental spin. "We both know that's not true."

"I signed a—"

"Stop," Gabby said loud enough for a few of the other people in the coffee shop to turn around. Then Gabby lowered her voice. "Before I figured out who you really were, before your law school antics, we were friends. Back then we studied together. Ate together. Then one night I drank too much and told you about Liam."

"About how you were engaged to the wrong brother? I remember." The tidbit Jessa knew that no one else did. It was the moment in law school when she realized Gabby thought they were much closer friends than they were. That unequal affection had given Jessa the upper hand.

"And years later, you told Baines, or at least told his attorney," Gabby said.

If it was a guess on Gabby's part, it was an educated one. And correct. Telling Covington had earned Jessa points, but not enough. She'd still ended up on his bad side and too many steps away from a partnership offer despite the risk she'd taken to divulge the news. "Why would I do that?"

"Because you're awful?"

Jessa didn't want to hear this. Not now, when her life was finally taking the right turn. She stood up. "We're done here."

"If I'm right, someone killed Baines. Maybe one person. Maybe a group. Then they attacked me. In my own home. Either way, Loretta Swain's name keeps popping up."

Jessa forced out a laugh. She'd heard about the home invasion but tried to pretend it was one of those horrible living-in-the-metro-area things and not a warning from the group. "I really hope you publicly accuse an appeals court judge of murder. That will work out great for you."

"Your name keeps showing up, too."

Jessa rested her hands on the table and leaned down, face-to-face with Gabby. "I know we're not friends, but I'm going to give you some advice."

Gabby sighed. "I can hardly wait."

"Stop this. Stop digging or looking for a better answer to what happened." Jessa refused to let Gabby derail her progress. "Your ex is dead, and I'm sure you have some feelings of guilt, but he's gone. Hanging out with a disgraced reporter and making outrageous claims that anyone can see are a bizarre overreach will lead you to a dark place. Get help for the attack and move on."

"Now who's threatening?"

Jessa stood up straight again. "You should thank me."

"And you should be careful. You like to be part of the 'in' crowd. That's who you are. You try to steal the shine of the people around you, but if I'm right, this 'in' crowd, these women, will turn around and destroy you."

Shot landed. Jessa felt the killing blow vibrate through her. Gabby's words made her look backward and question everything, and Jessa was done with that. She didn't want to face the worst parts of herself delivered by a person determined never to give her the benefit of the doubt.

Jessa grabbed her bag and her cup because it was time to make an exit. Forever. "Don't contact me again."

Chapter Forty-One

JESSA

JESSA GOT TO Retta's house three minutes early. She blamed Gabby for making her rush. For ticking her off. For saying things she didn't need to say.

Jessa knew who and what she was. She'd taken shortcuts. She'd made choices others might find wrong or even despicable, but that had grown out of necessity. The law didn't just come to her, like it did to Gabby. Picking out issues, putting the pieces together, seeing the bigger picture and forecasting possible problems—Jessa strained to make it all make sense. And when it didn't, she found workarounds, used tactics to ensure she survived.

She needed this life. Watching it crumble around her over the last few weeks had convinced her of how precious her achievements were. The years of being loved only as a stand-in for her dead mother and failing to live up to unreasonable expectations were behind her. But the idea of scrimping and clawing, of silently begging for more attention, haunted her.

The pendulum had shifted. People now viewed her as a hero. She was all over the news. *She'd* protected Ellie and Curtis. *She'd* faced down Darren Bartholomew and his powerful family. *She* had credibility and would cling to it, not letting anyone rip it away.

"Covington called. I hear your temporary suspension is over." Retta waited until her cook put a salad in front of her and one in front of Jessa and left the room before she continued. "That should be good news, but you seem distracted."

Gabby. Stupid fucking Gabby. "Sorry. I had a run-in with a person I'd like to forget."

"Is this related to the Bartholomew case?"

If she talked about it, issued the warning to Retta, then maybe she could forget Gabby and move on. "Law school, actually. Gabby Bruin, now Gabby Fielding, though she might have changed her name again since she's divorced."

Retta made a humming sound as she spooned out the salad dressing from a gravy boat then handed it to Jessa. "I know the Fieldings and read about her ex-husband's death. A tragic ending for a savvy businessman."

Jessa wasn't in the mood to hear anything that made Gabby a martyr.

"She's convinced there's some great conspiracy out there . . ." Wrong word. *Conspiracy* sounded negative, and Jessa regretted it the minute she used it. "Sorry."

Retta's eyebrow lifted. "About what?"

Jessa bounced back and forth between thinking she should and shouldn't tell. "You don't want to hear this."

"I remember Gabby." Retta smiled. "Very bright."

Perfect all the time. That was Gabby. "Uh-huh."

"Probably the smartest in your class."

Enough with the pro-Gabby chat. "But not very motivated. She got married and then got really weird."

Retta frowned. "My memory is that she used her degree to help her husband set up a very lucrative business. She reviewed documents and . . . Well, I'm sure you're not here to compare grades."

"She's convinced you're involved." Jessa blurted out the words. The need to dunk all that positive Gabby talk in a vat of reality overwhelmed Jessa. But then she saw Retta's face and her unreadable, unblinking expression. "I mean, it's not like the group did anything to Baines, right?"

"You aren't privy to any Foundation work that happened before you were considered for membership."

Jessa remembered that disappointed tone from law school. She'd overstepped. "Okay."

Retta put her fork down. "I'm also a little concerned about how easily you talk about the Foundation when you have neither information to draw conclusions about it nor a nuanced understanding of our work."

Time to regroup. Jessa realized she'd let hearing all the rah-rah stuff about Gabby's brilliance feed her rage and tried to pivot. "I was worried about you because she mentioned that reporter Rob Greene. It sounded like they—the two of them—were digging around in Baines's death and in other deaths."

An uncomfortable backpedal. The kind Jessa had promised

not to do again when she'd started at her current firm. Less blame-shifting and more responsibility. Shading the truth on that affidavit had taken her on a detour, but until the Bartholomew case she'd gotten back on track.

This time Retta pushed her plate to the side as if she was ready to deliver an in-depth, *this is going to sting* lecture. "Since we last met, your life has turned around. Do you regret that?"

"No, of course not."

"I told you there was a price associated with my assistance. Confidentiality. Dedication. Commitment."

Jessa made that her personal vow. "I remember and intend to give you all three."

"Let's hope that's true."

Jessa's brain shifted into overdrive. She tried to think of a way to ease Retta's fears and get back on her good side. "If you want, I could misdirect Gabby. Meet her and point her back to suicide, away from the Foundation."

Retta wore an unreadable expression. "Neither the Foundation nor the group behind the Foundation had anything to do with Baines's death. His death has nothing to do with our work."

This just got worse and worse. "Oh . . . right. I thought, but I can . . ."

"Ignore that reporter, Jessa. Talking the way he does, I doubt he'll be a problem much longer."

Chapter Forty-Two

GABBY

TWO DAYS LATER, when Gabby got the text from Jessa about meeting again, she almost ignored it. They didn't have a lot to say to each other, and Gabby hated being near Jessa. Something about her drove Gabby to lay out every fault and jump up and down on them. It was rude and unnecessary, especially because Jessa wasn't going to change . . . but she was punctual.

They met on the sidewalk out front of the coffee place Gabby liked. A different one from where they'd met last time.

She'd arranged to meet Rob at the same spot later. Since last time, she'd looked over every piece of paper he'd given her and was ready to talk. She'd also read articles about Tami. Seen their engagement photo. Felt the loss of a woman she'd never known.

Rob had to be trapped in a grief spiral. She knew how profound a shocking loss could be. But believing the words and having them be true were two different things. She'd originally suspected the former was at play, but now she feared the latter.

Gabby and Jessa walked to a small table on the patio out front without saying a word. Jessa finally broke the silence. "This is a courtesy meeting."

Good Lord. "I will never understand you."

Jessa made a strangled sound. "What is your problem this time?"

That fast Gabby flipped into offensive strike mode. The urge to lash out and take Jessa down swamped her. "With you? Do you want the list or are you looking for an abridged version?"

"Because you're so freaking perfect."

That stopped her. Jessa wasn't wrong. Gabby didn't exactly have the high road. She'd made plenty of mistakes, but the similarities between them ended there. She refused to believe otherwise. "I never pretended to be."

"Guess the rumor about how you gave in to your attraction to your brother-in-law and engaged in a fling does suggest you screw up now and then. Literally." Jessa smiled as she shook her head. "You should know that bit of gossip provided the law office with hours of speculation and amusement. Trying to figure out how you hid it, how you strung both men along. The logistics."

Don't react. Gabby repeated the refrain over and over until it echoed through her entire body.

"I thought you didn't hear anything about my case at the firm," Gabby said, desperate to bring balance back to the conversation and gain the control position. "See, this is what happens. You lie, you get caught. You get that look on your face. That one." Gabby pointed at Jessa's strained expression. "Then you crawl out of the hole by throwing other people in it."

"You wonder why no one liked you in law school," Jessa mumbled.

"That kind of childish taunting stopped working on me in junior high. We both know I had friends. We sat around and talked about how you magically passed criminal law after failing the midterm. Two tests in the class and you failed one, yet you ended up with an A." Every conversation seemed to bring them to a new, hateful low. Gabby despised who she was with Jessa and how the fury welled inside her and fought to break out. "Quite impressive."

"I studied."

One time. Gabby made a silent promise that she'd say this one time then let it go. She was closing in on forty and too old for this nonsense. "You stole the test, and when things got hot, you blamed someone else. What was his name? Grant? I can't remember because you got him expelled, the poor bastard."

"He cheated, not me." Jessa's words stayed calm, but she started to shift in the small chair.

All of it. Gabby decided to tell it all. To let Jessa know what shaped the negative view of her. "Then there were your private lessons with our contracts professor. Those certainly seemed to help your grade."

"What are you insinuating?"

Oh my God. "That you slept with him for a good grade. Wasn't that clear?"

"Sex shaming?" Jessa slipped into a chastising tone. "Really, Gabby? From you?"

"I don't care who you slept with or why." And that was the

truth. Gabby didn't have a problem with sex and clearly had made some questionable choices on that score in her life. She didn't judge others for that. "It was your condescending 'I get this class better than anyone else' bullshit. Strutting around like you were a genius when, in reality, you got an early peek at the test at the professor's house. That's a pattern with you. All that lying and cheating. It makes me wonder why you really left your first law firm. Did your partners catch you doing something very bad?"

"You're such a . . ." Jessa's voice cut off when she looked past Gabby. Whatever she saw made the color drain from her face.

The tone and mood morphed from taking shots at each other to what looked like panic. Gabby turned around, trying to see what had caused the shift. "What is it?"

"Is that Rob Greene? That reporter?"

"Probably. When you texted, I was already supposed to meet with him to talk about some information he gave me." Seemed reasonable to combine the two meetings, but then Gabby hadn't expected this odd, undefinable reaction from Jessa.

"Why here?" Jessa glared at Gabby. "Is the goal to ruin my reputation?"

"You're kidding, right?"

Jessa stood up, knocking her thigh against the table and making it wobble. "I'm not staying."

Gabby stood up at the same time. She followed Jessa's gaze and watched Rob ride his bike around a car idling in the right lane and then head for a rack with a lock in his hand. "That's your choice, but you might want to hear what he has to . . ."

Gabby couldn't get the words out. Couldn't shift fast enough to call a warning.

Tami's face flashed in her mind. That engagement photo. Her open and friendly smile. The break in Rob's voice when he spoke of her death.

Now it was Rob's turn.

The chaos broke through Gabby's shock. She started running as her mind shouted, *No, no, no.* "Stop!"

But it was too late.

The dark sedan that had been sitting, waiting, lurched to a start. Instead of going around or slowing down, it sped up and headed right for the bike rack. Rob looked up but never had a chance to run. The vehicle slammed into him, lifting him into the air, without hitting the brakes. A loud crack, then Rob flew over the hood. He crashed into the windshield before bouncing off and falling into the street.

The car sped up, tires squealing, and raced away.

For a second, no one moved. After a few beats, people watching from the sidewalk and in the café ran into the street. There were shouts about calling 911. People talked to one another and over one another. Someone mentioned CPR.

Out of breath and with injured ribs aching from the strain, Gabby pushed through the crowd until she reached Rob's unmoving body. Then she saw him. Eyes open and so much blood. It flowed from under his head, caking his hair. His hand lay limp, and his cross-body bag stuck out from underneath his side.

For the second time in only a few weeks, Gabby stared at a dead man.

Chapter Forty-Three

THE FOUNDATION

THE MEETING STARTED exactly on time. Tonight, they would vote on three action items. All called for assistance in dealing with evidence. Hiding it in one and creating it in the others.

The agenda included status reports on a few individuals they'd been watching, including the basketball coach who had been paying too much attention to his teen daughter's best friend. Offering to be her confidante. Grooming her.

Before that, another disturbing matter. This one required they listen to illegally obtained taped conversations between a professor and his teaching assistant, the third student he'd slept with in eight months then threatened when he thought she might speak out.

The bullying behavior shielded him from trouble in the previous two cases. One woman transferred, and another dropped out of college completely. This time, he had to survive an official university hearing on improper conduct and not just a laugh about "hot coeds" with his university president buddy over drinks in the office.

It had already been decided by the group that the professor's career would not survive the hearing. The university president was one of the group's targets as well. But the professor would lose his job, despite tenure. Settle for a quiet resolution, which would include payments to the young women involved. Not a perfect answer, but one that would take him out of power. Then the Sophies would watch him. This was his only chance, even though he didn't know they were allowing it.

But before that, another topic.

The leader started talking, knowing the room would go silent and all would provide her with rapt attention. "We have neutralized the growing issue."

They all watched her now.

"The reporter partners—both of them—now have been stopped. Neither can speak on the supposed existence of a group of vigilantes."

"Did he accept money?" The question came from the therapist who did testing and offered opinions in contested custody matters.

"There was an accident. Bike accident. He died on impact. Hit-and-run. There were witnesses, including Jessa, but no one agrees on what they saw, and the security cameras on the street didn't point to any identifying evidence. No license plates. No shots of the driver."

One hand went up. "The police will check garages for damaged vehicles."

"There's nothing left to find." The leader waited a few seconds, but no one asked any other questions. "As promised."

The greater good came first. That meant there would be

collateral damage from time to time. Regrettable but necessary. Rob Greene had been a problem for a while now. They had to stop him, and destroying his reputation hadn't been enough of a hint.

"I think we need to talk about our probationary member, Jessa."

"Is there another problem with her?" the child psychologist asked.

"Possibly."

Chapter Forty-Four

GABBY

GABBY'S GASPING TURNED to hiccupping breaths. After an hour answering questions about the accident she'd witnessed, she finally got to Liam's house. She barely made it to the kitchen before throwing up. Now she stood over the sink, mumbling and crying. She rubbed her hands raw. Scrubbed away the blood that dripped down the drain.

"Gabby?"

She could hear Liam's voice, but the blood wouldn't disappear. She took the brush and raked it over her skin.

"Wait . . . no. Stop." Liam came around from behind her. He knocked the brush out of her hands, sending it clanking into the sink, then held her fingers still as he turned off the water. He shifted her to face him. "What the hell is going on?"

"The blood."

His hold on her upper arms kept her from shifting around. She stayed still as his gaze searched her face. "There's no blood."

"Look at . . ." No red. Not this time.

"See?" He nodded toward the empty sink. "Water only."

"He's dead." The answer escaped on a whisper. She didn't have the strength to add more details.

"Who?"

"The car . . ." She closed her eyes and let her forehead fall against his shoulder. Blocking the vision that ran on fast-forward through her head zapped all her strength. "They killed his fiancée and now him. Two innocent people. All they wanted was to get to the truth."

Liam wrapped her hands in a kitchen towel and drew her close against his chest. "Who are you talking about?"

"Rob. Tami." There was no reason to hide his identity or separate herself from him. He'd died at the scene.

Liam didn't say anything for a few seconds. When he did, he sounded confused. "I'm not sure who Tami is, but Rob is the reporter, right?"

The unwanted movie reel started running in her mind one more time. "The car rammed right into him. Never even tried to brake or swerve."

"You were there?"

The questions made her head spin. She could no longer separate the facts she needed to hide from the ones she could tell. "I was meeting him."

Liam's hands flexed on her arms, but he didn't drop contact. "Okay, back up. You're not making any sense. I saw the news. The reporter died in a car accident."

"Not an accident. A hit-and-run." She grabbed on to the front of his shirt, willing him to believe her. "The car plowed into him. It was deliberate."

"Are you sure?"

"I watched it." The adrenaline had burned off, leaving her exhausted and craving quiet. "How many people have they killed?"

"'They' who?"

"There's a list . . . Baines is on it . . . or was. I think." She wasn't sure if she was making sense, but she kept trying. "What if they are getting rid of people who know?"

"Gabby, listen to me. I don't know what's going on, but you're safe here."

She shook her head. "You can't promise that."

"I have security. There's a doorman. Locks and security keypads." He exhaled. "Now tell me why you were meeting with that guy."

He stood so close. She could smell that distinct fragrance from his shower gel. The one she bought him every year for Christmas. The heat, the firm voice, his hands—it all comforted her. She'd been so careful, so protective of her secrets, but her defenses slipped. "He said he had information on Baines's death."

"Oh, Gabby . . ."

She couldn't stand to see the pity in Liam's eyes. It telegraphed how pathetic he found her right now. But she pushed on, trying to ferret out what he needed to know from the bits she needed to hide to protect him. "He has this theory. It's more than that. It's all this research about all these wealthy, connected men. They're all dead, including Baines."

"You know that sounds—"

"Ludicrous, I know. But I'll show you." She looked around

and realized that wasn't possible. "I don't have the documents here. I had to hide them."

The now-familiar look of concern spread over his face. "You have been under incredible stress. Baines's suicide. Walking in on it. The fighting with Kennedy . . . and me. The break-in, and now you watched a man get hit by a car. It's too much."

"You think I'm paranoid."

"No, Gab. I think you're burying your grief and sadness by running around after . . . I don't know what. Conspiracy theories? That's not like you, but I get it. Everything feels out of control right now."

She let her head fall to his shoulder again. Moved in closer, cuddled against him, promising that she would pull back in a few seconds. "I don't know what to believe."

"Believe me when I tell you I won't let anything happen to you," he whispered into her ear.

"You hate me."

"Never."

"I can't believe this." Kennedy's shout bounced off the kitchen walls. "You're disgusting."

Before Gabby could defend herself or explain that this only amounted to friendly comfort and nothing more, Liam jumped in. "Your mother—"

"Can't control herself."

Exhaustion gone, Gabby pushed away from Liam. "Kennedy, stop. Not today."

"You're all over each other."

The disappointment in her daughter's voice nearly knocked her down. "No, that's not what's happening."

"I can't stay here." Kennedy ran out of the room and up the stairs.

Gabby agreed. She needed Kennedy somewhere out of the fray, not in the group's direct line of fire. But they'd gotten that note to her. Gabby tried to reason it out and come up with the right answer . . . even if it meant risking Kennedy's hatred.

Chapter Forty-Five

JESSA

JESSA MADE IT back to the office, but she didn't know how. She'd been told to take a few days off as the Darren fallout cleared up, but today she needed to come in and sign a report the judge had requested from her. The question of her being removed had been settled with Ellie's admission that the allegations had been a lie. Now every issue had to be included in the record.

Jessa couldn't concentrate. She sat in her oversized leather desk chair and rocked. A slight movement that calmed the voices screaming in her head.

Rob Greene, gone. He poked around. He compiled information. He convinced Gabby, or, at least, made her believe he wasn't the conspiracy whacko the press made him out to be.

Now he was dead. Splattered in the street. Run down in what some called an accident. But Retta's warning kept repeating in Jessa's head. *I doubt he'll be a problem much longer.*

They killed him. She didn't know for sure, but she *knew*. He got too close, talked to the wrong people, refused to back down even after they incriminated him and ruined his career.

Alternate justice. Deep down, she understood that might include giving the green light to killing someone, but she'd thought about killing pedophiles freed by rogue juries or serial killers. The worst of the worst. Not some random reporter who walked into the middle of a secret case he didn't know was being assessed and decided around him. He didn't deserve the same ending as a man who hated and abused women.

She'd benefitted from the group's benevolence. Rob Greene had paid for questioning its existence. The juxtaposition of who they were and who protected each of them had her head spinning.

She leaned back in her chair and closed her eyes. Tried to block any thought about the people who loved Rob. About the pain caused in the name of confidentiality.

Her phone buzzed, and her assistant's voice came over the line. "You're needed in the conference room to review and sign."

Jessa didn't want to move, wasn't even sure she could. She'd been late coming in today, trapped by police questions and Gabby's vacant stare. No one scolded or questioned her about her tardiness. She hadn't mentioned what she'd witnessed or the halting steps that drove her morning.

How did she explain that she might have caused a man's murder? She'd talked about him with Retta, drawn the line between him and Gabby. She'd created all of this . . . at least in part.

Her phone buzzed again, and this time she got up without answering. She lumbered down the hall, forcing her legs to move even though the sudden heaviness in her muscles had her shuffling.

She opened the conference room door. It took a few seconds for the scene in front of her to register. Balloons and streamers. Every person who worked at the firm, from the support staff to the new associates to the partners, stood around, holding champagne and smiling.

There was a cake on the table and a banner stretched across the back wall. She tried to focus on it, but her brain kept misfiring.

Covington raised his glass. "Congratulations to Covington, Irving and Bach's newest partner—Jessa Hall."

Chapter Forty-Six

GABBY

GABBY MADE THE choice. Kennedy leaving would be safer than staying. Gabby hated that simple truth. Problem was, she didn't have any steam left to explain the potential danger to a disbelieving and hostile teen. The note found her at school, but Gabby realized the real target of that unveiling was her. Someone wanted Gabby to know they were watching.

Message received.

With Kennedy out of the fray, Gabby thought she might have a chance to figure out how she'd landed in the middle of this mess and, maybe, before anyone else got hurt, make sense of all the things Rob had told her.

Gabby dug deep into a well of patience that bordered on bone-dry. One attempt at being tactful, then she was playing the mom card and handing down a *because I said so*. "You are not taking the bus."

"Not *Don't go, Kennedy*." Kennedy used her most obnoxious mimicking voice to deliver that one. "What you're worried about is me being seen on a bus?"

Oh, child. Gabby wished *she* were on a bus right now. Anywhere but standing there, engaging in this ridiculous fight. She'd vowed to go easy on Kennedy as she worked her way through the information that had gotten dumped on her . . . but there were limits. "It's about safety. It's not safe for you to travel alone."

"Right." Liam nodded. "You need to stay here."

Okay, no. She and Liam weren't quite on the same page about this. "Maybe leaving isn't a bad idea, in general, but not alone on a bus."

Liam stared at her. "Why the change?"

Rather than chime in, Kennedy snorted. Gabby found that more annoying than the snide tone.

"Things have been . . ." Gabby tried to send Liam a silent message. "Weird around here."

Kennedy snorted again. "See? She wants me gone so you two can—"

"That's enough," Liam said, sounding very much like a dad, which was becoming a habit for him. "Your mother is right."

"Of course you'd side with her."

To his credit, Liam didn't flinch. "Your mom witnessed an accident today where the man died."

"What?" That quick Kennedy's mood shifted. Her voice morphed from dramatic teen anger to one tinged with genuine concern. "Were you hurt again?"

"No, baby. I'm fine." Gabby cupped Kennedy's cheeks, desperate not to burden her daughter with one more worry, then gave her a quick kiss on the head. "But between the break-in and the accident, nothing feels safe here right now. I need you away, in school, with security, and not near DC."

Kennedy slouched as if some of the fury ran out of her. "Is that really why? You told me that you weren't together, but you were kissing."

"No, we weren't," Liam said.

Gabby shook her head. "That's not what you saw."

For a few seconds, Kennedy's gaze traveled back and forth, assessing and decrypting. "You're pretty transparent. The way you two feel for each other." She visibly swallowed, looking young and vulnerable and too breakable. "I see it now."

That was not a road Gabby wanted to venture down. "That's in your head."

Kennedy rolled her eyes. "Right. I'm the one with the problem."

Gabby decided she preferred angry Kennedy to suffering Kennedy. "Your attitude needs a lot of work."

"But we agree I should go, so I'm leaving." She picked up the bag she'd packed and slung it over her shoulder. Her roller bag was in her other hand and ready to go.

Some of the tension had eased, but the energy in the room felt off. Awkward and uncomfortable. Liam was the one to break through it. "I'll take you back to school."

Kennedy shrugged. "No thanks."

"You don't get a choice," he said.

"And you don't get a say," Kennedy shot back. "You're not my father."

"Yeah, I fucking am." No anger or yelling. Liam stated it as a fact and made it clear he intended to stake a claim sooner rather than later. "Technically." He hesitated, clearly realizing the importance of what he'd just said. "So tone it down, and no more yelling and swearing at your mom."

"You just swore at me." Kennedy sounded stunned at the thought.

He shot her a half-smile. "Sorry about that. You're not the only one trying to adjust to a new reality here."

"Thanks for that, Mom." But she didn't sound angry either. More like she, too, was testing out the new world and finding it confusing but maybe not awful.

Gabby was ready for a few hours without either of them. "You two can spend the drive bonding over how awful I am."

Kennedy nodded. "Okay."

"That works," Liam said at the same time. "But you should call one of your friends. Have them come over. I'll be back by morning."

"I don't want to involve anyone else." Her friends had offered whatever she needed—distance or support—ever since she found Baines's body in his study. She wasn't great at reaching out and asking for help. They interpreted her inability as a plea for space when she really didn't know what she needed other than a few answers.

Liam looked like he was going to reach out and touch her arm but stopped. "I'm not comfortable with you being alone right now. Not today."

"I'll be in the car while you two figure this part out." Kennedy took off, without a goodbye or a hug.

Gabby tried not to react to being dismissed without so much as a hug. Her emotions bounced all over the place, and she tried to remember the sensations were even worse for Kennedy.

Gabby put on a smile for Liam. "You better go. With the mood she's in, she'll probably hot-wire your car."

"I'll talk to her. She's wound up and misinterpreted—"

"Thank you."

Gabby smiled as Liam picked up his gym bag and searched for his keys. It disappeared the minute he walked out the door. She welcomed the silence. She planned to fill it with research.

She needed to be ready because she had no intention of being the next victim.

Chapter Forty-Seven

JESSA

THREE DAYS AFTER the big office partnership surprise, Jessa wanted to go back to Faith's house, crawl into bed, and hide. Life came at her in flashes. She got thrown from one end of the spectrum to the other—shocked, lost in horror, as she watched a man get hit by a car, then flooded with happiness at finally meeting her goal at work.

The up-and-down exhausted her. But rest and hiding weren't possible. Tonight called for a celebration . . . or so Faith insisted. She'd reserved a small party room at one of their favorite Italian restaurants in Bethesda. It was supposed to be a surprise, but when Jessa refused to change back out of her lounge clothes after work and into something party-like, Faith rolled her eyes and spilled the secret.

Now Jessa sat at the bar as she pretended to wait for Faith to show up and their table to open. She ignored the entrance of a notoriously late-for-everything couple, more Faith's friends than hers, as they snuck in the door and slipped into the private room.

"Congratulations."

That voice.

No way. If Faith invited him . . .

Jessa turned on her bar stool and saw Tim. That pretty face and stupid grin. He cried out to be slapped, and she toyed with making that happen. "For what?"

He frowned. "The partnership?"

"Right. I forgot how you knew about things happening in my office at the same time as, and sometimes before, I did." She turned back to her drink, pretending like the blackberry mojito in front of her was the most interesting companion in the world.

He shifted his weight from foot to foot but didn't leave. "I know you worked really hard for this. It's a hell of an accomplishment. I'm happy for you."

"Uh-huh." She took a bigger sip than intended and had to fight off a coughing fit.

"Look." He slid his arm along the bar and leaned down until their faces were only a few inches apart. "We should talk about what happened."

"When you dumped me because I failed to fulfill your expectations of being perfect and maintaining a shiny reputation that made you look better?"

The bartender's eyebrow rose. She seemed to be hovering, listening in, ready to take on an obnoxious guy, if needed. Jessa appreciated the support.

"It was a temporary separation. Everything I said made you angry back then. You wouldn't listen to reason or any advice, really." Tim shrugged in his *poor me, what was I to do?* way. "I thought you needed some space to figure out your work issues."

Somehow, he made kicking her out of the house they shared when *she* was at her lowest point all her fault. He really was begging to get slapped.

"'Temporary' as in 'be out by tomorrow.' Those were your words, or close, right?" Jessa asked.

She thought she heard a slight hiss, the kind that might come with a dramatic wince, coming from the direction of the over-invested but supportive bartender. The reaction fit the moment.

Tim shook his head. "That's not what I said."

"Oh, Tim." Jessa shifted in her seat, putting a bit of room in between them and forcing him to stand up straight again. "My dear Tim."

"Okay, you don't have to—"

"No, you started this. You could have seen me sitting here and slinked out again, but you came over." With every word, she grew stronger. Power filled her. Rage turned to energy with the lethal force of a swinging sword. "So, for once, you're going to listen."

He let out a loud exhale. "Go ahead."

She thought about his abandonment. The hollow emptiness that left her reeling. His dismissal started a chain reaction, a screaming in her head that whined about how pathetic she was. A worthless loser who didn't deserve support. Then she thought about Retta and her warning and knew her mentor had never been more on target than in her assessment of Tim.

Jessa unloaded. "You need a woman who will hang on every word, praise you, stay in the background, and agree with everything you say. A pretty ornament who is allowed to have a life outside of you, but not much of one. Who enjoys a career, but only one that you approve of or even possibly pick for her."

"That's not who I am."

"It is, and I'm not her." She stood up, taking her drink with her. "I need a man. A partner. Someone who appreciates and supports what I want. That's not you. It could never be you."

He wore that *you're beneath me* expression that she'd once pretended didn't exist, but now it was all she could see. Retta and Faith had been right. She deserved better.

"Fancy speech. Are you done?" he asked.

"With you?" She downed the rest of the drink, deciding that it was too tasty to waste on throwing on him. "Yeah, I'm definitely done with you."

She had her friends. She had Faith. She had the Sophie Foundation.

A surge of energy pumped through her. Emboldened her. She carried a secret. The kind of secret that gave her power, and she refused to waste one more minute of her life on guys like Tim.

Chapter Forty-Eight

GABBY

GABBY SPENT ALL night rereading the papers Rob gave her. She'd copied them and stored one set in a safety-deposit box and mailed one to her great-aunt to put somewhere safe near her, along with orders that she give another copy to her attorney for safekeeping.

The woman had a backbone of steel. If Gabby had asked Great-Aunt Isabel, the woman who'd taken her in when her mom died, to drive here from Ohio and rip down the house with her bare hands, she would have. She was that woman. Strong. Decent. Pissed. A retired prosecutor and the reason Gabby had gone to law school in the first place. The perfect ally.

Gabby looked at the copies she'd kept. Wrinkled, with sticky notes posted all over them. Each death reviewed, analyzed, and cataloged. The companion list Tami had started about possible related cases led in more directions, added more fuel, but finding common denominators across the cases proved futile.

Some cases had one therapist, but just as many cases had other professionals, or none. Different judges and lawyers. Some of the deaths had nothing to do with a court case or divorce. In every single one, if she looked long enough, she found a nasty rumor or an allegation that eventually got dropped.

Melissa Schone popped up regularly as the detective, but she didn't have a say in calling cause of death in any case. Gabby also had to admit that Schone worked in the area. Her being involved in most of the Maryland cases made sense. They'd happened in her jurisdiction. A Dr. Downing had also made more than one appearance when kids were involved.

"This is getting me nowhere." She let out a yell loud enough to echo through the duplex but not loud enough to draw attention from the neighbors. She chalked the shouting up to a form of primal scream therapy.

With her concentration waning, her mind traveled to Liam and Kennedy. She'd worried about them all last night during their drive to New York. More than once, she'd called and talked with both of them. Not about important things like parentage or danger. About easy topics like Liam's terrible taste in music and strange love of fast-food tacos.

With them safe, or as safe as they could be, Gabby tried to focus on the papers in front of her, but the ink blurred. Her mind made connections then abandoned them. Her notes were a jumbled mess of nothing, or possibly something. The work involved meticulous knot untying and string making.

"This is impossible." She made the comment to the silent room as she stood to refill her coffee mug. Maybe the sixth cup would help her experience a breakthrough . . . or finally convince her that Rob saw a conspiracy where none existed.

Coincidences happened. All of that buildup amounting to

nothing was possible . . . except for his death. She'd tried to find more information about that on the Internet, but details were sparse. Everyone seemed to agree he'd died in a tragic hit-and-run that likely would never be solved. A horrible story but not an unheard-of one in a city.

"Even I don't believe in that much happenstance." She walked to the floor-to-ceiling windows and looked out at the front of the building.

Police. The word flashed in her brain as she watched two police cars pull up. Then a van turned into the horseshoe-shaped entrance. She couldn't read the side of it or the jackets of the people scurrying around down there, but she made out the word *forensics* as police filed into the building.

A woman got out of a sedan. She flashed something and talked with two men in suits. When she glanced up toward the window, Gabby jumped back, out of sight.

Melissa Schone, way out of her jurisdiction this time.

The police were here. At Liam's building. Walking into the lobby. Were they coming for her here? This didn't feel like another turn at asking her questions about Rob's death. The forensic squad suggested something bigger. Something other than a break-in and death that touched her tangentially but was not *about* her.

An itchy sensation of being watched, hunted, filled her. Hot, on fire, restless. Each one rolled through her.

I have to warn him, just in case. She reached for the phone to call Liam right as the doorbell chimed.

Chapter Forty-Nine

JESSA

THRIVING. JESSA COULDN'T think of a better word to describe how her life had turned. Being a partner came with a huge raise. More responsibility but less pressure for billable hours. She had lawyers beneath her now. People who answered to her.

She put a deposit down on an apartment. She loved Faith, but living together in a one-bedroom would get old fast.

She leaned back in her big chair and looked around her office. The bouquet on the edge of her desk, delivered less than an hour ago, came from Retta and Earl.

She'd spent her entire life on the outside, looking in. Never the smartest or the most popular. Attractive but not the prettiest or the thinnest. Always aching to be a bigger presence, more in control of the conversation—the person other people looked at and said, *I want to be her.*

Getting here required sacrifices. She'd made some decisions others would find questionable. She saw them as necessary. The climbing, the worrying, the jealousy. It had all paid off. Finally.

That's why the idea of being in a club and not knowing the rules didn't bother her. She'd work around them, follow them, or defy them, as needed. Being on the inside gave her that clout. Opened up possibilities.

She heard the knock on her office door and smiled. Her two-o'clock appointment had arrived, and she couldn't wait for this face-off.

Stan, Darren Bartholomew's attorney, stepped inside. He'd left his usual blowhard, *you're not worthy of my time* persona on the street, because this Stan was a subdued Stan.

She didn't bother getting up. "I bet you didn't think you'd be having this meeting anytime soon."

"About that." His forced smile hesitated while looking at the bouquet before settling on her face. "Of course, you know everything that happened in our case was a result of zealous client representation and nothing personal."

She treated him to a dramatic wince. "A backpedal that hard must hurt. Did you injure yourself?"

"Excuse me?"

She remembered he didn't have a sense of humor and tried again. "The motion you filed called me incompetent. That felt personal."

He laughed as if they were sharing a joke. "Darren is a difficult client. You know how it is. You're a partner now. You've had to deal with—"

"Is this an apology?"

"I didn't think I needed to make one." Some of the lightness left his voice. "Lawyers spar in the courtroom all the time without ruining their private relationships."

She was tired of being lectured to. "We don't have a relation-ship."

"Right."

Before he could say anything else, she jumped ahead. "I'm not leaving the Bartholomew case."

"There's been a lot of damage in this matter. Ill will and bad feelings. Things said that are difficult to forget. It might be bet-ter to have fresh—"

"No." Her fingers tightened around her pen. A little more pressure and she might snap it in half. "I will remain in as guard-ian ad litem, and if there are any more personal attacks against me, or my character, I will fight back."

He scoffed. "There's no need to—"

She waved her hand in the air. "You may leave."

Chapter Fifty

GABBY

GABBY STARED AT the search warrant. "You're a detective in Maryland. We're in DC."

"Right." Detective Schone stepped out of the shuffle of people in and around the condo to talk with Gabby. "That's why there's a mix of Metropolitan Police and Maryland police here. Out of professional courtesy and as part of a long-standing multijurisdictional agreement, I've been given the okay to take the lead on the search."

None of this made sense. Her house, maybe? But Liam's?

Gabby wrapped her fingers around the warrant, crinkling the paper in her fist. "What are you looking for? Why are you here?"

"Is Mr. Fielding home?"

A nonanswer, but it said a lot. She was coming after Liam. Gabby couldn't stop it, but she tried to slow down the hunt. Give him time to get here and call his attorney. "He's on his way back from New York."

Detective Schone stopped looking around the room and focused on Gabby. "Why was he there?"

Nope. Gabby refused to play the game where she answered questions and Detective Schone dodged hers. "Is this about Baines or the missing money . . . ?"

"You should wait outside."

"No."

Detective Schone smiled as if she enjoyed every minute of the discomfort she caused. "Excuse me?"

"He's not here to watch over this, so I will." Not that she had any right to be there. They could remove her, but she got the sense Detective Schone wanted her to experience every second of the building panic and insecurity. Gabby couldn't stop anyone or ask a bunch of questions. She had to stand there and take it, even though seeing strangers paw through Liam's personal space made her queasy.

"Are you claiming to be his attorney?" Detective Schone asked.

This woman always had a comeback. This time, Gabby refused to get sucked into a nonsense conversation that rambled in circles. "No, but Baines was my ex-husband."

"Why do you assume this search relates to his death?"

Something in the detective's tone touched off an alarm bell. It rang and clanked inside Gabby's head, warning her to tread carefully. To not talk too much or say the wrong thing. "What else would it be?"

"You were attacked. You witnessed a hit-and-run. There are money issues of concern at Mr. Fielding's business." The detective shook her head. "Drama follows you."

Her, not Liam, which is why this search still didn't make any sense. Courts didn't approve search warrants just to shake people up. Judges needed probable cause, which meant something Gabby didn't know about touched off this sudden need to poke around Liam's life.

But she couldn't shake the conclusion that all of this circled back to Baines and his death. Gabby didn't see the connection, but she glanced around, analyzing what the team picked up and placed in bags and boxes to try to get a clue. "Are you saying those incidents are related?"

"I'm saying no matter where there's trouble lately, you show up."

Gabby snorted at that. "I was thinking the same thing about you."

A younger man came down the stairs holding an evidence bag. "Detective Schone? We found this."

"What is that?" Gabby could make out a bottle and a needle but not the label. While she didn't know every part of Liam's private life, she didn't remember any health issues or medicine. She'd been staying at his place for three days and hadn't seen him take a single pill.

"This?" The detective's smile grew wider. "This is a very big problem for your brother-in-law."

Chapter Fifty-One

GABBY

"**WHAT THE HELL** is going on?" Liam stood in the doorway, overlooking the carnage of what once was his pristine family room. He held a duffel bag and his keys as two officers took positions on either side of him.

Battling sensations of relief and sympathy warred in Gabby. She wanted to say something smart. Something that would ease the tension. Nothing came to her. After a few seconds of collective staring, she forced a few words out. "Thank God you're here."

"You're back from New York," the detective said. "I'm going to need to ask you a few questions about your trip."

"Answer mine first." He took a step forward, but one of the officers held him back.

The detective waved the man off. "It's fine. Mr. Fielding can come in . . . for now. But take the bag."

Liam stood there as the police stripped the duffel off his shoulder and motioned for him to go farther into the room.

"We're going to need your car keys. Your vehicle is covered by the search warrant," the detective added.

The situation worsened with every word. Gabby struggled to keep from retching. Anger. Full-fledged rage. That was the only way to survive the constant spinning: to focus all her energy into rugged indignation. "Stop treating him like he's a criminal."

"He's being treated like anyone else would be in this situation." The detective motioned for the officers to keep searching.

"I'm here now. What is this about?" Liam stopped scanning the room and stared at the plastic bag in the detective's hand. "What are you holding?"

"Methohexital."

Liam shrugged. "Okay. And?"

"A sedative."

Confusion flooded Liam's face. "Where did you get it?"

"I was going to ask you the same thing," the detective said.

Gabby wanted to jump in, to use that expensive legal education to save or at least protect Liam, but the fuzziness in her brain refused to clear. Sedatives. Searches. She hated that her secrets had ripped her family apart, but now she wondered about what Liam had been hiding.

"The sedative isn't mine." Liam stepped back as if standing too close to the bag might incriminate him. "I take a vitamin and a pill for high cholesterol. That's it. No other medicine."

The detective made a humming sound. "That's an interesting response."

"Why?" Anxiety churned inside Gabby. She had to bite back

all the words floating through her brain. Babble could only cause trouble here.

But the detective kept talking directly to Liam. "We found the bottle and syringe in your bathroom upstairs."

His bedroom . . . but drugs? Gabby couldn't make those pieces fit together no matter how many times she pulled them apart and tried to make them fit together again.

"Not possible." Liam pulled his cell out of his pants pocket. "I'm calling my attorney."

"Go ahead. Your sister-in-law is holding the search warrant."

Liam froze. "Why me? What brought you here?"

"We have information that you may know more about your brother's death and your sister-in-law's attack than you previously told us." The detective's gaze traveled from Liam to Gabby and back again, assessing the stunned reactions in real time.

Liam shook his head. "What the hell? You can't be serious."

"Who gave you this so-called information?" Gabby asked at the same time.

The detective shook her head. "Not relevant."

"Of course it is." Gabby hated this woman. Yes, she had a job to do, and a difficult one, but she seemed to relish it. She enjoyed launching into lectures and delivering killing verbal blows.

"A second review of the autopsy—which you, Mrs. Fielding, requested and fought for—showed a needle mark at the back of Baines's neck." The detective raised her hand, showing off the needle in the bag.

Liam sat down hard on the armrest of the couch. "Wait . . ."

"A mark in your *brother's* neck."

"Yeah, I'm aware of who Baines is." Liam spaced out the words. Talked slowly and firmly even though he looked ready to drop.

"You mean *was*. And toxicology confirmed the presence of a sedative." The detective still held the bag in the air. "Which is why this is important."

"You're saying . . . What are you saying?" Gabby stood there unable to move. She listened as the detective jumped to impossible conclusions. She might be overplaying her hand, but it sounded like . . . God, Gabby couldn't put the horror into words.

"Nothing yet." The detective didn't break eye contact with Liam. "But sedating your brother would make it easier to kill him."

"No." Gabby didn't know she'd said the word until she heard it. "You are looking in the wrong direction."

The detective faced Gabby. "And easier to subdue you, Mrs. Fielding, when you just happened to walk in on the scene."

Chapter Fifty-Two

JESSA

CHINESE FOOD NIGHT. Faith had declared cooking a bore and ordered takeout. The noodles smelled good, and if Jessa could crush the whirling sense of dread that something terrible lurked in the darkness, waiting to lunge, they'd probably taste good.

"For a person who's in the middle of the best week of her life, you sure seem distracted," Faith said before scooping up another bite out of the white container in her hand.

Right. Time to act fine. Jessa had been doing that on and off for most of her life. "I'm a big-time partner now. You need to talk to me with respect."

Faith rolled her eyes. "You're not my partner."

"I've seen your previous girlfriends. I don't think I'm your type." Faith liked the put-together, buttoned-up-but-naughty-underneath type. The kind who knew what they wanted and didn't flail around, waiting for disaster to strike.

"Wrong type of partner, but you're not that either. What's up?"

Faith sat sideways on the couch, with her shoulder pressed

into the cushions and her focus on Jessa at the other end. That made it tough for Jessa to duck or hide her expression or even sigh without it being dissected.

Jessa gave up on trying to eat and set the food container on the coffee table. "Do you ever get this dragging feeling, like things are about to take a turn for the worse? Like it's all too good and a downslide is inevitable?"

Faith groaned. "Jessa, no."

"What?"

"Do not mess this up. You are on a roll. You are on the verge of having everything you ever wanted."

"Or momentarily lucky." But she knew *lucky* was only a small piece of the explanation for having her world turn right again. Retta. The backdoor dealing. The evidence that appeared or disappeared at her whim. Right now, the whim worked in Jessa's favor, but what if it didn't in the future? What if the tiny bit of control she'd wrangled out of her job and her life crashed down on her?

"Look, I know you're still upset about Tim, but that scene in the bar was spectacular. The fact you dismissed him. Literally waved him off." Faith laughed. "The bartender will be telling that story for a year."

The thing Jessa couldn't say nagged at her. On seeing Tim, she'd experienced a spark she didn't want, followed by a momentary pulse of power . . . then it faded. "I thought I'd feel something else when I saw him."

"Hate?"

Jessa ignored the sarcasm. "Sadness. We left so much unfinished between us."

Faith stabbed at the noodles but stopped eating. "Is this some sort of fear-of-success thing? Because if it is, we're going to buy you a self-help book or get you a therapist. You can't self-destruct right now."

"I don't intend to."

"But . . . ?"

"I'm assessing who I am and if I can be better." Some days the Sophie Foundation sounded like the right avenue. Other days the weight of the responsibility pressed down and Jessa's resolve wavered. She had blind spots in her personality. The surge of power fed a sleeping need inside her, but that might be the worst part of her.

Right now, she could recognize the light and dark, the undertones and the pitfalls. Potentially losing that perspective scared her. She didn't want to be Darren Bartholomew or his family or anyone like them.

Faith balanced the container on her lap. "Explain what you're thinking."

"You're a compassionate person. You worry about the women at work. You fundraise and do whatever you need to do to be there for those families." Faith had dedicated her life to untangling people—mostly women and children—from abusive, shocking, and unthinkable situations. She pleaded and educated, pulled and guided. Jessa couldn't imagine believing in anything so much. "I've been here and watched you struggle with depression and devastation when a woman went back to her abusive spouse."

"I suck at losing, but people are not always ready for help. They want to believe their partners can change or feel too guilty or are too beaten down to believe they deserve better. It's a long-term process to break that hold."

"And that pain and damage, it pricks at you, tries to change you, but somehow you manage to separate their decisions from your life and move forward." Jessa envied the skill. She looked back and reran every failure in her head, tortured herself with the instant replay of her poor decisions. "Look at the Young case."

Faith sighed. "That family name seems to keep coming up lately."

"You were accused of hiding the mother, helping to kidnap the child, and you stayed calm. Instead of flipping into denial, you stood in front of the press and gave a speech about how easy it is to violate a protective order and put everyone's attention back on the husband and abused spouses." Jessa stepped around the accusations and the ongoing sense more than one family lawyer held, that Faith had assisted the wife in some unknown way.

"Maybe, but I still couldn't save them. He killed them. I'd bet everything I have on that, and it's the debilitating part of the job that I keep to myself. Thinking about it, reliving it, would make doing this work impossible." Faith shook her head. "But I'm still lost about what any of this has to do with Tim."

"Nothing, really." Jessa rested her head against the cushions. "It's more like . . ."

"Just say it."

I'm a terrible person. "I watched a man die. Before that, I listened to Gabby unravel." *A vicious, empty person consumed by my own needs and getting ahead.* "I felt nothing."

"Okay." Faith sat up a little straighter. "I think it's more that you don't let feelings in."

"I feel pretty annoyed at Gabby. That snuck in without trouble. You pointed out that we were close once. Not like Gabby thought, but . . . I don't know. I guess I'm just in this position where good things are happening, but all around me there's chaos."

"Except with me."

"Yeah, you're solid. You're always solid." Decent, smart, beautiful, focused. Jessa should hate her, but Faith never judged. She accepted and supported, providing the type of unconditional love Jessa had spent her whole life chasing.

Faith shrugged. "You're not empathetic, in general."

Ouch. "That makes me sound like a psychopath."

"No. I'm not making a good-person-versus-bad-person comparison. I'm saying you don't take on other people's anger and pain. You watch from a distance, not letting their emotional upheaval unbalance you." Faith leaned forward, reaching her hand across the blanket, and touched Jessa's foot. "It's not a bad thing. In fact, in your job, where you deal with so much hate and the blurring between fact and fiction, it's a necessity."

"I wish Gabby hadn't appeared in my life again." Dealing with her, getting stuck between the position she wanted at work and a past relationship she wanted to forget, had thrown Jessa off stride and she never regained her balance. She'd been tripping and crashing and wallowing in self-doubt and a borderline case of self-loathing since she'd signed that damn affidavit.

Faith sighed. "She makes you feel bad about yourself. She always has."

"So she's the jerk." Jessa really wanted Faith to agree.

"When one person in a duo thinks you're great friends and the other doesn't, it's sort of incumbent on the one who doesn't value the relationship to safeguard the person who thinks you're friends. I don't mean stay friends with someone you don't like or don't want to invest in, but to come up with an exit strategy that lets you both walk away as close to whole as possible."

"And I didn't do that." She'd failed spectacularly in her handling of the Gabby issue. No question.

"You dealt with the problem by pretending she didn't exist, which is human. Maybe not the best way but understandable. Who wants drama? Unfortunately, now you're experiencing the fallout. She views you a certain way, and you hate it."

As the enemy. Worse, as irredeemable. "All true."

"Her life is on a downswing, and yours isn't."

And still Jessa felt nothing. "How does that help me?"

"Honestly, it's time to break contact. It's been years, so, maybe, forgive yourself and move on." Faith picked up her chopsticks again. "If she needs help, let her find it somewhere else. You can't solve Gabby Fielding's problems."

Chapter Fifty-Three

GABBY

FOUR HOURS. **THAT'S** how long it had been since the police started questioning Liam. He walked through the locked door separating the waiting room from the rest of the police station, then nothing. Hours and hours of nothing.

All she could do was stare at the entry pad and steel door, willing it to open and for him to come out. By the end of the second hour, her nerves had ramped up, and she fantasized about clawing and punching her way into the restricted area, but she stayed still. Didn't draw attention.

When she looked up for what had to be the hundredth time, Liam stepped out. He would have rushed right past her if she hadn't stood up and blocked his path. "Finally."

"Gabby?"

They met in the middle of the busy room. He tugged her out of the fray when a man came in yelling. She couldn't make out the words, but something about his neighbor. Officers listened and one escorted him away from the crowd of vending machine users and waiting visitors and into a back room.

She didn't see anything else because Liam walked them outside. They traveled down the ramp to the parking lot before he started talking again. "What are you doing here?"

"Waiting for you."

"Probably not a great idea." He glanced up at the station's second-floor windows before looking at her again. "They think I killed Baines. Hanging out with his ex might send the wrong message."

She refused to apologize for caring about him. Past or not, he was family. "I'm still your sister-in-law."

"Right, and if they think we're having an affair, they might think we colluded and killed him."

The words screeched across her brain. The leaps, assumptions, and what-ifs Detective Schone would need to make to land there were breathtaking. The thought of being under that much scrutiny without knowing it shook Gabby. "What did the detective say?"

Liam leaned against a metal railing. "She asked a hundred questions, all trying to pin me down and blame me for Baines's death."

Every time Gabby tried to make that connection, to think it through and play the timeline, her mind balked. "That's unhinged. Why would you hurt your brother?"

"Because we were fighting over the business." He broke eye contact for a few seconds, watching a police car pull into the lot and park instead. "That's what the emails say."

She stepped in front of him, forcing him to deal with her. "Emails?"

"They have a series of emails where I threaten Baines to tell me about the missing money or I'll force him to talk. They say other things, too . . ."

"About us?" The tight control she had on those secrets, on those days when she grappled with the worst decision she'd ever made, unspooled.

Liam stuffed his hands in his pants pockets. "They think I followed through on my warnings but then lost control or something went wrong. Either way, the view is I went too far and killed Baines, then set the scene to look like a suicide."

Liam as a killer. *No, no, no.* "You can't . . . but . . ."

"None of it's true, Gabby. I didn't know about the money until after he died. I never sent the emails. Hell, I've never seen those messages before." He kept moving around, almost frenetic, as he explained. "This is . . . I don't even know what this is."

"It will be okay." She had no idea if that was true, but she thought he needed to hear it.

"Will it?" He yelled the question. "What the fuck is going on? I'm serious. What? This is absurd. It's like I'm being set up, but who would do that? And why?" He shook his head. "I can't even grieve for Baines because I'm too busy being pissed at him and at . . ."

At me. She knew that's how he wanted to end that sentence. "Liam . . ."

"Is someone trying to destroy me? I would never hurt Baines or you. I mean . . ." Words flowed out of him as his voice bounced back and forth between confusion and fury. "That medicine bottle. The bogus emails. It's all garbage."

Evidence faked and planted. She remembered Rob's notes and all his warnings. All those cases where a piece of information would appear, somehow missed and suddenly the only answer to fill in a blank. "Can't they track that sort of thing and verify the emails are fake?"

"They're not inclined to help me right now. They want me to confess so they can clear the case, answer the concerns you made public, and be done."

She'd pushed and talked about bringing in lawyers and the media. She lit a match, and now it burned in a line headed straight for Liam.

"This is my fault," she said, knowing they both thought it.

He pushed away from the rail and moved closer to her. "Of course not."

"The fake evidence . . ." Rob had warned her about this happening. Exactly this.

Liam wasn't listening to her. He kept talking. "I don't know what's going on in that detective's head, but they didn't arrest me, and right now I'm grateful for the breathing room. I need to find an expert to discredit the emails and prove I'm being set up. Clear my name then sue the fuck out of this police department for harassment."

"You think someone planted the evidence then tipped them off to point the finger at you." That happened. It was the only explanation.

"But how?" Liam shook his head. "The person had to get into my condo. Into my computer. The only two people in there are you and Kennedy, and neither of you did it. It really doesn't make much sense."

Only someone with power and access could accomplish this. Someone who could pay experts. "Earl Swain."

Liam frowned. "What about him?"

Maybe not him, but his wife. Loretta Swain, the woman with a secret society at her command. "The stolen bid. Maybe that pushed him over the edge. He has money, so I'm sure he has connections."

"I have money, and I wouldn't hire people to frame someone." Liam's flat tone told her how little he thought of her theory. "No, he doesn't gain anything by ruining my reputation. He battled with Baines, but Earl and I get along fine."

"Okay, but—"

"Sure, he wins a few contracts, but he's a guy who likes competition. And he's not unhinged."

She had to be careful. Liam appreciated practical solutions. He didn't go off on wild wanderings. He would have hated her searches and snooping. But Rob Greene had predicted all of this. He'd warned her. Nothing else made sense. Liam hadn't killed anyone. Hadn't threatened anyone. She may not have really known what Baines was capable of until it was too late, but she knew Liam. Him being set up was part of a bigger plan. A message to her.

She got it, but she didn't intend to lie down and take it. They'd gone too far. Liam and Kennedy were off-limits. She'd get the evidence to clear Liam's name and protect her family. Somehow.

It was time for her to fix her mess.

Chapter Fifty-Four

THE FOUNDATION

MOST OF THE Foundation's meetings centered on reviewing files and discussing actions. The work didn't leave a lot of room for socializing or enjoying time together. The women came in and sat down, dealt with hard topics, sometimes life-and-death topics, all while locked under a dome of security and trapped in the tension of the moment.

This once-a-year meeting had a different focus—a silent auction. The annual event they used to raise money for their public causes. Truth was they campaigned all year. They had a full-time staff of two, unrelated to the confidential backroom workings of the Sophie Foundation, who, along with volunteers handled the funding and paperwork, regulations and thank-you notes.

All year, the charity pushed an agenda aimed at assisting and, at times, rescuing women and children in danger due to violence and abuse within the home. The silent auction was the charity's shining moment. A dressy event catering to influential people with fat bank accounts, willing to pay five thousand dollars for a table then vote on various donated items. The event allowed for mingling and talking and check writing and, most important, the honoring of the Foundation's namesake.

Retta both loved and hated this weekend. She'd vowed long ago not to let Sophie and Claire Kline be forgotten. Not to let the reason for Sophie's murder—her abusive, mean, pathetic husband, Adam—slip into the quiet safety of history. This event ensured the accumulation of needed funds, but it also prevented anyone from "cleaning up" Adam's reputation or even mentioning his name without also stating in a full-throated and clear voice that he was a dangerous animal who'd killed his wife and child.

He was not forgiven. His history would not be scrubbed clean, or the edges dulled by the weight of time or insulting explanations. Any attempts at blame-shifting or suggesting Sophie had invited the violence or played a role in her own killing would be squashed and the person voicing the opinion ridiculed.

This year's auction had one other benefit, and that one related to Jessa.

"She understands the importance of this event." Retta had engaged in more than one conversation with Jessa on that topic, so she felt comfortable making that blanket statement. "She believes I will be assessing her ability to work a room and assist in fundraising for the charity."

A hum of agreement traveled around the room. Heads nodded.

"I have been clear that the charity and the confidential work we do are two very different things, so she won't know she's being assessed by all of you as well."

"I'm concerned about your wavering support. The vote to

consider Jessa for membership didn't pass twice. Only your lobbying enticed some of us to agree during the third round," the child psychologist at the back of the room said. "Her history suggested we be wary, and now, suddenly, you are. I'm wondering what's happened between then and now."

"My support hasn't changed. She has the potential to be our most devoted member, and we need new members. Women who are making a name for themselves and in a position to help." Retta reiterated her reasons for thinking Jessa should have a seat at their table. "Remember, I have a personal history with her. I've seen her struggle. Seen her be ruthless, when needed."

"I understand that, but—"

Retta refused to concede the floor. "Her history prepared her for this type of work. She knows the world isn't fair and has always been willing to bend the rules to get what she needs. She has the fire and the drive. She can justify what others might find unjustifiable. She only needs time to prove herself to us."

"And until then?" The psychologist pressed her point. "You know if the concern keeps growing, we'll need to—"

"Yes." Retta didn't let the other woman spell it out. They all understood the severe price of failing during probationary status. "I know exactly what will happen."

Chapter Fifty-Five

GABBY

GABBY NOW UNDERSTOOD the phrase *fish out of water*. She'd been to the Sophie Foundation annual auction fundraiser before. Baines moved in this crowd. Back before the company hit its stride and the money started rolling in, he yearned to belong, so even when they couldn't spare the donation, they paid for a table and placed bids.

She remembered winning a spa day one year because Baines insisted that they bid on something, and an overpriced afternoon at some place she'd never heard of was the cheapest auction item she could find. The next year she'd nearly fallen over in relief when someone outbid Baines on a flashy new speedboat.

This year, even with her place in this crowd relatively secure, she had to deal with a steady buzz of awkwardness. No one knew what to say to the former spouse of a man who'd allegedly committed suicide. The lack of chitchat worked for Gabby. She didn't want to share her sadness and confusion with anyone in this room.

She attended because she couldn't miss the opportunity to stalk Loretta and her husband. She'd done some investigating, and they were the two who started this charity. The Foundation was their baby. If Rob was right about the vigilante side work the Foundation did, then the Swains were behind the attempts to upend Liam's life. Gabby wanted to show them she was right there, standing in the way and ready to fight.

Jessa Hall stopped circling around her and walked over, wearing a black sheath that managed to look both simple and extraordinary at the same time. It showed off her long, lean frame, and the halter top with the slim bow around her neck added a certain charm.

Jessa handed Gabby a glass of champagne and cradled one of her own. "Congratulations on being the hot topic of whispered conversation."

Gabby scanned the crowd and saw more than one pair of eyes quickly avert her gaze. "That's more your move than mine."

They stood, looking out over the country-club ballroom and the small groups of people hovering around each auction item. Gabby depended on the swell of music and the mumble of conversation to drown out their words. The fake smiles they both wore would perform most of the heavy lifting in convincing the room they got along without sniping at each other.

"Not many women would think attending a big, flashy party a few weeks after their husband died was a good idea." Jessa gave Gabby's dress a quick up-and-down. "Did you win that in the divorce? Pretty."

Gabby ignored the instinct to glance down at her lacy navy

cocktail dress. "Former husband. And even your firm thought I should be allowed to keep my clothes."

"An oversight, clearly. But I'm confused how showing up here is a good idea." Jessa took a quick sip. "Unless you like the attention."

"Remind me, are you a big hero or a dangerous, incompetent wreck this week? The press can't seem to pick a side. A debate among people who clearly don't know you."

Jessa smiled and gave a little wave to someone across the room. "You're not a lawyer, so you don't—"

"I actually am." Gabby turned to face Jessa then, thinking a confrontation, small as this was, might make her shut up.

"Right. You live off your dead ex's money and don't work, so—"

"You seem obsessed with my ex-husband. Should we talk about that?"

Jessa didn't say anything for a few seconds. "Why are you here?"

"It's a good cause." The adrenaline racing through Gabby slowed. She could do this. A party like this, being among the people possibly manipulating behind the scenes to rip her family apart, demanded all her control and acting ability. Lucky for her, pretending and tolerating were the two things she excelled at lately.

Jessa's smile widened. "There's a rumor in my office that your brother-in-law was questioned in Baines's death."

One hard smack. That's all it would take to knock that satisfied grin off her face. Gabby really thought about entertaining the crowd and doing it, but Liam needed her. He didn't know it and certainly didn't believe it, but he did. "Did you start that rumor, Jessa?"

Jessa drained her glass and picked a second glass off a passing tray. "You're exhausting."

The slight dip in her voice. Gabby heard it and dove in. Hate Jessa or not, Gabby had to try. Had to push and, maybe, save Jessa from her terrible choices . . . this time. "This group you're in or trying to get in with is very dangerous."

Jessa's saccharine smile finally slipped. "I have no idea what you're talking about. It's a charity. Nothing more."

"For someone who habitually lies, you're not very good at it."

Jessa's fingers tightened around the thin glass stem. "You should stop this."

Not as collected and in control as she pretended to be. Gabby saw that truth and noted it, not sure what that meant about how deep Jessa had gone into the darkness. "Define 'this.'"

"Poking around. Buying into outrageous conspiracy theories."

People walked around them. A few said hello, but no one tried to get in the middle of their conversation. Jessa thrummed with a strange sensation. Gabby thought it might be panic, but maybe that was wishful thinking. Jessa lacked that little voice that warned about going too far. About crossing a line.

If this group's activities shook Jessa, Gabby feared for Liam and Kennedy. The only option might be to work *with* Jessa, which sounded almost too daunting to be possible.

Gabby lowered her already soft voice to a whisper. "Tell me why the police are going after Liam."

"Ask the police."

"What is your group afraid I'll find? Bigger question, why did Baines need to die?" Gabby watched the swagger drain from Jessa. "If you don't know, tell me how I can find out."

"You're insane." Jessa's fingers clenched and unclenched around the glass as she talked.

She'd found a weak spot. Gabby didn't know why or what had Jessa spooked, but she leaned into it. "This group has killed people. Mostly men. Mostly shitty men. That doesn't make killing okay, but it does explain why no one is questioning the deaths. They view the loss of life as a benefit to the community, which is how I assume you justify murdering people."

"You should stop drinking."

Gabby hadn't taken a sip, and they both knew it. "I have a list of names. Men who have died under suspicious circumstances."

Jessa stepped back and ran right into one of the many men in navy suits walking around the room. They both apologized before Jessa turned her anger back on Gabby. "Maybe you need a hobby."

Unraveling. Gabby saw it and heard it. With anyone else, she might have used more care, but she knew this was a temporary opening. Jessa's defenses would rise again, and she would rally. Gabby had a limited amount of time to get through.

Loretta and her husband watched from across the room, so Gabby sped up. "Baines made mistakes—some big ones—but he wasn't a pedophile or a rapist. He didn't attack women, which makes me think making him a target was a mistake."

"You're talking in circles."

Jessa seemed to be staring at Loretta, so Gabby moved, blocking Jessa's view of the room, and forcing eye contact. "Imagine thinking you have the right to decide who lives and who dies. That you're entitled to hold that much power. Now imagine what happens when it all blows up."

Energy wound up inside Gabby. She was on the right track. Rob hadn't been wrong. He'd predicted Jessa was a new member. The ties to Retta, the sudden law partnership, and the uncharacteristic lack of crowing about the accomplishment made Gabby believe.

Jessa looked at the floor. "I'm going to mingle."

"You can't control this or lie your way out of it, but you can help me get to the truth."

Jessa's head snapped up. "We're not friends."

The air changed in a flash. The charge running between them and around them vanished. Gabby didn't know how she'd lost it. She made one last try to reach Jessa. "For your sake, I hope you realize when it comes to this group you need an ally. Let me be that for you."

"I'll pass." Jessa shoved her empty glass into Gabby's free hand and walked away.

Chapter Fifty-Six

JESSA

TROUBLE. SHE WAS in deep trouble. Jessa knew the second she saw Earl Swain headed her way. He cut through the crowd, barely acknowledging those who wanted to touch him or talk to him. Retta mingled and smiled across the room, acting every inch the perfect hostess. She didn't even glance in Jessa's direction, no matter how much Jessa willed her to do so.

Earl nodded toward the empty table to Jessa's left. She took that as an order to sit down.

He'd always been protective and decent with her, but people spoke with almost a sense of awe about his ruthlessness. He was known to take a position and refuse to bend during intricate business negotiations. He viewed compromise as a synonym for getting his way.

Covington talked about Earl's background in hushed, respectful tones. Retta referred to three brilliant brothers raised by a single mom who had to balance getting a nursing degree with boys running in every direction. One brother excelled at sports and went on to play in the NBA. The other was a well-known playwright. Earl was the successful one. The one who made the most money.

Earl succeeded because it was expected. Because his competitive drive didn't let him lapse behind his older brothers. That kind of determination made him tough and practical. And right now, he looked pissed. Other people probably couldn't tell, but Jessa could. The usual welcoming smile he wore when he saw her was nowhere to be seen.

He sat across from her and stared down a man who ventured too close but then wisely scurried away before bothering him. "Do you know what I would do to protect my wife?"

"Probably—"

"Anything." He folded his hands together. "Don't let the money and the big house fool you. She and the boys are everything to me. Nothing threatens them. Do you understand?"

His smooth, clear tone had Jessa's insides shrinking. He made his point without ever raising his voice. "I would never harm them."

"Gabby Fielding."

Jessa hated this topic. "Yeah, she's everywhere these days."

"The divorce is behind her." Earl glanced at Gabby with what looked like reluctant respect. "She's no longer in Baines's shadow."

"She doesn't believe he killed himself." Jessa blurted that out and regretted how much it sounded like tattling. The last thing she wanted was to come off as insecure in front of Earl.

He stared at Jessa, not saying a word. He stalled long enough that Jessa had to fight squirming. The relentless attention made her wither, but she tried not to let it show.

Finally, he spoke. "It sounds like Gabby is someone you should avoid."

"I'm trying." She never thought Gabby would pop up here. This should have been a safe non-Gabby space.

"Good." Earl stretched out in his chair. He had a medium build, but he managed to take up a lot of space. "You're on the verge of accomplishing the goals you set out for yourself years ago."

A topic change. Not a great one, but Jessa grabbed on to it. "I'm afraid to believe it."

"You plan and prepare. Swallow setbacks and other people's doubts. Make mistakes that derail you and try to break out of a life you never wanted before it can define you." He tapped his fingers against the table. His expensive watch caught the light. "Then one day, an opportunity drops in your lap, and you have to decide if you're willing to make the sacrifices needed to grab that opportunity."

Sacrifices. Retta had used that word, too. This wasn't a lawyer discussion. This was about the Foundation, or, more accurately, about the *other* work of some members of the Foundation. Jessa still didn't know what she could and couldn't say and to whom.

"It should be easy to take what you want. You ache for it. Dream about it. Taste disappointment and regroup. Find a new way." He made a fist. "But making that final jump is a different thing."

A lecture . . . a warning. She couldn't tell where this fell, so she made her position clear. "I already said yes to Retta's offer."

"Words are easy, Jessa. True sacrifice, the kind that will quench that thirst and make all your choices and all that drive worth it, is about action. About earning trust."

Forget a friendly conversation. This was a warning. His expression stayed open and friendly. His voice never rose, but her body reacted. Her nerves jumped to life, and restless churning started in her stomach.

She'd been caught messing up before. Her last law firm, the one before Covington, caught her lying to a client about documents being filed when they weren't and hours billed that ran a bit too high, and confronted her. Fired her. Agreed to a nondisclosure agreement and silence only when she threatened to expose a partner's habit of sleeping with every female intern. The younger the better.

This moment felt a lot like that one. Pivotal and life-changing.

She had to swallow twice before talking again. "Did I do something wrong?"

"That's a good question. Did you?" His eyebrow lifted in the same accusatory way his wife's did.

"Is this about Gabby? Because we're not friends." Jessa refused to get pulled under by Gabby's deadweight. "Our lives intersect in places, like it or not, and I don't, but that's all."

"Retta and I share everything. I support what matters to her. So your doubts about taking the next step are my concern because they threaten Retta, and I can't allow that."

Jessa hated that he saw through her and tried to hide her shifting thoughts. She wasn't someone who got bogged down in the "rightness" of a decision. If it worked for her, that was enough. But going full vigilante came with risks. She knew if someone in the group had to be sacrificed, it would be her, and signing up for that level of responsibility had her backpedaling.

"It's not that I think I can't or that I'm unworthy, but I've never been good at blind trust. I like to know what's expected before I jump in, think through the options, before . . ." She almost said *committing*, but she *had* committed, so she just let the sentence hang there.

"In other words, you only said yes so that Retta and others could rush in and save you. That's disappointing."

His frown. That tone. She'd grown up getting inundated with the *you failed us* vibe, trying and failing to make everyone happy, and she didn't handle it any better as an adult. The space above her left temple started to pound. A migraine would knock her flat before the night ended.

She tried to talk over the banging in her head. "That's not what I meant."

"Your reputation is intact. You're a partner in your firm, or will be as soon as the paperwork is done." He sat up, all signs of an informal discussion gone. "Did you think those were gifts?"

A ringing joined the banging. She struggled to keep her words clear and slow despite the chaos erupting inside her. "I fully intend to honor my pledge to Retta. I believe in the cause."

"What cause?" When she didn't immediately answer, he made a humming sound. "That hesitation is a problem."

She reached out and touched his arm. "I can do this."

He stared at her fingers until she moved them. "I'm not the one you need to convince."

Chapter Fifty-Seven

GABBY

SHOWDOWN. THAT'S THE only way Gabby could describe the scene when Retta came over to greet her. They shared an un-emotional hug, and both smiled, though Gabby thought vomiting would be more appropriate.

Retta stood back but kept her hands on Gabby's upper arms. "It's good to see you, Gabby."

"Judge Swain."

"The formality isn't necessary." She gave Gabby's arms a final squeeze then dropped her hands. "I haven't been your professor for more than a decade. You can call me Retta."

The law-school version of Gabby would have killed for that honor. Gabby knew better today. No matter what it might look like to the crowd, this was not a friendly chat. She expected it to take a turn, and fast. "I buried the awkward-and-unsure-student part of me long ago, but my gut reaction is to balk at the idea of being that casual with you."

"I remember a very different student. One who was always

learning and questioning. You didn't pretend to know every-thing, which allowed you to be open to discovering new ways of analyzing and assessing." Retta clasped her hands together in front of her. "Do you still question everything, Gabby?"

Gabby fought not to babble. She needed to keep her answers short and distinct, not show any sign of weakness. "When the pieces don't fit together, yes."

"That can lead to trouble."

There it was. The start of a subtext battle Gabby would never be able to win. She aimed for keeping up. "I rarely think of the discovery of the truth as dangerous."

"Snooping around, making up theories that you can't pos-sibly support with evidence. Those behaviors invite a kind of scrutiny that can turn your life upside down."

Not the most subtle threat. But if Retta came out fighting like that, she might have something to hide.

Gabby pushed a little. "For example, I don't buy into the idea that Baines killed himself. The theory doesn't fit with who he was or how he was in his final days."

Retta stopped talking long enough to say hello to a couple and nicely shoo them away. "If, hypothetically, you disagreed with the police and the medical professionals and the official cause of death, you would be alone. Vulnerable."

Vulnerable. Gabby hated that word as much as she hated the sensation and lack of control. "Truth is the most important thing, don't you agree?"

"Closure."

"What?"

Retta kept nodding to people who walked by, saying hello. "People need closure. Sometimes that means bending the truth."

"That sounds like situational ethics."

The whole conversation was surreal. They talked about menacing, awful things with happy smiles and warm waves.

Retta frowned. "When did we start talking about ethics?"

Yeah, that was the problem. For some reason, the judge didn't appear to recognize the subject. "Right and wrong. When you should cross the line or not."

"I fear I failed in teaching you, because there isn't a line. There's a vast gray space. What you'll tolerate and what proactive measures you take determine where you land in that space."

"I don't know, Retta." Gabby emphasized the other woman's first name, making it clear for this discussion, at least, she was not a student being taught about some new theory. "That sounds pretty convenient. Like an excuse for not following the rules."

"Who sets the rules?" Retta's smile reappeared.

"Isn't that obvious?"

Retta sighed. "No, but your answer brings us back to the idea of danger."

Her family's safety meant nothing to Retta. Gabby didn't have to guess. Retta was making that clear.

"We all have secrets. The things we did, decisions we made, that changed us. We push them down, bury them deep, cover them with other truths and greater needs. Hope no one knows." Retta shrugged. "But someone always knows, and that's not a bad thing. It guarantees balance."

"Sort of an 'if you do X, then Y happens' thing."

Retta nodded. "Well put."

"Is it? That sounds like one big, horrifying game to me." Like sending a note to a kid, knowing it would turn her life upside down and push her to an awful place. Retta was a mom. How did she put other kids in danger and still sleep at night?

"It's a good thing we're only discussing a hypothetical." Retta winked and walked away.

The conversation proved one horrible truth to Gabby. Like Jessa, regardless of the potential fallout and collateral damage to others, Retta slept just fine.

Chapter Fifty-Eight

JESSA

THREE DAYS LATER, Jessa sat in Retta's conservatory. The glassed-in room overlooked the expansive backyard and a pool too pristine to use. Not a towel, pool toy, or human in sight.

Today wasn't about the auction. This counted as day one of Jessa's official training to join the group. She bumbled her way through most of her interactions with Retta, hoping to say and do the right thing. The facts she didn't understand about the organization, who was in it, or exactly how the work got done, struck her as huge holes she needed to fill.

They'd already engaged in a few minutes of filler conversation. Done the whole tea-versus-coffee thing. The anxiety burning through Jessa signaled it was time to jump in. "Is the group publicly tied to the charity in any way?"

"No, not publicly. I always think of our private group as the foundation behind the Foundation. Two distinct organizations with very different priorities and values. One files paperwork and is subject to all sorts of disclosure laws. The other not beholden to any sort of formal rules or regulations."

Not the kind of details Jessa had hoped for, so she tried again. "So none of the members attended last night?"

"A few did." Retta crossed one leg over the other. Today's pantsuit was an emerald green and fully professional, as if she'd just stepped off the bench and into a designer's swanky dressing room. "But I wonder why that matters to you."

"I'm inquisitive." When Retta's expression didn't change Jessa knew that wasn't the right answer. "I'd like to know who else is in the group. That's a normal reaction, isn't it?"

"You know what you need to know at this point in the process."

She was off-balance and flailing, but she was starting to suspect that's exactly what Retta wanted. Jessa felt the pull, like being reeled in until it was too late to shake loose. "How long is the membership process?"

"As long as it takes."

Okay, then. A conversation where she poked around for answers and Retta threw a roadblock up with every answer didn't exactly bring clarity. Jessa hoped a discussion of the cases Retta gave her to study might help. The fact scenarios were varied, some horrifying, dealing with children and abuse. One about a father who killed the man he thought kidnapped and murdered his daughter.

None of the fact patterns matched Baines Fielding's suicide, but Retta had already stated the group wasn't involved in that. Trying to reopen the discussion only invited Retta's wrath.

"I read the sample cases you gave me." Jessa didn't have them because that's not how this game worked.

She'd read the cases on a tablet Retta provided. One with

limited access and a keystroke program that mapped what she looked at and when. The whole process had been monitored, according to Retta, and as soon as Jessa read a file it disappeared. She couldn't go back and review anything a second time.

"The idea, like with law school, is to ask you a few questions and get an idea of how you process information. As your former professor, I have some idea, but you have legal and world experience now. It will be interesting to see how that maturity has shaped your views over the last fourteen years." A folder balanced on Retta's lap. She ran a hand over it but didn't open it. "Let's start with general concepts. How far would you go to keep a rapist off the street?"

Jessa wasn't ready for the question. "How far?"

"Would you accept a jury's finding? A judge's finding?"

"Yours, I would." That seemed like a safe answer.

Retta frowned. "Don't pander."

The pressure closed in on Jessa. The walls didn't move, and the air continued to flow, but a tightness wrapped around her chest. A crushing suffocation that had her fighting for steady breath. The confidence of being picked, of being in contention, gave way to a familiar panicked, out-of-control sensation.

Jessa rubbed her hands together even as the *you can do this* mantra that had been flowing through her head began to fade. "What are the options?"

"Why be limited to a set of possible punishments?" Retta shifted in her chair. The simple act served as a reminder that she wasn't trapped in this conversation. She could move, even leave, if she wanted to. "Remember, this is a different justice system. A private one that benefits the victims and recognizes that many people when faced with confinement would say, or do, anything to avoid punishment. How would you prevent that sort of threat to justice?"

Jessa had no idea. Every answer struck her as wrong or illegal or not strong enough. "I . . . You could . . ."

Retta let out a little sigh. "Would you vote to make inculpatory but irrelevant evidence disappear?"

Jessa attached to the *irrelevant* part. "Yes."

"Would you manufacture evidence?"

"What type?" The interrogation technique reminded Jessa of law school. She didn't love being under fire, but she could handle questions. Those gave her a chance to see where Retta might want her to go. She could fake it . . . or redirect the questions to ones she could answer.

"Why does that matter?"

"Do I create the evidence? I don't understand how this would even work."

Retta stared at her, as if assessing how much information to provide. "We have members, in law enforcement and laboratories, with the power to impact the formal justice system. Scientists, forensic experts, and others who are sympathetic to our cause. Some judges who will make certain rulings or assist in jury selection in a nontraditional way."

Jesus. That suggested large numbers of people who could be activated to serve the group's will. A conspiracy that extended into different disciplines.

Jessa weighed the cons of taking a position. Answer wrong

and . . . Hell, she didn't want to think about the consequences. "If I knew someone was guilty, I wouldn't, in this parallel system, let a technical violation of the law keep a person from being punished."

Retta frowned. "Tepid."

"I prefer to think of the strategy as careful."

"In this case, the same thing." Before Jessa could respond to that, Retta moved on. "Could you vote to pressure witnesses, pay them off, or even *find* witnesses you needed to prove your case?"

She knew the answer Retta wanted now and gave it to her. "Yes."

"Could you, if you saw no other way, look at someone who had engaged in a series of horrible acts, and say that they had forfeited their right to freedom?"

Jessa thought about Darren and his threats. About some of those case files Retta provided, all filled with abusive men. Killers. Pedophiles. The facts made the answer very easy. "Yes."

"Could you vote that they forfeited the right to continue their behavior?"

Such careful wording. All the blame fell to the person accused of acting in a certain way. No mitigating circumstances, no questions about fairness or evidence. That leap, huge . . . daunting, tested her resolve. "You mean kill someone? How is that possible?"

"Again, we have people who assist us. Others, for specific acts for which we don't have a resource, are contacted through sources, are paid, and never know who handed down the sentence or why."

Hired killers. Could she really mean that? This was more than evening the playing field and eliminating technicalities. This hubris allowed for death sentences. Sitting in judgment of other humans and deciding their fate based on information in a file.

Jessa needed to know more. "But if these other sources get caught—"

"They don't."

She thought about Gabby and that new article about the break-in at her house. "But if they, say, were in someone's home and the owner came home, would they attack or even kill the person? Are you okay with that type of collateral damage?"

For a few seconds, Retta just sat there. She didn't respond or take the question out of a hypothetical and into real life. Tension pounded on them when she finally spoke. "The most important rule—the number one rule—is to protect the group's work. What we do is bigger than any nonmember or member, even me. That means recognizing the gravity of the work through confidentiality, secrecy, careful selection, studied decisions, and, if needed, personal sacrifice."

The last sentence hung between them. They wouldn't hesitate to sacrifice her. She could be signing on as potential fodder for their vengeance machine. Their exit strategy.

Jessa asked the one question she had avoided. "Now that I know about the group, about the actions you take, am I a liability?"

Retta didn't blink. "Nothing is permitted to threaten the group, and that includes you."

Chapter Fifty-Nine

GABBY

GABBY STOOD AT Baines's front door, waiting for a police escort to arrive. She had a key and could walk right in again, but with all the scrutiny she decided to play by the rules. She regretted that decision when she saw Detective Schone get out of the car.

Any other police officer would be fine, but Gabby was not that lucky.

Gabby had come alone because she didn't think she needed to hire yet another lawyer to handle yet another part of her life. She already had a divorce lawyer bill equivalent to Kennedy's future college tuition that demanded attention. One was enough. But the idea of dealing with Melissa Schone one-on-one made Gabby rethink that choice.

Neither woman said a word as the detective opened the front door and escorted her inside. Gabby didn't wait around for idle conversation. She headed for the second floor but barely made it up three stairs before the detective started talking.

"We've subpoenaed your divorce attorney's file and notes."

Gabby stopped in midstep and looked down at the detective. "Nice try, but all of that is protected by attorney-client privilege."

"Not if your discussions include information about the commission of a crime."

"What crime?" Gabby tried to think if anything on the list Kennedy had asked for last night was worth being here.

"Your brother-in-law killing your ex-husband."

Gabby's hand tightened on the bannister in a grip that turned her fingers a chalky white. "He didn't."

"You're the one who insisted someone else was in the room." The detective glanced in the direction of the study. "We investigated and followed the trail to Liam."

This was the nightmare. She wanted answers, and the police had punished her for it. Worse, they were punishing Liam. "You're wrong."

"There was no sign of a break-in here the day Baines died, and the alarm was switched off. You and Liam had keys, as did your daughter, but we've ruled her out because she was at school." Detective Schone smiled. "Well?"

"Thanks for clearing my teen daughter." Gabby started walking again, determined to get to her daughter's bedroom and get this visit over with as soon as possible.

Detective Schone followed behind, laying out her case piece by piece. "You claim you didn't know about the added security. Liam did. The alarm company technician says Liam was here when the system was installed. That would explain why he isn't seen on the house's security video. He would have known where the blind spots were."

"Wait a minute."

They stood on the landing, facing each other. The accusations piled on top of one another until they built into a sturdy stack. Not devastating, and nothing that shook her faith in Liam, but combined, they had impact.

"Money issues at the company. Baines hiding business dealings from Liam. Liam having a key. Liam knowing where the cameras are. No self-defense wounds on Baines because he likely trusted his brother and didn't see the attack coming."

So many coincidences, and all of it circumstantial but compelling. Even Gabby had to admit that. "Liam wouldn't—"

"Then there's the sedative illegally obtained and found in Liam's home, which he would have used to disable you, so you didn't see him lurking in the room." The detective's gaze dipped to Gabby's arm. "Have you checked? For needle marks? They should have faded by now, but did you back then? Was there a part of you that sensed what really happened in that room?"

Gabby forced her hand to stay at her side. Her ribs still hurt, but she'd checked after the police found the needle. Used her magnifying mirror and contorted and swiveled around until her body ached. Looked in case someone—not Liam—had debilitated her that way. She didn't see anything.

"Liam was at work when Baines died," Gabby said. "That destroys your entire theory."

The detective shook her head. "He wasn't. He says he had a meeting at a potential warehouse site, but the individual he was supposed to meet with never showed. We haven't been able to locate that individual to verify Liam's account."

The fact scenario got worse and worse. "You have this all wrapped up and solved."

"We're getting there." The detective walked past Gabby and stepped into Kennedy's room. She stopped by the window, but her gaze never stopped scanning. "Which is good for you. If Baines was murdered, you get your insurance. A substantial amount. A four-million-dollar policy."

The amount sounded huge, but her attorney had insisted she needed the insurance. Now that Gabby wasn't getting a dime, she wished her attorney had required a few more protections on the money. She'd be fine, but not where she was before. She'd already started looking for legal jobs she might be qualified for after all these years of not practicing. "That amount was to cover future alimony and expenses for Kennedy and—"

"And it provides motive."

"Wait . . . *me*? You just spent five minutes laying out a case against Liam."

"I never said we thought he did it alone."

The woman was relentless. And wrong. Gabby would be the first to admit she'd made mistakes. She'd been furious with Baines and his attitude during the divorce. She'd used old photos and recounted family stories to remind him of their life together, of all those years, but no plea blunted his need to grind her down.

But their marriage, all those years of friendship, meant something, and that's why she couldn't blindly agree to the suicide ruling. Now the entire family would pay for her persistence.

The juxtaposition of Detective Schone standing in front of a wall of posters, a sea of young male entertainers Gabby couldn't identify if someone put a gun to her head, made it hard for her to concentrate. "At least you finally agree Baines was murdered."

Detective Schone picked a stuffed teddy bear off the shelves above Kennedy's desk. She fiddled with something in the back of it.

"What are you doing?" Gabby thought about grabbing the toy out of the other woman's hands but settled for the question.

"We had to be proactive after *someone* ignored the police tape and came into the house a few weeks ago." The detective held up a black square. "Can't be too careful."

"A camera? What is wrong with you?"

"There's an easy way to end this, Gabby." Detective Schone dropped the bear on the desk. "If you agree and point the finger at Liam, all this goes away. You get your money. You get your life back. You might even get this house, depending on how the facts go."

A devil's bargain. Her financial well-being in exchange for Liam's life. Gabby couldn't believe the detective thought that game would work. "He didn't do it."

"This is a simple answer to a complex problem." The detective leaned against the back of the desk chair, looking calm despite the sick ideas she spewed. "I'm sure Liam can be convinced to confess if it means saving you and Kennedy. Then all those nasty secrets you want to keep hidden, stay hidden. No one knows your business. The dirty laundry doesn't get dragged out for all to see, dissect, and whisper about."

Nasty secrets. Gabby didn't know how she'd missed it before. It seemed so obvious now. "You're one of them."

The detective lost her satisfied smirk. "Stay focused."

"You're part of the group. You don't uphold the law. You use your badge and your position to maneuver around it. Manipulate it. Lie, cheat, do whatever twisted act, and then later rationalize it all as being in furtherance of some greater good." God, it was so clear. Gabby saw it all now. This woman didn't appear everywhere because this was her jurisdiction. She was there to manage and report back. She acted as Retta Swain's right hand. "Rob was right. The tentacles are everywhere, even in law enforcement."

"You sound paranoid, Gabby." But Detective Schone didn't sound as confident now. Her voice lacked that calming, almost condescending cadence that telegraphed she was in control.

Gabby hated her. Seethed with hatred of her. "It's Mrs. Fielding to you. And get out."

"Sometimes a car accident is just an accident. Sometimes it's more, and if it is, you should take that as a sign and be careful."

This bitch. "Clearly threats and killing aren't beneath you."

"I'm pointing out that secrets have a way of getting out, even those you think no one else knows. Ugly family secrets." The detective hesitated, clearly to make her point. "Think about that before you make your final decision."

The stockpile of evidence against Liam sounded strong, but Gabby now understood how easily evidence and circumstances could be twisted and distorted. She silently apologized to Rob for doubting him and to Tami for having paid such a steep price to find the truth.

The idea of condemning Liam to save herself . . . Never. But Gabby got the message. Comply or her life would explode into a nightmare.

She needed leverage and had an idea where to find it.

Chapter Sixty

JESSA

JESSA'S WELL-ORDERED AFTERNOON schedule blew up. She waited until her assistant left her office to unleash on her unwanted visitor. "You can't be here."

Gabby didn't flinch, but she did pace. She walked back and forth in front of Jessa's desk. "I left messages. When that didn't work, I hunted down your cell number, and you ignored those calls, too."

"Some people would take all of that as a hint."

"I would have gone to your house, but I have no idea where you live these days."

"That's a relief." Jessa tried to maintain the snide volleys because that had become their sole means of communicating, but she messed up and looked at Gabby's face—pale. Mouth in a line. Rigid muscles. A tiny bit of sympathy crept in. "What happened?"

Gabby dropped into the chair across the desk from Jessa. "Do you know Detective Schone? We talked about her before, right?"

"Unfortunately."

"She's going after Liam, my brother-in-law."

Jessa still didn't understand the reason for the meeting. "Okay."

"For killing Baines."

"Oh, shit." No more shots. This was serious and way out of Jessa's experience. She reached for a binder where she kept a referral list. "I'm a divorce lawyer, but our firm often pairs with excellent criminal defense—"

"He has a lawyer."

"Then I don't understand why you're here."

"Retta. The group."

Jessa leaned back in her chair and prepared to be annoyed. "Not this again."

"You can stop pretending it doesn't exist and that you're not a member or trying to be one."

Gabby was so sure, and so right, that Jessa wasn't sure how to react. Gabby took the existence of the group as a given and plowed forward from there. That left little room to maneuver, but Jessa tried to anyway. "This conversation is exhausting."

"Do you understand what's happening?" Gabby rested her arms on the desk and leaned in. Unspent energy buzzed around her. "They killed him, for whatever reason. And now Liam could go to jail. He would be ruined. Wrongly imprisoned. And my life . . . well, there are things I don't want . . . known."

Out of control. There was no other way to describe Gabby's fidgeting and rush of words. It was the best position for a nemesis or frenemy or whatever she was, but Jessa couldn't call up any enjoyment. Seeing the usually even Gabby frenetic and desperate didn't bring any satisfaction.

Jessa tried to wade through the words and figure out what exactly was happening in Gabby's world. "Is Liam really Kennedy's dad? I know I said the things about the rumors, but I was messing with you. Baines referenced getting a DNA test but then refused to talk about it. He made it clear to Covington that Kennedy was his daughter, and no one could take that from him."

Gabby nodded. "For all his faults, he did love her."

"Covington saw a way to score points and potentially turn a judge against you. He also wanted to eliminate Baines's responsibility to pay child support, which would amount to a lot of money, but Baines wouldn't agree."

"The Liam and Baines question is . . . delicate."

So, yes. "You, the person who drags up my past and pummels me with it every five seconds, have naughty secrets to hide about your brother-in-law? What a shock."

"I've made mistakes. I thought I had good reasons, but none of them matter now."

The honest response threw Jessa off. She had the ammunition and the power but lacked the will to use them. She'd never thought of herself as the all-talk, no-follow-through type, but that's where she landed when it came to Gabby, and that realization had Jessa fumbling.

She tried not to let it show, but she had to ask. "Did you ever think I might feel the same about my mistakes?"

"I'm trying to figure out why you care what I think about you at all." The comment came out more as an honest question than an accusation.

"Because you won't shut up about things I did."

Gabby's shoulders fell as a bit of the dramatic tension spinning around her dropped off. "I could have spilled every sin in a motion during the divorce. You filed your false affidavit, and I didn't come after you or your law license. My attorney begged me to write out what I knew about you and attest to it under oath, but I didn't."

"Why?" That's the part Jessa never understood. Because she would have used every salty bit. She would have gathered even the most inconsequential pieces of intel and shot them right at Gabby if their positions had been reversed.

"Believe it or not, I don't want to destroy you. I understand being raised with very little and having to fight for attention and resources. We both got to the same place—that law school—and figured out different ways not to squander the chances we had."

Part of Jessa hated finding this common ground. Holding on to the anger and being able to insult Gabby, both in silence and to Faith, had become habit. A more comfortable and familiar choice. "You constantly judge me."

"Maybe I do. That's fair. I didn't agree with your methods, and I still worry about how easy it is for you to lie, but my real problem was that you've always pretended your achievements were based on merit, and we both know that's not the truth." Gabby shrugged. "Then you abandoned me. When I said I was going to marry Baines during our last year of school, you cut me off."

"I don't want to be that person anymore." That was the bottom line. The words Jessa said but didn't act on, but she meant them. Here, she did.

"Then help me." Gabby's voice grew louder as she made the plea.

Jessa motioned for her to whisper, or at least not yell. "I can't."

"If this group is willing to frame Liam, an innocent man, what else are they capable of?"

Jessa refused to think about that. More accurately, she wanted to *stop* thinking about that. Since meeting with Retta, the idea of being shoved into the role of scapegoat for this group was Jessa's biggest worry. "Do you know Liam didn't do it? Maybe it was a heat-of-the-moment thing."

"He's better than both of us. And Baines didn't use the information about Kennedy against her, or Liam, or even against me in the divorce. So why would it have been such a big issue that it resulted in his death all these years later?" Gabby glared at Jessa as she said the words. And she couldn't have been clearer.

"Damn, Gabby. Your life is as messy as mine."

"Liam could go to jail. Hell, I could go to jail. Detective Schone made it quite clear I should support the allegations about Liam or risk something even worse."

"All I know is what I was told." Jessa sucked at tiptoeing through tough topics, but she tried. "No one I know had anything to do with Baines's death."

"Be specific. You're saying the group didn't order or arrange for his murder?"

"I'm not saying there's a group. You never heard me confirm

the nonsense you're spewing. Do you understand me? I will lie, cheat, and leave you flat if you try to say I did confirm." Despite the carefully chosen words, Jessa blew past the point of plausible deniability. If Retta found out . . . Yeah, Jessa didn't want to think about that. "But no hypothetical group I've ever hypothetically heard of killed Baines. You're wrong about that theory."

Instead of feeling anxious, Jessa experienced a pulse of relief. If anything awful happened to her, if she did end up being sacrificed for some greater good she still didn't fully understand, Jessa knew the one person other than Faith who might question her end was Gabby. A woman who would fight this hard, risk this much, for an ex who'd spent most of a divorce trying to destroy her would fight for the truth no matter what.

"Retta's husband and Baines were locked in some sort of business fight. Baines had stolen documents," Gabby explained.

"I don't know about that and don't want to." Jessa was already in too deep and breaking all the rules. "This conversation—the one that never happened—is over. We both said things that no one else can know."

"Agreed." Gabby rubbed her head as she stood up. "I know you won't to listen to me, but get out of that group now. Feign an illness. Fake some sort of emergency. Whatever you need to do. Save yourself before it's too late."

Jessa heard the concern in Gabby's voice and knew it was genuine. "I have it under control."

Gabby shook her head. "Neither of us believe that."

Chapter Sixty-One

GABBY

THE NEXT DAY, Gabby hurried back to Liam's house. She rushed inside and dropped her keys on the entry table, not expecting to see him standing in the middle of the family room. "Why didn't you wait? I came to the police station to get you."

She'd lost count of how many rounds of questions he'd answered. This time, his lawyers had stopped the meeting and shut off access. The next move belonged to the police and prosecutor, which meant they could drag him away at any moment.

"I needed to get out of there," Liam said. He still didn't move. His disheveled appearance, with his tie undone and hair sticking out here and there, suggested the questioning had not gone well.

"What's your lawyer saying?"

"The police are mistaking coincidences for evidence."

"Okay, well, that sounds promising." Not really, but he looked rough enough without her adding to his anxiety. "I guess."

She could see a storm raging around him, inside of him. His

usual unruffled, can-handle-anything demeanor faltered. His slumped shoulders pulled at her. She debated going to him, hugging him, telling him they'd get through this, but all affection carried a taint now. Could she touch him without creating an odd vibe between them, or worse, reigniting whatever feelings they once had for each other? Neither of them could afford that, but they did need each other. He might not see it, but she did.

"You're worried about the business, and I get it. But the news hasn't leaked. I've been all over the Internet, and there's nothing." She skipped over Jessa's offhanded comment at the charity auction because it suggested someone knew. Other lawyers. People in the courthouse. Someone with access to the prosecutor knew and had been whispering about Liam.

He stopped staring at the floor long enough to shoot a *what's the matter with you* glare in her direction. "Do you really think my lawyer and PR team can contain the scandal forever? Everyone will think I killed Baines. My own brother."

Detective Schone all but promised that. Gabby blocked that thought. It invited trouble, and they had more than enough of that right now. "No one that matters."

"Kennedy."

Her greatest weakness and his. She closed her eyes as pain whipped through her. She understood the reason for his self-punishment now. He'd just found out he had a daughter, all brokenhearted and really ticked off, but he had one, and she might believe the unthinkable and pull away forever.

Gabby had to pretend that wasn't a possibility for his sake and for hers. "She won't believe it. I know you didn't kill Baines and you would never hurt me."

Gabby held on to that. The evidence pointed one way, but the man she'd known for most of her life had never been a man who could kill for personal gain and without one ounce of remorse. Maintaining that trust took all her energy. The medicine bottle . . . planted. She also had once thought of Baines as steadfast and honest, but he'd turned. She'd watched it in real time. Lived through it.

Liam was different. He had to be, and she had to believe it. Anything else would destroy her, shatter any possibility of finding normal again.

Forgetting the what-ifs and *what could happen* issues, she started to go to Liam, desperate to offer comfort and steal a tiny bit in return.

"My sister," he said.

Gabby stopped, all thoughts of finding a moment of peace gone. "Natalie? What about her?"

He folded his arms in front of him and faced her. No more looking around or seeming dejected. His expression was unreadable and not at all open. "Detective Schone suggested Natalie's death may not have been an accident."

Oh no . . . The anxiety simmering inside Gabby ratcheted up, bringing darkness and panic with it. "She's reaching. It's what the police do. They find pieces of your past and try to make nothing seem like something. It's . . . I mean . . ."

"You're babbling."

His flat tone touched off a renewed round of alarm. She struggled to keep her voice even, not letting the outside mirror the terror inside. "I'm upset."

"About what?"

Pivot, pivot, pivot. The word screamed in her head. "How can you ask that?"

"Detective Schone told me you knew more than you were saying about Natalie's death. That you have information you were hiding from me."

Not this. Not now. Gabby tried to hold on. "I don't know what she's talking about."

He didn't move. "Tell me the truth about the fire."

Chapter Sixty-Two

JESSA

JESSA WAS IN hour four of running through scenarios and case examples with Retta. So far, getting invited to full membership with this group was harder than getting through law school.

They'd been locked in the office Retta and Earl shared at their home for most of the afternoon. Not the most enjoyable way to spend a Saturday, but Jessa couldn't exactly say no. Retta insisted this was part of the process for a potential new member of the foundation behind the Foundation, or whatever the group's official title was. Jessa was too tired to ferret that out.

Retta left to take a call with her sons. Something about a family trip over the holidays. The break trapped Jessa in a room full of books when she really wanted to find the kitchen and get something to eat.

Talking with Retta burned through Jessa's reserves. The granola from this morning was long gone. The anxiety and fear of being wrong stole her energy. So did the control needed to not ask about Gabby and Baines.

Gabby. Jessa wanted to put her old law-school chum and her problems in a box on the shelf and forget them. Gabby's problems were not her problems . . . but they did overlap. Sort of.

If the group called for Baines's death, a solution Jessa believed should only be used for the most extreme cases, she couldn't make the choice make sense. Retta lying about it only made her want to dig for more details.

Damn it, Gabby.

Jessa glanced at the open door to the hallway then back to the desk. No. She couldn't. She didn't even know what she'd be looking for. But still . . .

She walked around to the desk chair and pulled it out of the way. Another look to the doorway, but no one stood there. She listened, straining to pick up a hint of footsteps or talking. When she didn't hear either, she brushed her hand over the top of the desk, shifting one stack of papers then another. Looked like trade magazines and other nonsense but nothing important.

Of course, it couldn't be that easy. She hadn't expected top secret documents and a map of Baines's house to spill out, but come on. A little luck would have been nice.

After another peek at the door, she pulled out the long middle drawer. Did she have to worry about fingerprints? Just in case, she picked up a pen and used the end to move the contents around. Nothing but the usual paper clips and notepads in there. Breath mints. Random business cards. A key to . . . something. She grabbed it and immediately regretted it.

Okay, time to speed up. She opened the drawers on the left.

File folders. So many file folders. A quick run through the labels didn't turn up any names she recognized. Fine. Now the right side. And . . . bingo! A locked drawer.

She took out the key and opened the lock. A tiny voice in the back of her head said getting in had been too easy, but she kept going. Diaries? No, they were calendars. She tried to think if those would be helpful. A few small notebooks. She paged through one, and the scribbles weren't in sentences. Numbers and dates only.

The lack of incriminating evidence explained why the key had been so easy to find. This isn't where they hid things that needed hiding. There wasn't much of a need to lock down stuff that didn't matter.

She reached around, patted the inside of the drawer. Felt around, let her fingers smooth over every edge as she snuck looks at that damn door. Under it? Nope. Behind it? She felt . . . something. She winced at the thudding sound as she slipped the drawer out to get better traction.

Tape and another key. *Great.*

She shoved the drawer back in and jumped at the unexpected thump that sounded more like a bang when she closed it. "Shit!"

She froze, half expecting Retta to walk in with a gun in her hand. A few seconds ticked by, and the doorway stayed clear. She heard the muffled sound of Retta's laugh and realized the call raged on. "Thanks for staying in touch with your parents, boys."

Jessa stood up and looked around the room with the key

pressed against her palm. Something in this room required a
key. A small hard-to-find key.

Paintings. Furniture. Bookshelves. Her first thought was a
hidden safe, but she hoped not, because how in the world would
she find that? It didn't look like a luggage or safety-deposit key.
They had a few outbuildings on the property, but she couldn't
exactly ask for a tour of the potting shed.

"This is ridiculous." She went back to the desk, hoping something obvious would come to her.

The key had to matter, because why tape it to the back of
a drawer? *Important* didn't mean the hidden lock was in this
room. She didn't know what to try next.

"What are you doing?"

That voice. Retta. In the doorway.

The nightmare scenario. The worst possible ending to this
day. Jessa struggled to form words, to come up with a good
explanation—any explanation—for standing behind the desk.

Then Jessa remembered that weird little notebook she'd
picked up. Where had she put it?

Chapter Sixty-Three

GABBY

NATALIE AND THE FIRE.

Gabby had spent years avoiding and outrunning this topic. For a long time, she'd thought the secret would burn through her and seep out. But she'd kept it tucked away, separate from every other part of her life. Disconnected from her thoughts. When her mind did wander into the shadows and dip into that day and what she'd heard, she kicked the memory away. Out of the light. Now Liam was trying to reach in and yank it out.

"Gabby? Answer me."

Telling would ruin everything. Raise questions. Pile on more doubt. Make him hate her. Once she unlocked this box, she'd never be able to slam it shut again.

"The detective is trying to divide us. Work on our loyalty to each other." And that was true. Detective Schone knew the truth . . . which seemed impossible, or she guessed. She could have had access to attorney records, though Gabby couldn't imagine Baines sharing any part of this topic with anyone. It gave people power over him, serious power, and he never conceded the high ground.

"Why would she do that?" Liam asked.

"If you don't have my support, you're weaker. But if we're fighting, it plays into her wrong assumptions about us." Gabby tried to stop talking. She didn't want to tiptoe through any of this, and here she was stomping her way around the facts.

"Fill me in on the assumptions."

Gabby went with a version of the truth. The pieces were right, but if he fit them together he'd get the wrong picture. "She tried to get me to agree with her about you and Baines being in a fight. About you killing him. She told me to turn on you to save myself."

Liam shook his head. "Why do you need saving?"

That's not what she expected him to grab on to. She needed him angry about the violation of his privacy, not standing there all stoic, as if waiting for her to hurt him again. "The thing . . . You know, what she said. The thing about us. Together. Our past and what that meant. What we might have done. That we came up with a plan. For Baines. I don't know why we would, and we didn't, but . . . To hurt Baines and then kill him."

He shook his head. "You know you have a tell, right? The way you talk changes when you're worried or under fire. We've joked about it, but still you're trying to lie to me."

The babbling thing. She'd had it since she was a kid and never kicked it. She'd even taken speech training classes and saw a therapist about anxiety. Nothing helped.

"The last few weeks have been a terrible ride." An epic understatement, but not a lie. "I barely held it together, then Kennedy got so angry and refuses to be near me. Now she's gone. Then that reporter and the accident. The attack, which I still don't get. Was it a coincidence that it happened so soon after Baines . . . died? I haven't had the time or space to grieve for anyone." She could feel her nerves firing and her words picking up speed. The anxiety swelled, and she tried to take a breath. Tried to slow down. "Kennedy and I are trying. We talk at night, and—"

"Gabby."

A sharp, buzzing pain started above her eye. "Liam, please. This is all too much. We're not on solid ground. We can't do this now."

"I'm giving you a onetime pass." He held up a finger as if to emphasize his point. "You tell me now, and I'll figure out a way to let the fact you hid whatever this is from me slide. But this must be the last time, and you must tell me now. No more stalling."

Not this. The secret was too big, too horrible. "You can't control your emotions like that."

"Jesus, how bad is this? What do you know about Natalie, the sister I loved, took care of, and watched over, that I don't?"

"Nothing, really." The statement was true, but she heard the softness of her voice and knew she hadn't sold it.

"Gab, honestly. I'm a patient man, but you are testing my limits."

"You'll hate me," she blurted out.

"Do you really not understand what I feel for you?" His arms dropped to his sides as he took in a deep breath. "I'm forty-three.

I've been in love with you since I was eighteen. Through marriages and divorces, through lying about Kennedy and depriving me of a chance at being her father. I still love you. It pisses me off, but I do. So, no, whatever you aren't telling me won't make me hate you. I've tried. Trust me. The hate doesn't hold."

Breath left her body. Longing battled with despair. The rawness of his voice and the sweet honesty of his admission pricked at her. She whispered his name because that's as much energy as she could muster right then. "Liam . . ."

"Gabby, now. Please." The pleading moved into his voice. "It can't be as bad as you're making it sound."

Wrong. "Baines killed Natalie."

Chapter Sixty-Four

JESSA

THINK. SAY SOMETHING . . . *anything. You stood up for a reason. You're in front of her desk for a reason.* The directions ran through Jessa's head, one after the other. She needed to pick a few words, a simple excuse, and run with it. *Stay calm. Don't flinch.*

Gabby had called her a liar. Well, it was time to perform.

"Is your call over?" Jessa couldn't believe her heart could hammer that fast and that hard without her needing a hospital.

"The boys are headed out for dinner." Retta set two cups of tea on the edge of her desk. "Now tell me what you're doing."

Finding the damn notebook I tried to steal.

"Looking for a pen." Reasonable. An easy-to-remember excuse.

Retta looked at the penholder sitting next to her computer and lifted one out. "Like this?"

"I was looking right at it. Sorry!" Her voice was too high and tight. Jessa could hear it and fought to modulate it. "I think reading about murderers and pedophiles scrambled my brain."

"That's understandable. The fact patterns are meant to have an impact. We'll look at a few more with less egregious behavior and see what your thoughts are." Retta smiled. "May I have my chair?"

"Right. Sorry . . . again." Jessa stepped out from behind the desk, taking the time to look around, searching for the stupid notebook.

By the time she got back to her chair, her mind had switched gears. She'd put it back in the drawer. She'd never picked it up or moved it around. She had not screwed up.

But she knew none of that was true. She'd had it in her hand and then—

"Do you need a longer break?" Retta asked.

"I'm good." Scattered and a little panicked, but otherwise . . . not okay. At least Jessa thought her voice sounded more natural that time.

"I need your focus, Jessa. These matters are too important."

"You have it." Her foot hit on something. She ran the bottom of her shoe over the lump a few times and heard what sounded like a crinkle. She made a quick lunge for her coffee cup and banged it against the desk to cover the paper sound.

"Why are you nervous?" Retta used her full judge voice on that question.

"You said we were switching to different scenarios. I'm just getting ready for the change." She trapped the lump under the toe of her shoe and dragged it toward her.

"The nonegregious cases are the most difficult in some ways. They can be hard to assess, but the decisions need to be as grounded and justified as with harder fact cases."

"That makes sense." Jessa looked down and spied the crumpled notebook and put her whole foot over it to hide it. "But do cases like, let's say, business agreements or general arguments require a look from the group?"

"We don't deal with business disagreements or petty squabbling." Retta stared at Jessa for a few extra disquieting seconds. "Ever."

Another confirmation about Baines that pointed to Gabby being wrong. Jessa refused to ask a more direct question. She was taking enough chances.

She dropped the legal pad Retta had given her to take notes in the room only. One slip and Jessa grabbed the notebook, tucking it between the cardboard back and the yellow pages of the pad before sitting up and securing it on her lap.

The adrenaline pinging inside her refused to stop. Her breath rushed out, and she had to gulp a few times to keep from visibly panting. "Maybe I should use the bathroom before we start again."

"Of course." Retta finally looked away, but only for a second. "The notepad stays here."

"Sure." Jessa was halfway up, balancing the notepad and the hidden notebook, and a load of misfiring nerves. "Do you need more coffee?"

Retta tipped her mug to peek inside, and Jessa jumped on the opportunity to fix her mess. She slid the small notebook into her pocket. She'd secure it under her clothing in the bathroom, but for now keeping a hand over it should hide the extra bulk.

Retta shook her head. "I'm still good."

"Excellent." Between the inane chatter and the intense fear of being found out, Jessa's muscles had tightened with tension. She waited for a wave of exhaustion to hit her.

"And Jessa?"

Shit. Jessa turned around right at the doorway to the hallway. So close to freedom. "Yeah?"

"We haven't discussed this, but it should be clear. Stay away from Gabby Fielding and her ridiculous theories about Baines's death."

Jessa intended to do exactly that . . . very soon. "Done."

Chapter Sixty-Five

GABBY

"WHAT ARE YOU talking about?" Liam's voice sounded more stunned than angry.

Gabby knew that would flip after a few minutes of explanation. But she needed time. Spitting out a family-destroying secret like this took preparation. She'd had three years, but since she'd never intended to tell she wasn't ready. "Can we sit down?"

"No."

Okay, fair. "I'm going to back up so that you can understand all of it."

"I don't care how you tell me, just tell me because right now I don't know if I should kick you out of my house or take you somewhere for therapeutic help."

She tried to remember how to breathe. "You think I'm making it up."

"I fear you've had some sort of break."

"Look at me." He hadn't looked anywhere else, but that's not what she meant, and she thought he understood. "Do I look unhinged or out of control?"

"Just tell me."

A calmness she'd never expected fell over her. She'd spent years running from this topic, burying it, and trying to pretend it away. She'd assumed if she was ever forced to tell, the impact would be the equivalent of a crash landing. Chaotic and fumbling, racing and terrifying resignation.

"Baines always talked a good game about becoming a millionaire and getting invited to the right parties. The drive started out as wanting to be in a place where we didn't have to decide between heat and food on a weekly basis, but it grew into something very different," she said, trying to lay a foundation.

Liam didn't move. "I was there. I know how much financial security meant to him. To both of us."

But he didn't. For Liam, the need and determination remained healthy. His competitive nature had never tipped over into a can-never-have-enough pounding need.

She tried to make the disclosure clear. "Our marriage, which was already built more on nostalgic love and deep friendship than romantic love, began to falter."

"I don't get what this has to do with Natalie," Liam said.

One had grown out of the other, but he wouldn't understand until she'd guided him through all the steps. "He became obsessed with having enough money to start the business with you. You were both working at other places. Baines struggled because he wanted to be in charge and could be belligerent to those who were. We didn't have any money back then. Neither did you. Then your aunt died, and the impossible became possible."

Liam nodded. "She left us enough to buy our first warehouse and some land. Enough to get us started in a business of our own. And?"

She could tell Liam was running out of patience, so she tried to speed up without missing the important pieces. "You two got starter money. A lot went to charity. And the remainder, including ongoing royalties from the children's series she'd written, went into a trust for your sister."

Liam shrugged. "She needed extra help."

Gabby knew the truth. The family lived on the edge of danger. Their father's antics had bankrupted them. They'd lost a house and friends. The constant uncertainty had impacted Natalie the most. She'd grown up scared and wary. With absent, uninvolved parents, Natalie hadn't gotten the services and help she needed, even though so much would have been provided by the state if her parents had reached out.

The learning issues compounded Natalie's tendency for self-isolation, and the unraveling sped up the older she got. Her increasingly cloistered life and crippling anxieties demanded intervention. The money helped because it paid for a house and services. For therapy that Natalie used only on and off because her paranoia would flare and she'd block everyone, except her brothers, out of her life.

Here was the hard part. The unforgivable part. "But if anything happened to Natalie, the money from the trust went to you and Baines."

Liam shook his head. "No."

"No?" She knew she had those facts right because she'd sat in on meeting after meeting about the estate and about Natalie's care.

"He didn't kill her for money." Liam stepped back, continuing to shake his head. "We took care of her. We were her guardians, but more than that, her protectors. For her whole life."

The Fielding brothers. One of the reasons Gabby loved them both so much was because she'd seen them with Natalie. No one could make fun of her or hurt her. But Baines eventually broke her trust in the worst way possible.

"Baines started to . . . blame Natalie. She called him a lot. Took up a lot of his time."

"We didn't care about that." Liam practically shouted the denial.

"*You* didn't. You saw Natalie as a loving sister and accepted the responsibility. Baines began to think of her as a drain. I saw the toll her demands took on him. Natalie, fatherhood, work, me. It was a lot for him to handle. So, I tried to be the one Natalie went to, to be the go-between, but after so many years of leaning on the two of you, especially Baines, she couldn't switch gears. Not fast enough to suit Baines."

"You make him sound like a fucking monster."

She didn't say the obvious response. When it came to Natalie, at the end, he had been.

"A man started coming to our house. Baines would go outside with him, into that little shed we had at the back of the place we rented in Bethesda during the construction on our house." She'd never seen Liam so pale, almost listing, as he stood there. "The guy was creepy. The kind of man who looked right through you, and you realized he was nothing but an empty, evil shell. No empathy or feelings."

Liam still didn't move. She wanted him to sit or lean against something. To prepare him for the blow she'd only partially landed so far.

"One day I followed them. Listened outside." The memory ran in Gabby's head. She could see it and tried to blink it out, but it shouted at her, demanding her attention. "Baines talked about how Natalie was running through the money too fast. How the royalties weren't what they'd once been. How there wouldn't be enough."

Liam went back to shaking his head, as if he could physically stop the words from penetrating his mind.

"The other man said something about spreading a rumor. About how if people thought Natalie had money in the house she might get robbed. She could be the victim of a home invasion, and that would solve 'the problem.'"

"You're wrong," Liam said. "She didn't keep money there. Not more than a few dollars. She didn't need to carry money because she didn't go anywhere."

He sounded so rational. She needed him to understand this was anything but. "We know that, but this was a *story*. Subterfuge to explain what happened next. They were talking about your sister and not being able to get access to her money, and 'problem' was the word they used. One week later, Natalie's furnace malfunctioned. All the fire alarms also malfunctioned."

"Stop."

Talking about this slowly killed her, and she could see it was destroying him, too. Chipping away at what he believed and replacing it with something too sinister to bear. "The forensic pathologist referenced sleeping pills. Baines insisted she'd been self-medicating, but we both know she didn't take pills before that. She drank to self-medicate, and there was no alcohol in the house. The nurse had gotten rid of it. Only Baines had ever seen her take sleeping pills. You didn't buy them. Neither did her nurse."

"I said stop." Liam swallowed a few times before talking again.

She closed her eyes because that was easier than looking at him. "You asked me to explain. I'm trying."

"Did you confront Baines with your suspicions? Did you try to stop whatever you thought was going to happen to Natalie?" he asked.

Her shame, all that guilt over her failure to step in, never lessened. It burned as bright today as back then. The *what if* thoughts that ran in a loop in her head. "I asked him about the man. He lied, insisting it was a guy coming around, asking to do odd jobs around our house for money."

"But that's not what you heard."

"No." She had nowhere to hide on this. "I knew Baines loved Natalie, so I thought I'd misunderstood. Baines was so clear. Lied to me without blinking, made me think I'd gotten it wrong. But the conversation never left my head. The coincidence was too big, which is exactly what I told Baines when I said I wanted a divorce."

"That was, what, almost a year later. You knew for six months and stayed there. Married to him and pretending he didn't kill our helpless sister."

And that made her a monster, too. She heard the words even though he didn't say them.

"It took me that long to be brave enough to go." She knew Liam would never understand that just walking away sounded so much easier than it was. She remembered moving money to accounts in her own name and packing up Kennedy's things. Planning and waiting for the right time. "I thought he might kill me, too. That I knew too much, overheard the wrong thing. What would have stopped him?"

"Me." The word sat there for a few quiet seconds. "You didn't say a thing to me. I was right there. You had to know I would have listened to you and stopped him."

She hadn't known who he would believe. She'd picked Baines over him. She'd made her terrible choices. "By the time I put together what I heard, along with his talk about possible expansion of the business despite a lack of funds, the fire happened. That week was a chaotic rush filled with fear and confusion. Me, searching through the house, trying to find any concrete evidence that would prove my theory about what had really happened to Natalie."

"I was . . ." He rubbed a hand through his hair as even more confusion wormed into his voice. "God, I was a mess. Furious that something as simple and ridiculous as a furnace check could have saved her life. Do you know how guilty I felt?"

"Yes, because so did I. For different reasons."

"Baines mourned. I would find him sitting in his dark office at night, crying. Hell, he rushed into the building to save her," Liam insisted.

"Guilt, probably. Remorse. I don't know." Gabby heard her cell buzz. A text, and she ignored it. "I worried you'd kill Baines if you knew, and I'd lose you, too, so I stayed quiet."

"I would have gone to the police."

She toyed with that, too. But there was nothing to grab on to. "I had pieces of an overheard conversation that he denied and insisted I got wrong. After the fire, I confronted him again, and he said I needed to stop lying or I'd lose Kennedy." She gulped in a breath, hoping it would calm her, but it didn't. "Conjecture and theories. His word against mine. There wasn't any evidence. The police and fire investigator stated there was no foul play. I asked and pushed for a report on the fire then waited for the results. The conclusion came back as a horrible accident."

Some of the color returned to Liam's cheeks. "But you knew differently."

Her phone buzzed again. "I believed, and I still believe, Baines paid someone to kill Natalie. That man in our yard or someone that man knew. I'd never seen him before and not since. Baines denied and tried to use Kennedy against me, but it was too late. I no longer trusted him."

"You shouldn't talk about trust." When his phone buzzed, he looked at it. "It's Kennedy."

"What?" Gabby scrambled to grab her cell. The message on the screen made the blood drain from her head.

A reporter called. He knows the truth about Liam being my real dad.

Chapter Sixty-Six

JESSA

AFTER A WEEKEND with Retta and thinking about Retta, Jessa was ready for work on Monday. Today was a big day. Her assistant had marked it off on her calendar for "partner orientation." Jessa wanted to celebrate, but her mind kept getting dragged back to Retta's home office.

Jessa had paged through the small notebook she'd stolen several times. It fit in her palm. After repeated tries, she still had no idea what the lines of letters and numbers meant. Some sort of code, clearly, but why?

The bigger problem was the key. Now Jessa had it, when it should be taped to the back of a desk drawer. She had no idea how she was going to return the items without getting caught or when Retta and Earl would notice them missing. The first time had been scary enough. She didn't welcome a second round of covert stalking.

"With the partner meeting scheduled and associate oversight rules done, we can move to some related issues." Covington led her from the small conference room where they'd been meeting with the office manager and bookkeeper to the file room.

Jessa was surprised Covington even knew where this room was. He didn't exactly search out his own supplies and case files. The man had two assistants and everyone at the firm on speed dial to answer to his demands.

"You're familiar with the client filing codes," he said.

"Of course." The folders were color-coded and divided by age. She'd learned about that early in her tenure at the firm, so she didn't understand the need for the replay now.

He turned to the door across from the supply closet. "This is the partners' file room."

She'd always assumed the unmarked locked door had something to do with computers. No one ever went in there. "Why is this room separate from the rest?"

Covington typed a code into the keypad next to the door. "The office manager assigned you a security code. It's in that manual she handed you."

She'd gotten stacks of binders since becoming a partner. She'd signed papers and heard more about the retirement plan than she'd ever wanted to know.

"We keep specific files in this room. Problematic ones. Most cases, after they finish and the bill is paid, and a certain amount of time has passed, are closed then moved to our off-site storage. Other cases, ones we believe will circle back or could result in further litigation with the firm, stay here."

"Further litigation?" She looked at what seemed to be a wall of safes, and a surge of *what have I done?* hit her.

Covington rested his hand on a door with his name on it. "Some cases are of a nature where we can't risk losing track of the files, so we keep them close."

As a partner, she had partnership liability, so she found this room terrifying. For the first time, it hit her that running the firm came with responsibility and not just new benefits and more income. "I guess I'll have a locker or safe, or whatever you'd call these."

"Specifically designed safes. And, yes, all partners do. Past and present. We kept these old-school and use keys."

Past included Retta. Retta and a locked cabinet. Jessa couldn't ignore the obvious. "Do I get a key?"

"Of course." Covington drew one out of his pants pocket and handed it to her. He pointed to an open door. "This one is for you. The partners may suggest you put certain cases or documents in there from time to time, but you should use it as you see fit. If you need more room, we can give you a second space. I have three."

Four supersecret vaults hidden in a wall. Jessa tried to understand why someone would need one, never mind three.

"I wouldn't put money or jewels in there, but I have my will and other family and business documents in one of my spaces." Covington smiled. "Consider it a safety-deposit box of sorts."

Jessa looked at the space marked LORETTA SWAIN. She used to be a partner in the firm, so it made sense she had old files here. But what else?

Two hours later, Jessa walked back into the supply closet, through to the "special" room. She'd kept the key from Retta's desk on her at all times. Part of her didn't want it to open the door. She wanted to be able to call Gabby and say she'd tried, but she'd hit a roadblock, and good luck . . . *and please never call me again.* But part of Jessa knew the key would unlock the cabinet, and then she'd have a new mess to clean up.

She walked over to Retta's space. The vault with an equal potential for disaster or nothing. Jessa slid the key in and turned it until it clicked. Unlocked.

It figured this one time she was lucky.

She sifted through a few files with a series of case names. Nothing stood out, so she moved to a large envelope, which appeared to have personal papers and some information about accounts for Retta's kids. Private information. The kind many people would keep in a home safe, but Retta had here. Away from everyone.

Jessa looked at the back section. Files without names. Labels with numbers.

For a few seconds, she just stood there. Walk away and lie. That was one option. The other was to step deeper into Gabby's claims.

Jessa wanted to do better, be better. To not skate through difficult situations by ignoring them or maneuvering around them, leaving them for someone else to handle. But why? She regretted so much and could easily step away and add this to the pile. What was one more lie?

She texted Gabby, cursing herself as she did it.

Chapter Sixty-Seven

GABBY

IN THE WORLD of terrible choices, this was her worst. Gabby sat in an uncomfortable wooden chair in the waiting area in Loretta Swain's office. Just Gabby and the judge's assistant, a fifty-something woman in a black wrap dress who had insisted the judge didn't see walk-ins without appointments until Gabby made it clear she wasn't going anywhere.

She didn't think she had a choice but to wait. Her world had crashed down around her, and the judge had the power to hit the stop button and turn off all the chaos. She might pretend she didn't, but Gabby knew better. The ups and downs of her life matched too neatly with the times when she asked difficult questions. Just as Rob had told her they would.

No, this vigilante group existed, and the judge ran it, or at least held a lot of power in it. Gabby would bet everything she had on that fact, and she was doing exactly that with this visit. It could go sideways fast, but Gabby couldn't imagine anything worse happening to the people she cared about. So if the judge wanted a sacrifice or a deal, Gabby would make it.

"She's on her way back and asked that you continue to wait," the assistant said into the quiet room.

Since the assistant hadn't answered a phone, it was unclear how she'd talked to the judge, but fine. Gabby had been there for forty minutes. A few more didn't matter.

Ten minutes later, Loretta walked into her office with a young man, likely her clerk, trailing behind her. She smiled at her assistant as she dropped off an armload of papers and files. She said something to her clerk that had him scurrying from the room through a door to . . . somewhere.

The judge finally turned and looked at Gabby. "I wasn't expecting you today."

"I apologize for bursting in and demanding to see you. It's an emergency."

Loretta made a humming sound. "Right. Well, I only have ten minutes, but they are yours. Melinda? Hold my calls."

Right as Gabby stood up, her cell phone buzzed. She looked at the screen, half expecting to see another message from Kennedy that teetered between panic and fury, but this one had come from Jessa.

Call me

Gabby put that on the list of things to do right after she convinced Liam and Kennedy not to hate her and came up with the best way to hide from neighbors who, thanks to social media, now knew she'd slept with both Fielding brothers and lied about who was Kennedy's dad.

Loretta sat down at a round table in a small conference room. She folded her hands in front of her as she waited. Gabby tried not to be obvious about glancing around for hidden cameras, but she did look.

"You seem to be a regular in the news these days," Loretta said.

"Yeah, lucky me." Gabby's cell buzzed again. Another text from Jessa, which Gabby didn't take the time to read before sitting down. "That's part of why I'm here."

"How can I help?"

An interesting conversation opening. Gabby jumped on it. "You can make it stop."

Loretta's eyebrow lifted in the same way as it had back in law school when a student gave a wrong answer. "Excuse me?"

"Feeding stories to reporters and social media sites, or news, or whatever we call them. Telling my secrets to the public on a steady drip. All of it. Stop." Gabby didn't beg because she didn't want to give the judge the satisfaction of having that much power over her, even though she did.

Loretta shook her head. "I'm confused about what you think I've done."

"Oh, please." Gabby's cell buzzed again, and she wrapped her hand tighter around it. "Liam being Kennedy's father. The truth about Baines. The false evidence planted at Liam's house."

"I'm still lost, Gabby. What are you asking me?"

Gabby had to keep from screaming. "Can we skip the denial part?"

The phone buzzing came in spurts now.

Loretta glanced toward Gabby's hand. "Do you need to take that call?"

"Ignore it. It's just . . ." Gabby looked down at the screen. Jessa's last three texts said the same exact thing.

SOS!!

"Well?" Loretta asked.

Gabby didn't know if Jessa was trying to save herself or if something actually had happened. For a few charged seconds, Gabby toyed with ignoring the message, turning the damn phone off, and continuing with the confrontation. Then Jessa sent one more text.

I found what we need.

Gabby stood up. "I have to go."

"You waited all afternoon to see me." Loretta's voice stayed even, but she was a smart woman. Her eyes gave her away. So intelligent. Savvy.

"My mistake." Gabby was almost at the door.

"Sit down, Gabby. We'll talk."

Gabby ignored the order and walked faster. "There'll be time for that soon."

Chapter Sixty-Eight

THE FOUNDATION

THE WOMEN GATHERED in their regular meeting space, only with more fidgeting and whispering than usual. A restless energy filled the air. The tension wound and tightened even as they greeted one another.

Before the leader could start the meeting, Dr. Downing, the child psychologist, spoke up. "The ongoing need for emergency sessions is a grave concern."

"Would you rather not be informed about the latest issues?" Retta asked.

"Your attitude doesn't ease my worries."

Retta exhaled, clearly trying to bring her annoyance at being questioned under control. "My apologies. This has been a very trying few days, dealing with the fallout."

"We all voted for her conditional membership," another member, this one a prosecutor, said. "We all bear responsibility for our choice."

Retta relaxed, settling back into her chair. "We've been monitoring our potential member's email and phone conversations.

She's been under surveillance, and her mood is much improved since our intervention, but, despite warnings, she is engaging in behavior that could have a negative impact on the group."

"How so?" Dr. Downing asked.

The job of answering the questions fell to Retta because she was the member who had submitted Jessa's name for consideration. More than once. As the sponsoring member, Retta had to answer for Jessa's actions. "I brought transcripts of the communications. The originals are in this folder, along with some photographs."

The women leaned in, each examining the evidence Retta had brought to the table. Their expressions ranged from unreadable to concerned.

"We need to take another vote." Retta handed a thin file to each member. "We should take some time to walk through the gathered evidence to avoid making a second mistake."

The women started reading. A few rechecked the original emails. All studied the evidence.

"We must act quickly." Retta hesitated before continuing. "But this needs to be our final decision on the issue of Jessa Hall."

Chapter Sixty-Nine

JESSA

JESSA ARRIVED BACK at Faith's place just after eight with a briefcase filled with documents and her laptop. She'd been using both since her brief call with Gabby earlier in the afternoon. They had to meet, but Jessa needed a few more hours to make sure she covered everything, then she'd call Gabby.

Tomorrow. The fallout discussion could wait until then.

Exhausted from the internal battle over betraying Retta and a day of racing around, filling in every possible hole she could think of, Jessa was ready for wine and fluffy slippers. She opened her car door and slid out. Faith had two parking spaces—one underground near the elevator, and one in the back by the storage lockers, where Jessa parked. It was a pain trying to maneuver into the tiny space, but Jessa appreciated avoiding a daily spar for on-street parking.

Her space sat under a light, but today the row nearest her car had blinked out again, bathing this half of the parking floor in a shadowy gray haze. Second time it had happened since she'd been staying with Faith.

She slung her bag over her shoulder as she locked the car. Awareness tingled to life. An initial rush of adrenaline vibrated through her. She shook it off. Keys in hand, ready to do battle, she turned toward the door to the building and gasped.

Darren Bartholomew. Right there. In the private garage. In front of her.

She dropped her keys as she bit back a yelp of surprise. When he put his foot over the key ring and kicked it away, she almost drowned in the panic flooding her. The kind of terror that made her teeth click together as if she'd been plunged into an icy lake.

She should have switched from heels to sneakers before she'd gotten in the car, but she'd been in a hurry. Now, outrunning him sounded impossible. She backed up against the car, slamming her body to the door. Putting what limited space existed between them.

"Darren." Her voice sounded hoarse.

He smiled. "Surprise."

She looked at him, heard that soft, coaxing voice, and understood his wife's fear. The sensation of being trapped and having to scrape and claw to survive filled Jessa. She looked around, scanning, hoping to see anyone. With or without assistance, she'd run and scream, hit and kick. Do anything to avoid him. But, for now, she was alone in the closing darkness.

She tried to clear her voice, force some firmness into it, but failed. "What are you doing here?"

"Don't you want to ask why I'm not in prison?"

"Fine. Explain that." She tugged on the door handle, but she'd locked the car, and the fob must have landed just far enough away to keep her out. Someone should have called and warned her about him being out. Detective Schone showed up unwanted here and there, but not when she was needed. "When did you get back?"

"Today. A few hours ago." Hate pulsed off him. Those flat eyes didn't show an ounce of fear or regret. "On a technicality."

And he came to find her. He didn't need to say it because his feral expression said it all.

Jessa knew the truth about why he walked free. Retta. The group. The unseen hand of assistance he didn't even know he'd been lucky enough to receive. He had a group of women who despised him, and who he probably saw as beneath him, to thank for an unexpected release.

"I decided to see you first. Next stop, my wife and son."

He was going to kill them. "You should see your lawyer, Darren. Get his advice."

"He's lucky he got me out. Another day in there and . . . well, you don't want to know." Darren slapped a hand against her car, right next to her head, standing far too close.

A kick. She didn't care where she landed it so long as he went down. She tried to focus. Forced her lungs to breathe. "There's a restraining order. You can't go near—"

"Stop acting like you're in control." The rage boiled up and came out in an uncharacteristically choppy tone. "You messed up. Despite my warning, you sided with my stupid bitch of a wife."

She ducked too late.

He hit her. The heel of his hand rammed into the side of her face. Her head banged against the car window, and her vision blinked. Before she could drop or yell, he grabbed her arm and twisted. Her skin burned under his fingers, stealing her breath.

"You didn't listen to me," he said, just inches from her face.

No! She wound up, gathering every drop of energy inside her, and screamed. He flinched, and that tiny bit of space let her inch away. She lifted her bag. Nailed him with one shot to his chin, letting the weight of her laptop do most of the work.

A car pulled around to this side of the garage. The headlights moved over Darren as he bent over, screaming about how she would pay. When the car horn sounded, Darren froze then ran. He sped by the car, shutting the driver's-side door right as it started to open. Then he was gone.

The world began to sway. Jessa dropped to her knees. She hit the cement with enough force to hear a crack. Aches started to surface. She heard voices around her and Faith yelling her name.

Jessa focused on one thing—she'd won this round, but she had to move or Darren's family would lose the next.

Chapter Seventy

GABBY

GABBY PACED. SHE'D been pacing for what felt like hours. After receiving the emergency SOS from Jessa and having a brief conversation about her finding some vault, all communication ceased.

In any other circumstance, Gabby could console herself, saying Jessa needed time to extricate herself from the office and call again. But between the truncated visit with Retta and Liam's ongoing legal issues, the danger and uncertainty ratcheted up.

Gabby's inbox had been flooded with nasty emails and requests for interviews. Some true crime podcast already jumped in and speculated she and Liam had killed Baines to get him out of the way, and now an army of social media warriors were running with the unfounded garbage. Picking through their lives. Drawing conclusions from random photos they found online.

She wanted to say, *Well, at least Kennedy is out of the fray*, but her school had already called. Other parents were concerned about Kennedy's attendance. The administration didn't know if it could keep the students from bullying Kennedy. The dean even used the phrase *young women can be mean*. Yeah, well, some older ones sucked, too.

In only a few weeks, every wall had come crashing down, each carefully placed brick, all the outer barricades of protection. Baines had stolen business secrets. Baines had moved money. Baines likely had killed his sister. But everyone demanded *she* pay the price.

She couldn't stay here and wait. She needed to *do* something, even if that meant bothering Jessa.

Gabby picked up her purse and her cell and headed for the front door. She'd stake out Jessa's house and . . . Wait. She still didn't know where Jessa lived. That left driving around in circles, repeatedly texting Jessa in a pathetic grab for attention.

Fine. She'd do it. She'd do whatever she had to do.

A knock at the door stopped Gabby's mental sputtering. Liam lived in a security building. People couldn't get upstairs without being buzzed in.

"Mrs. Fielding? Open the door." Detective Schone's voice.

No, no, no. Gabby's heartbeat turned to a gallop. It pounded through her, in her ears, in every muscle. A tiny warning voice in her head told her not to open that door. Not to go anywhere near Melissa Schone until Jessa called with more information.

Gabby backed away. She'd never ignored law enforcement before, but she was going to this time. The detective was here for the group, not on official business. Jessa repeated that fact in her head as she drifted down the hall, not making a sound and never breaking eye contact with that front door.

Another knock. This time louder.

Liam's building was the type where people had live-in help. Some of his neighbors or the builders thought the assistants should use a different door than the residents. Gabby thought the whole thing was insulting. So did Liam, which was why he never used that back entrance. No one did . . . until now.

She walked through a doorway that led to the laundry on one side and a small bedroom on the other. It had been advertised as the au pair suite, and the size felt claustrophobic compared to the rest of the rooms in the spacious condo.

Liam used the area for storage. Knowing she only had a little bit of time, she locked the door to the bedroom behind her and started moving things around. She shoved an old desk aside and some boxes that Liam had probably moved from one house to another as he'd left each of his marriages. She finally unburied the back door, the so-called servants' entrance, which she viewed as a safety hatch.

After putting her ear to it and not hearing a sound, she opened the locks and peeked outside. Detective Schone's voice echoed down the floor. She was talking to someone and banging on the front door around the corner. Gabby ignored it all and, as quietly as possible, opened the emergency exit door and followed the stairway down to the lobby.

Three excruciating minutes later, Gabby hailed a cab, the harder transportation option for the detective to trace, or at least she hoped so, and left the neighborhood.

Chapter Seventy-One

JESSA

TWENTY MINUTES LATER, Jessa still hadn't calmed down. She called Ellie Bartholomew and her attorney and warned them. Jessa refused a call to the police or an ambulance for help because she didn't trust either. She couldn't afford to get trapped in a small room or hauled away to a cell that she'd never break out of again.

No, Darren being out, finding her at an address he shouldn't have, was a message. Retta was no longer protecting her. The group was cleansing itself. They didn't care if Darren killed her, so long as she stayed quiet.

Jessa had no idea how her life had come to this. She'd always been so careful. She hadn't drawn attention. Sure, she'd bent the rules sometimes. She'd let others do most of the heavy lifting in law school and at work. But she didn't deserve to die for that.

"Here's another cup of tea. The other one has gone cold." Faith sat next to Jessa with an arm wrapped around her. "I think we should call that Detective Schone. She knows about Darren, and—"

"No!" Jessa couldn't slow down her pulse or control the jumping inside of her. She knew Faith was scared for her and trying to help, but Faith didn't understand. "I told you. We can't trust her. This is so much bigger than you think."

"Okay." Faith squeezed Jessa even tighter. "You've been through a horrible thing. Your mind is racing. Those neurons are firing. I need you to breathe."

The comfort suffocated her. Jessa jumped up from the couch. She needed to move, to burn off the frenzy of emotions bombarding her. "This isn't really about Darren. It's about a group of women."

"That doesn't make sense."

"A vigilante group."

"Jessa, sit." The trace of pain in Faith's voice was hard to miss. "Please."

"No, no." Jessa sat down with her hand on Faith's leg then shot up again. She couldn't afford to be at ease. She needed this energy. She had to store it up and get to Gabby. "They found me here. I'm so sorry. I should have warned you, but I wasn't allowed."

"I don't understand."

Of course she didn't. She couldn't. "Someone knows I'm staying with you, and that person told Darren."

Faith winced. "Was it a secret? I think I told—"

"You didn't do anything wrong. This is . . ." Jessa ran through her memories, trying to spot someone following her. She didn't see how a camera could have been planted in here, but she looked around anyway. Her gaze fell on her bag, and it all made sense. "They have some sort of tracker on me."

"We need to get you to a hospital. I'm worried about a head injury." Faith's soothing voice contrasted with Jessa's sharp, staccato one.

Jessa ignored the comment as she dove for her bag. She pulled out her cell phone. The GPS. If the group could uncover all these secrets about the men they targeted, they could trace her. "I need to get the chip out."

"What?"

"They can find me through this." Jessa held up her phone, knowing she verged on sounding paranoid. But she was right. They knew too much. She couldn't make it easy on them to gather even more intel. "I need this one number, but the rest of what's on there doesn't matter."

She repeated Gabby's number a few times, sinking it into memory. When that didn't work, Jessa grabbed a pen and wrote it on her arm, then she ripped at her cell, trying to take it apart. Her hands shook, and her muscles ignored the orders from her brain.

"Let me help." Faith used her fingernail and took out a tiny memory card. "This?"

Jessa snatched it out of her hand and ran to the bathroom. She flushed it.

"Jessa, what the hell?" Faith stood in the bathroom doorway with her hands over her mouth. Terrified, confused. Her expression suggested she was a few seconds away from calling for help.

That couldn't happen. Jessa could almost hear the clock ticking as her time ran out. "I can't be here. It's not safe for you."

"I'm fine." Faith motioned for Jessa to come out of the bathroom. "Let's sit down and talk."

"I need a new phone."

"Do you want mine?"

She'd already put Faith in danger. That had never hit Jessa until right now. Taking her phone would only compound the problem. "No, I can buy one."

"Wait." Faith disappeared for a few seconds.

Jessa used the time to grab her bag and a few things she needed. "I'll call you as soon as I'm safe."

"Here." Faith held out a phone. "I have a stack of these. We give them to abused spouses. It's a way for them to have an emergency line and to speak without their abusers watching or tracking them. But you need to stay here and—"

"No." Standing there, talking, only made Jessa more anxious. Her knees and cheek ached, but she didn't have time to baby the injuries. "It's better this way. You won't know where I am."

Faith's mouth dropped open. "I want to know where you are!"

"I'll tell you everything, things you really don't want to know about some powerful women in the area, but not yet. I need to do something first."

"Jessa, I'm begging you. Stay here and rest. We'll snuggle on the couch and—"

Jessa grabbed Faith and wrapped her in a tight hug. She never cried but could feel her control slipping away. "Trust me. I just need a few hours. Please don't call the police or anyone else."

Before Faith could hold her or argue, Jessa pulled away. She could hear Faith calling for her as she stepped into the hallway. One glance at her hand and Jessa texted Gabby.

It's me. Jessa. Meet me where it's safest.

They'd talked about this so briefly. She'd made a side comment about not seeing each other in the open, about going where no one should be. Now she had to hope Gabby got the hint.

Chapter Seventy-Two

JESSA

THE FRONT DOOR was unlocked by the time Jessa arrived at Baines's house. She stepped into the grand foyer, expecting Gabby to be right there to greet her for their clandestine meeting. She didn't know her way around the dark house, but she saw a light in one of the rooms.

"Gabby?" Jessa whispered the name, but the marble floors caused her voice to echo.

She slipped into a room with a desk. Probably an office or library. The space looked inviting enough, with a big leather desk chair and shelves lined with books and personal photos.

She picked up one of Baines and Kennedy sitting by a pool. Kennedy did look like him, but now Jessa knew that was due to him being her uncle. She did not in any way envy Gabby dealing with that messed-up family situation.

Jessa's head thumped, and the adrenaline shooting through her had her a little out of breath. She wanted this over, and fast. They didn't know who they could trust, but Jessa knew who they couldn't rely on—Retta. And Darren could be anywhere, so Gabby needed to stop rattling around this gigantic house and show her face.

The creak behind her filled her with relief. Being excited to see Gabby was a first, but Jessa welcomed the sensation. "It's about time. I thought . . ."

A man stood there. A familiar one. Taylor or Tom. Something like that. They'd met outside of Retta and Earl's house that night with the reporter. His being here didn't make sense. No one knew she was here. She didn't have her phone. She'd changed bags. She didn't say or type the address anywhere.

"What are you doing here?" But she feared she knew the answer. She'd said too much, dug around in the wrong places.

She saw the knife. He held it low, right against his leg, but the light bounced off the blade.

Think! Her mind raced with possible solutions. There appeared to be one door, and it was behind him. Window. Closet. Where was that cell phone from Faith?

"Is Retta with you, or is she coming later?" she asked in the calmest voice she could muster.

The question had him frowning. "What?"

His name came to her. If she could keep up the ruse while she figured out an exit plan . . . "Retta told me to meet her here. I assumed you drove her. Trent, right?"

"How do you—"

She turned and reached for the nearest object. Hardcover books. She grabbed them double-fisted. Lobbed one then another at him. Slammed the first into his head. Aimed for the knife but hit his stomach with the second. She screamed as she threw. Dodged around the desk, racing as fast as she could for the door.

She touched the knob right as he grabbed the back of her shirt.

"Not today!" She kept moving, dragging him with her. "Gabby!"

She slipped on the marble but managed to stay on her feet. Only a few steps to the front door and freedom, but his hand clamped down on her shoulder. A stinging pain had her stopping.

He was on top of her then. A muscled arm wrapped around her waist and lifted her off the floor. Dark spots blurred her vision as she lashed out, trying to smash the back of her head into his face. She clawed at the arm banded around her. Her fingers slipped as he whipped her around in the air.

One minute she was on her feet, the next she hit the ground. Hard. A harsh sound escaped her. She knew it came from her because the noise vibrated through her.

Dazed and dizzy, she lay on her back and looked up at her attacker. Trent stood over her with the knife. Blood dripped off the end.

"Stabbed?" She'd sliced him? That had to be it.

She tried to kick out, but her body refused to move. A strange numbness moved through her. Her hands felt wet. Lifting her head grew impossible as the sound of labored breathing registered in her brain.

Her eyes closed, and she forced them open again. She was so tired. The exhaustion crept up on her and stole all her strength.

She strained to get up but couldn't move. As the minutes ticked by, the last of her energy drained away. Her right hand slipped off her stomach and fell to the floor beside her.

The wetness. Blood. A slick fiery red covered her closed fist. She couldn't remember making a fist but couldn't stop. Her hand remained clenched even as she fought to open it. More red. Running out from under her, around her.

She heard a click and what sounded like a sharp intake of breath. Gabby was here. *Finally.* She would fix this. Jessa couldn't form the words, but Gabby knew the truth. She knew everything.

Rest now. Peace. Quiet. Jessa savored the soothing comfort of both. This time she let her eyes close, but they opened again at the sound of Retta's trembling voice.

"No! What did you do?"

Chapter Seventy-Three

JESSA

THERE WAS AN odd sucking noise that made it hard for Jessa to hear the words. Retta entered the room, all animated and yelling. More emotion than Jessa had ever seen from her. Retta shoved the man . . . What was it again? Trent? Yeah, that was it.

Retta's pantsuit today was a Wedgwood blue. Jessa had no idea why that mattered or stuck in her mind. Her eyes were so heavy. The blue popped through the fuzziness.

"You had no right," Retta yelled.

He probably shouldn't be here. That made sense. Jessa struggled to remember why she was here . . . Where was she? She focused on the leather chair and ottoman in the far corner of the room, but they didn't look familiar. Faith had once joked that she couldn't afford real leather, so not hers. Maybe Tim . . . Wait, no. That wasn't right.

The wheezing grew louder. Like a gurgling. The sound bounced around Jessa's head.

Where is that coming from?

She opened her mouth to ask and started coughing. The thick, rattling kind. That probably explained the wetness on her cheeks. But her stomach and back? The odd pulsing. She faded in and out, but the pain only increased.

Retta and the man watched her now. Neither moved or said a word. The look on Retta's face . . . Was it guilt? She had her fist to her mouth as she shook her head.

A rush of strange sounds, then a voice broke through. "What happened?"

Jessa smiled, or she thought she did. Gabby's voice. About time she got here. The dramatic entrance was . . . typical.

"Jessa! Oh my God," Gabby said as she slid to her knees beside Jessa. Gabby held her hands in the air, like she wanted to touch or comfort.

Jessa wasn't sure why, but she needed to sit up. There was something she needed to do. She'd come here for a reason. A really important project.

The wheezing came in short, painful puffs now. The sound came from her. She'd finally figured it out.

"Did you call 911?" Gabby shouted at the other people in the room. "We need to get someone on the phone to help until the ambulance gets here."

Too late. The words rolled through Jessa's head. They were all too late.

She was dying.

Not yet! I promised to be a better person. Let me try.

"Open your eyes, Jessa. I need you to stay with me," Gabby pleaded.

Are my eyes closed? Jessa could have sworn they were open a second ago, but Gabby sounded sure, so now Jessa didn't know.

Gabby's words rushed out, and she held something against Jessa's stomach. The pressure throttled up the pulsing. The pain stabbed and sliced now. Jessa wanted to push Gabby away, but her hands lay limp.

"Jessa, can you hear me?"

I'm sorry. For the lying and for all the horrible things I said behind your back. You deserved better. Jessa wasn't sure if she said the words out loud, but she didn't think so.

Jessa couldn't tell how many minutes passed since she'd gotten to the house. A few? Many? She mentally pushed and shoved her way through the darkness slowly enveloping her. She had one more thing to do. That's why she needed to make that fist. The small move swallowed up all her concentration, her last drips of energy, but she would get this done.

A push and another. No, her fist wouldn't open. But she could make it tilt. The back of her hand knocked against Gabby's arm. Once . . . twice. Gabby finally took her hand.

There.

Done.

"Jessa, no!"

Chapter Seventy-Four

GABBY

GABBY FELT JESSA slide something small and hard into her hand. Against her palm. Gabby didn't have time to look because Jessa's body went limp as the last beats of her life drained out of her.

Gabby struggled to remember CPR and first aid. She pressed her other hand harder against Jessa's blood-soaked shirt, desperate to stop the bleeding. Red stained the floor and her skin. The memory of finding Baines in the same room whipped through her. Death sank into every inch and every corner and festered there.

"Do not move."

Gabby heard Retta's order. She didn't know if it was meant for her, but she couldn't go anywhere. She had to sit there and protect Jessa until the ambulance arrived. Hold her hand on the gaping wound and hope Jessa still had a chance with a flurry of machines pumping air and blood for her.

"Gabby?" Retta's voice floated through the quiet room.

Gabby ignored the soft-toned outreach. Mentor, judge, supporter. She'd done this. She'd stalked Jessa, followed her here, and killed her. Brought a man with her to finish the job. A man Gabby recognized from the grocery store parking lot all those weeks ago. The man who had intervened when Rob tried to give her information. Retta had had him following her all along.

"Gabby, listen to me." Retta kneeled across from her, on the other side of Jessa's still body. Retta reached out and checked for a pulse.

When Retta's hand fell limp on her lap, Gabby knew.

"She needs help." Gabby felt rage *for* Jessa instead of *at* her. Jessa's life could not end this way. Not during one of the only times she'd taken a chance for someone else. For her . . . Gabby hated it, but Jessa was only in this house, on the floor, because of her, which meant she'd done this. She'd made demands and said awful things about who Jessa was, pushed her to help. And now she was dying.

Gabby looked up, ready to scream the house down, until she looked at Retta's face. Tears ran down her cheeks, as if she cared. As if she hadn't ordered this.

The need to spew hatred and vent about blame poured through Gabby. "Where is the ambulance? When did you call?"

"No one is coming."

No one . . . "What? How can that . . . How could you . . ."

Retta sighed. "We need to come to an understanding. Right now."

"Screw that." Gabby fumbled, trying to remember where she put her cell. Pocket, right. She took it out, but before she could hit a button, the man behind her stole it out of her hand. "What are you—"

"There's not going to be any miracle here. Jessa will die today." Retta wiped her cheeks, sounding ragged and a bit lost. So quiet and forlorn, and totally uncharacteristic of her. "How she will be remembered and who will take the blame is up to you."

"Don't put this on me." Gabby started to rock back and forth. She tried to stop, but her body refused to obey.

"Your phone number is written on her arm, not mine." Retta touched the fading pen marks on Jessa's skin. "That's what the police will see."

Gabby blocked that truth out. She had to if she wanted to keep moving. "She idolized you. She would have done anything for you, and you betrayed her."

"I asked her to stay away from you."

Guilt pressed in on Gabby from every direction. She hadn't known this would happen. She'd never wanted this. She hadn't caused this . . . but a tiny voice in her head kept saying, *Liar.*

"That's why you killed her? Because she called me?" Gabby turned around and stared at the man looming behind her. His face lacked any emotion. He acted like nothing happened, like he hadn't sliced the life out of the woman lying dead in front of him. "You can't tell me this was an accident, that he killed the wrong person on your command."

This was a purposeful kill. Premeditated and carried out with precision by a man who served as the trigger for a woman who couldn't tolerate losing her public image or being bested by her former mentee.

Gabby's breath hiccuped inside her. "This is your fault."

"This was not supposed to happen, but it has, and we have to deal with it," Retta said.

So bloodless.

"You do." Gabby harnessed all her guilt and sadness and turned it into rage. Aimed it at the woman across from her. "You're the leader of your pathetic little group. You make the rules and give the orders. You don't get to have regret now."

"I am the co-leader. This order didn't come from me."

Earl. That explained Baines and the papers she'd found. Gabby couldn't believe a business battle had led to three dead people, but it sounded as if it had. "Then let Earl explain this. Where is he? Is he going to show up in his fancy suit and fix this?"

When Retta held up a hand, Gabby braced herself, waiting for the man behind her to grab her or plunge a knife into her. But nothing happened. Nothing physical. Instead, he spoke. "We're out of time."

Gabby sat back, finally breaking her hold with Jessa's ravaged stomach. Gabby didn't want to die, but she would not beg. She tried to figure out if she could lunge and knock Retta down, use her as a shield for whatever Retta's bodyguard enforcer had planned.

"Stop strategizing, Gabby. I'm not going to let Trent kill you, and you're certainly not going to touch either of us." Retta stood up, rising like a phoenix from the ashes. "There is a relatively simple way to handle this. Darren attacked Jessa earlier."

"What? How is he even out of jail?"

"That part *was* my doing, I'm afraid." Retta's calm assurance returned. All signs of losing it and crying disappeared. In their place, the cool, collected, scary judge. A woman every inch in control of the room. "Your brother-in-law, or boyfriend, or whatever he is to you. I don't really care, but he is in trouble. Evidence points to him for Baines's murder. I know because I gave approval for the planting of that evidence."

"You bitch."

"We're now in Baines's house, and this murder could easily be roped around Liam's neck, too. You would likely be implicated as well. Unless you choose otherwise."

Adrenaline whirled to life inside Gabby. She jumped to her feet, ready for any attack. "You're insane."

"Darren made plans to kill his estranged wife. He wanted to hurt Jessa. He's not a good man, and with his family's reach and resources he could threaten many more women in the future," Retta explained.

"How is that relevant?"

"Those are the hard facts. I have evidence to support every statement. But there is an option where he goes to prison for Jessa's murder. We can defuse him and clean this up at the same time."

Jessa lay dead, and Retta only cared about how bad a guy this Darren person was. Gabby didn't care. "Why would he be in Baines's house? That's ridiculous."

"If Darren did it, Jessa didn't die here. She died back in that parking lot where he attacked her. He threatened her earlier then came back and followed through on his threats. Under that scenario, Jessa is remembered as another tragic statistic. We will celebrate and honor her." Retta glanced at her watch. "But time is of the essence. We need a decision from you."

"Me?" Gabby needed Retta to say it out loud. To put her heinous plan into words so there was no confusion.

"Darren or Liam—you choose."

"Leave Liam and Kennedy out of this." No, more than that. "Stay away from my family, or I swear I will kill you myself."

Retta nodded. "So you choose Darren."

"I didn't say—"

Retta looked past Gabby. "Make the arrangements. We need this done immediately. And take Jessa's bag with you. Gabby won't be needing whatever Jessa brought for her."

"Yes, ma'am."

Gabby heard his footsteps and watched him leave the room. She turned back to Retta. "What is wrong with you? How did you go so far off track? You don't get to decide who deserves to die."

Retta stood up. "Lucky for you, right now I do."

Chapter Seventy-Five

GABBY

THE STAIN WOULDN'T come off. Gabby stood in the shower and scrubbed until the water turned cold. She used Liam's soap, at his house, but all she could see was Baines's office. The bodies piling up. Jessa's unblinking eyes, begging her to do . . . something.

Liar. Cheat. Untrustworthy. All the slams she'd made about Jessa over the years, and said directly to her face, ran through Gabby's head on an endless cycle. The guilt ratcheted up, washing over her in a slime of filth she'd never be able to break out of again.

Tears mixed with the icy water. The spray pounded her with a thousand tiny needles. Her only thought as her body shook was about how close she'd come to being the group's latest victim.

They all begged her to shut up and go away, but she wouldn't let Baines's death go. Liam told her. Detective Schone told her. Jessa told her. But she'd been so sure she knew better. She thought she could find justice for Baines as a final gesture of affection for the life they'd shared, but all she did was break her daughter and invite danger and death in for everyone around her.

God, Jessa. I'm so sorry.

Baines, Tami, Rob. So much loss.

Gabby slid down the tile wall. Wet hair covered her eyes as she gulped in air between sobs. Jessa had lied on an affidavit to make herself more important at work, and in a roundabout, messed-up way she'd died for that mistake.

Gabby sat there until the bumps on her skin shouted at her to get up and turn off the water. Strength abandoned her. All she could do was look into the rainfall and wonder what to do next. Thoughts swirled in her mind. Solutions. Options. Ways to work around the secrecy of the group and find a person not on the inside, not beholden, and not a believer in the scheme.

Minutes passed before she could finally lean forward and turn off the water.

She didn't know how to live with what she'd started . . . except to finish it.

TWENTY MINUTES LATER, Gabby sat at Liam's dining room table. She opened her hand and stared at the memory stick Jessa had passed to her as she died. The little piece of plastic that had cost Jessa everything.

Retta had taken the papers Jessa brought to Baines's house, but in the end, Jessa had outmaneuvered her mentor. Jessa had taken the risks and would have the last word.

Gabby vowed to make that true.

Chapter Seventy-Six

MILLIONAIRE BUSINESSMAN IN CUSTODY—
Potomac, MD

Darren Bartholomew, 46, son of philanthropist Malcolm Bartholomew, was arrested late Tuesday at his uncle's home on River Road, in Potomac, Maryland, for the murder of Jessa Hall, the court-appointed guardian ad litem for his minor son.

Bartholomew, a former high school and college lacrosse standout and the current vice president of Bartholomew Holdings, was recently incarcerated for violating a protective order in place for his estranged wife, Eleanor Bartholomew. He was released due to a technical flaw with the written order. On the day of his unexpected return to the area, Bartholomew allegedly confronted Hall in front of witnesses then fled the scene. Hall, a highly regarded domestic attorney in Montgomery County, Maryland, survived that confrontation but Bartholomew returned, and Hall died from a stab wound shortly thereafter.

A friend of Bartholomew who asked not to be named said Bartholomew had been inconsolable about the breakup of his marriage and his limited time with his son. He spoke often of his negative views of the justice system and its lack of concern for fathers in custody proceedings.

Malcolm Bartholomew has stated he believes his son's unfair treatment caused serious harm to his mental state. The elder Bartholomew and his wife, Marian, are well known in the metro area for their charitable pursuits and sizeable donations to the arts community and to research technology at the University of Maryland.

Hall's law partners and colleagues are in mourning for the loss of a person they call "an expert in her field," a lawyer who was dedicated to her clients and friends.

Bartholomew has been taken into custody. His attorney could not be reached for comment. The police advise the investigation is ongoing.

Chapter Seventy-Seven

GABBY

ATTENDING JESSA'S FUNERAL turned out to be almost as stressful as watching her die in secret. People who claimed to know and love her took turns standing up and gushing about her talent and personality, her drive and commitment to truth. Her law partners welcomed guests. Retta stood stoic and motionless at the back of the church, with her husband, Earl, by her side. Jessa's best friend, Faith, didn't say a word, but the tears streaming down her cheeks spoke to her pain.

Gabby didn't want to be there, shouldn't be there, but she felt obligated in this last moment to honor Jessa. Not like the news stories, which focused on poor Darren rather than the woman he killed. Not like the people praising her during this ceremony. The mourners' spokespeople talked from an impersonal distance, sounding as if they were reading from sympathy cards rather than talking about the real Jessa.

Gabby knew who Jessa was. Savvy, flawed, self-focused, and desperate to be better. That last part truly defined her. It was the piece Gabby would hold on to because it showed that people could want to change and take real steps to make the shift happen.

After all those years of blaming Jessa, Gabby had to own up to her own failures. Her lies. She and Jessa were more alike than Gabby wanted to believe. Liam and Kennedy could attest to that. While she didn't deserve absolution, Gabby vowed to atone, or at least try, and she silently thanked Jessa for showing it was possible.

Forty minutes of songs and speeches, and the service finally ended. Gabby wanted to bolt from the room and put the entire nightmare behind her, but she couldn't. The combination of Faith's despair and Retta's caring façade played out in front of her. Both strong women. Both major influences on Jessa and the woman she became.

Only one played a role in her death.

Gabby couldn't let it go. Staying silent about what really happened at Baines's house protected Liam and Kennedy but damned her. Jessa, despite being thoroughly annoying at times and lying her way through trouble, deserved a better ending. The news named Darren as the suspect in Jessa's death, but the window was still open for Retta to change targets and blow up Liam's life.

So much lingering danger. So much damage.

The mourners filed along the pews and into the aisle. One by one, the attendees made the slow procession to the outside. The warm sun bounced off the marble stairs. Gabby drew in a deep breath. Let it calm the nerves pulsing to life inside her.

She watched Earl kiss Retta on the cheek and walk over to shake a man's hand. It all looked so normal. So professional and honorable. A perfectly packaged cover-up that depended on her playing her role and not making trouble.

Faith and Retta passed each other on the way to greet other people. Gabby would have guessed they knew each other, but they didn't acknowledge each other in any way. No nod or simple *I'm sorry*.

Jessa's ex, Tim, was there, looking lost. He didn't wander around. He stuck with a group of other men in dark suits, likely the high-priced lawyer crowd.

Gabby took it all in, knowing she should go. Walk out and not let the jumble of words clogging her throat come out. Let Jessa die in peace with her sacrifice unknown.

Should.

Retta smiled at something the person talking to her said. They both quickly switched moods and did the serious nod thing, likely as the grief of the moment hit them again.

Don't do it. The words kept repeating in Gabby's head even as she followed Faith away from the crowd. Watched her circle back and get a drink of water then stand alone and take a shuddering breath.

One word. Nothing to give away the truth. Gabby could do that. It made sense for her to comfort Jessa's best friend of close to twenty years. Gabby doubted the sincerity of some in the crowd, but not Faith.

"Excuse me. Faith?"

Don't do it.

"Gabby, right?" Faith's smile came and went. Her face remained pale and drawn. "I remember you from some of the parties Jessa used to have with law-school friends."

Friends . . . Yeah, Gabby let that go. "We'd reconnected recently."

Faith frowned. "Really?"

Gabby understood the confusion. She'd bet money Jessa hadn't said a decent thing about her in . . . well, ever. "She didn't tell you?"

"She had a lot going on. The breakup with Tim. The partnership. The big case that got knocked off course by bad press and then—"

"I'm so sorry." Gabby regretted the blurting but not the sentiment. "It's . . ."

"A shock."

"I just . . ." What did she say next? How did she dip into the truth without revealing it? "Things aren't quite . . . I'm not sure . . ."

Faith put a comforting hand on Gabby's arm. "Are you okay?"

"Nothing is what it seems." *Don't do it. Don't do it. Donotdoit!* "With her death, I mean."

Faith glanced around before lowering her voice to a whisper. "Gabby?"

Oh, shit. Gabby's speech picked up speed, matching the dramatic thunder of her heartbeat. "I think you should know the truth. You're not going to believe it because it's not believable. It took me a while to . . . well . . . There's this group of women and they wanted Jessa to join, but . . . I know this sounds impossible, but . . . it's not."

"You're upset. You should stop."

"I know. I get it. You don't believe me, and I wouldn't either if I were you." Gabby took in a deep breath. "You'll hear Darren killed her, but he didn't. They did. Because . . . she . . . she knew too much."

There. She'd said it in a rambling, stumbling way, but it was out there. Faith could choose to believe her or call her *that paranoid woman at the service* or whatever. Gabby didn't care because she'd said the words.

The sick part was that she'd piled her mess on Faith, and a part of Gabby hated that, but this woman had loved Jessa, had been her best friend through everything. She had a right to know Jessa tried to be better. She'd tried to do the right thing. Gabby wasn't sure if she'd made that clear or not, but she let the conversation sit there. Let Faith have the next word.

Faith let out a labored exhale. "You never learn. I told Retta you couldn't be trusted to keep quiet, and I was right."

Chapter Seventy-Eight

GABBY

GABBY'S MOUTH DROPPED open. She could feel it hanging there. She'd stumbled through a messy explanation, expecting Faith to pat her on the head and walk away. Not this. Never this.

"So you're saying . . ." *Nope.* Gabby's mind still couldn't get there. "What exactly are you saying?"

"This supposed group you're blathering on about doesn't exist, because of course it doesn't. It couldn't. But if it did, what good would hitting me with that word vomit do?" Faith no longer wore the sad and despondent expression of a mourner. She looked and sounded pissed. "You need to be smarter and a hell of a lot more careful."

Not the first time Gabby had heard that. "Right . . ."

"Why would you make your family a target after you just moved them out of the firing line? Do you want Liam to go to prison?"

"I don't . . ." *Good Lord.* What was she supposed to say? Gabby had no idea about the etiquette or proper response to being sideswiped by a near stranger who might also be a killer.

"You sound paranoid. No one will believe you and your stories about phantom deadly groups, so stop." Faith hesitated as if waiting for a response. "Do you understand me? Yes or no? Say something."

Gabby decided to give her one. "Okay."

"You caused this. You shamed Jessa into helping you. You wrapped up all her insecurities and fired them back at her. Your judgment wore her down. Got her talking about being a better person, as if she needed your permission to exist." Faith held out an arm. "Now look where we are."

They'd separated from other people, but Gabby finally got the point. Most of the haze had cleared, and in its place . . . clarity. "You're one of them. Part of the group."

Faith rolled her eyes. "Do you not know what 'stop' means?"

Gabby willingly shouldered part of the blame for Jessa's death, but the vast majority went to someone else. The person with the knife and the person who'd sent him there. "Did you know Earl was going to have Jessa killed?"

"Earl? What does he have to do with this?"

"I thought he . . . you know . . . the other . . ." Gabby couldn't rein in her babbling response.

"Why are you crediting a man for any of this?"

"Retta said her co-leader, and I . . . Oh, God." Gabby's stomach flipped. A queasy feeling swept over her. She wanted to throw up and run and wake up and have all of this be a nightmare she could wash away with a scalding hot shower. "You. The co-leader. That's you, not Earl."

"If the group existed, it would exist *because* of me. Because of me going to Retta after a terrible case, a life-changing case, knowing she would listen because she'd buried her murdered best friend years before."

"Excuses."

"No, reality. Retta knew on an intimate, painful level about the system's failures, law enforcement's ambivalence, and the public's short attention span." Faith's voice never lifted above a harsh whisper, but fury rattled through it. "You have no idea what it's like to help someone only to have the system that's designed to protect them suck away their hope then fail them."

Gabby didn't want to hear justifications and sad stories. "You knew what would happen to Jessa when she got to Baines's house. You sent Trent."

"We protect the group at all costs."

Not a denial. "That's madness. Do you hear yourself?" Gabby looked around, hoping to see reinforcements, but then would she even recognize them? Anyone could be in this group or related to it or working for it. The tentacles seemed to have endless reach. "You explain away the things you do with an end-justifies-the-means mentality while gleefully playing judge and jury."

"Are you done talking yet?"

"Never mind that innocent people, people who aren't part of the abusive crowd you want to eliminate, get hurt and killed in the process. Rob and Tami. Do you remember them? The reporters. They'd just gotten engaged. Baines. Poor Jessa." Gabby could see how the hideous process justified itself, but this was too much.

"Regretful but necessary." Faith's expression didn't change. "But the group didn't touch your precious ex."

This woman. "I guess you accept a certain level of collateral damage. Is that how you justify the string of deaths? Do you pretend they aren't really people? Write their lives off to the good of the cause and keep on making judgments?"

"You don't know anything about us or what the group believes. We live and die by these decisions and grieve every loss." Faith tapped her hand against her chest. "We fix the mess others create and make it safer for you to travel around in your insular, wealthy world without fear. So you're welcome."

"You talk a good game, but you ordered the murder of your best friend." Gabby saw Faith flinch and kept going. "Who does that? You can argue about justice and the system's failures all you want, but how can you justify a betrayal like that?"

"I had no choice. *You* gave me no choice."

Gabby would not take on that responsibility. She had always been honest—maybe too honest—with Jessa. "You sound like one of those abusers you hate so much."

"She had been warned over and over. She knew she was being tested and ignored every alarm and warning, including mine." Faith shook her head. "She didn't know about my role, but she made it clear she was under fire, and I gave her support. She promised she would stop engaging in dangerous activities, but you kept dragging her back in."

Gabby could hear what Faith didn't say. There was nothing accidental or heat-of-the-moment about Jessa's death. She'd been hunted by her best friend's paid killer. "Was I supposed to die, too?"

"The cause comes first." Faith separated each word, emphasizing the horror. "And listen to you being all high and mighty, above it all, and disdainful because you don't like the results this one time."

Faith didn't see how the power had corrupted her. Gabby didn't know how a smart woman could miss it. "You think a lot of yourself."

"Hypocrite." Faith shook her head. Let out a heartless little laugh. "When it came time to make a deal to save your daughter and brother-in-law, you jumped right in. That result was fine."

"I didn't agree to that."

"Maybe you weighed the pros and cons for a few seconds, and the guilt eats at you a bit, but when the decision was to keep all your secrets and guarantee your family's safety, then—what a surprise—justice wasn't a bright line. You shifted your beliefs and assigned blame to Darren. You probably felt justified doing it because a part of you decided Darren deserved being taken down."

Gabby hated the ring of truth in those words. She had looked the other way when she figured out what Baines had done to his sister because proving it had seemed too daunting. She'd limited Liam's role in Kennedy's life because it was easier.

Still, she didn't want to be lumped in any group with Faith. "I would point out I was blackmailed by Retta. That's why my line shifted. She shifted it."

"Poor you," Faith said in a mocking tone. "And don't throw around legal terms when you know better. You were faced with a *decision*, not blackmailed. You needed a way out, and you took it. Screw courtroom justice."

Gabby refused to let that be true. "You've been doing this too long. You can't separate out truth from fiction."

"Retta and I were faced with similar decisions. Could she live with the murderer of her friend and godchild being made into a martyr? Could I live with women and children being used as legal fodder to ensure their powerful poor-me husbands remained free?" Faith let out a harsh laugh. "See, when you're the one who needs to answer, you revise the question. Your sense of what's right and what's justice slides because the system doesn't work."

"Then change it from the inside." Gabby knew it was a lame response. A knee-jerk one people threw around on social media when they secretly knew a good solution didn't exist. "What you do is vigilantism, not justice."

"If you do the former correctly, it becomes the latter."

Gabby got it now. There wasn't an argument she could make to convince Faith. This wasn't about reasoning with her or showing her logic inconsistencies or problems in her thinking. The system had failed, and Faith had given up on it. She'd created a new way where she could bend it to her satisfaction.

"What happens now?" Gabby asked.

"That's up to you. Are you done with your crusade? Are you willing to go back to your precious little life with your boyfriend or brother-in-law or whatever he is to you these days and keep your mouth shut?"

Gabby refused to take the bait about Liam. Refused to respond at all.

Faith smiled. "And here's a hint—there's only one right answer."

Chapter Seventy-Nine

THE FOUNDATION

THE WOMEN AGREED to meet on an emergency basis. Again. The rule about being careful and spreading out visits had been abandoned in favor of triage. The downward spiral of blame and fighting between the founders had the group careening toward chaos. Here, chaos looked more like practiced control, but the result was the same—something had to change.

Retta scheduled the discussion but asked Faith to arrive early. Their personal issues had spilled over into the group and threatened its existence. Both believed they were in the right. Neither would concede. They had to compromise before they lost control.

Faith walked into Retta's home office through a flurry of household activity. A woman delivered a tray of tea to the corner of Retta's desk before rushing out of the room again. Music played but shut off when the door closed, plunging the room into silence.

Faith being Faith, she stayed singularly focused on the woman who had been her protector and ally for more than three years. "We have a problem."

Retta had her own agenda for this private meeting. "Do you have any remorse for Jessa?"

The comment made Faith stop in midmarch and lift her head. "Excuse me?"

"The love and friendship didn't only run one way. I know how much she meant to you, so explain why you gave the order to have her eliminated after the group voted to give her another chance." Retta's anger at being boxed in and not advised still burned white-hot, but the grief would hit. The loss, the waste, the betrayal. Retta packaged it all up and ignored it for now, but the sadness would break through, and waiting for the rush of unwanted emotion made her furious with Faith.

Not one to be brushed off or yelled into submission, Faith pulled out the chair across from Retta and sat down. "How do you think I feel?"

Retta didn't care. "I'm not convinced you feel anything at all."

"She was my best friend. I loved her more than anyone."

Retta snorted. "You had an odd way of showing it."

"I told you from the beginning Jessa didn't belong in the Foundation. I begged you to listen to me because I feared this would happen. Not exactly this, but a bad ending." Faith's firm voice faltered for a second before regaining strength. "She didn't have a strict internal code. She was a survivor but not a believer."

"The entire group made the decision to begin the membership process, not just me."

"I voted against her membership twice and only relented on

the third and final vote because you asked me to, as a favor." Faith shook her head. "Lie to Earl, to yourself, but not to me. You wanted her in the group. You liked how much she worshipped you. You knew you could control her. That she would have given you a guaranteed vote. You wanted her to trust you more than she trusted me."

"Your memory is very selective. Your vote was your choice, unless you're saying you worshipped me and wanted to please me, too."

"Is this really what you want to talk about?" Faith asked. "Because I can think of—"

"No." Retta rushed on before Faith could launch into an argument that would eat up all their spare time before the other women arrived. "It's the ease with which you ignored the vote of the group and sent Trent after Jessa."

Faith rolled her eyes. "And, being your lapdog, Trent immediately called you to tattle on me."

Retta was ready for that move. "But not before he killed her. On your order. You didn't have the authority. You overstepped the will of the group."

Faith leaned back in the chair, clearly not intimidated by Retta's stature. "Funny you should argue that, since I got the idea to use Foundation assets and resources to solve a problem from you."

Retta noticed Faith wouldn't deal with her decision about Jessa head-on. She'd compartmentalized her order, separating it out from her love for her friend. Retta worried that mix of deflection and denial would backfire on Faith at some point.

Sentencing a man based on his heinous acts was a very different thing from ordering a murder of someone you loved.

"You might remember we also had a vote about Baines Fielding. Months ago, but we did, and you lost. You couldn't prove your accusations about him killing his sister and being a possible danger to Gabby and the brother-in-law," Faith said. "The group's decision was to watch him but do nothing."

"I remember."

"But then he killed himself, which we both know is not what really happened." Faith stopped, as if waiting for a longer rebuttal that never came. "That choice started all of this, Retta."

Retta didn't regret that decision. Maybe that the timing had threatened Gabby's financial future, but not that it was done. Baines needed to be stopped. No one threatened her family. She and Earl had agreed on that and cut a few corners by using group assets to make it happen.

She refused to plead her case to Faith and went with a simple explanation instead. "Baines was a wild card. He had started paying someone to follow my sons. Stolen medical and academic records. Invaded their privacy, and if the photographs we saw were any indication, his investigator got far too close to my boys." That was the piece that had tipped Earl over into action. He could handle being stalked but refused to let anyone near his sons. "Baines, out of whatever mixed-up business hatred he had for Earl, also hired someone to dig around for dirt on Earl and on me."

Faith shrugged. "These are personal problems."

Retta saw the danger as far more pervasive. "The investigation could have led back to the group. Look what happened with the reporters."

"Okay, but your guy killed Baines with a witness in the room, and then that witness—the ever-present and determined Gabby Fielding—went on a rampage that could ruin everything."

Retta couldn't argue with the timeline, so she pivoted to the more obvious point. "Gabby isn't that powerful."

"You should tell her that, because she's acting like she is. Thanks to her, a reporter and Jessa are dead." Faith poured a cup of tea. "Which makes me wonder why Gabby is still alive. Enlighten me."

"We've had too much collateral damage. We've failed to keep a low profile and follow our own rules. Both of us. If this continues, someone will start poking around, and we won't be able to pivot out of it."

"You mean someone *else*. Gabby is already poking." Faith stared at Retta over the rim of her teacup. "I told you about our confrontation at the funeral."

One more thing to keep Retta's anger in the almost unmanageable range. "She's not going to talk. She has too much to lose. Too many family secrets she wants to keep buried."

"You exposed the biggest one. The one about her daughter's real father." Faith snorted. "It didn't even slow her down."

"I was trying to do damage control when I had my man contact the daughter at school."

Faith rose in her chair before settling in again. "You *created* the damage!"

"You're lashing out. We had been tracking Jessa, but she'd

almost snuck away. She wanted to hide and thought she could, but you gave her a phone that let us track her one last time. And then you sent Trent." Retta admitted lulling Jessa into thinking she could have privacy then exploiting that trust had been brilliant. "You set her up then knocked her down."

Faith's bravado took a hit. "You would have done the same thing. You didn't see her after Darren attacked her. She'd unraveled. She wasn't going to keep any of our secrets."

Retta could guess how that played out. Letting him loose might have been too much. She'd assess that later when she assessed every other move she'd made. "Listen, we've been doing this for years without a problem. We can correct the current trajectory and fix this."

"It's too late to handle this only between us. We need to be honest about the choices we both made outside of the usual process." Faith slowly lowered her teacup to the desk. "I'm also asking for a vote to wrap up the one remaining loose end so that we can move forward with some sense of stability."

"Gabby."

Faith nodded. "We both know what needs to be done."

Chapter Eighty

GABBY

GABBY CONCEDED TO the body search. Not that she had much of a choice. Retta had picked Woodend Nature Sanctuary in Chevy Chase as the location for the meeting and brought a bodyguard with her. Wisely, not Trent.

When the man took Gabby's bag and cell phone then started the patdown, Gabby eyed Retta. "Is this necessary?"

"Clearly."

Retta looked out of place at the picnic table in her designer pantsuit and thin diamond bracelets. The table had been moved away from the Sanctuary's mansion and all the trails until it was nestled in a circle of trees. Children ran in the distance, screaming with excitement as adults watched. They were far enough from crowds to have privacy. Gabby assumed Retta had called in a favor or was part of the Audubon Society that ran the place. Either way, it was just the two of them and her enforcer.

Gabby waited for the spot check to finish before sitting across from Retta. "I was surprised you called."

"There have been some developments," Retta said.

Gabby hated that wording. It suggested her fears had been warranted. "Let me guess. Faith is upset you let me live?"

Retta made a sound that came close to a groan. "Blame your stunt at the funeral for that."

Stunt seemed strong, but Gabby didn't deny it had happened. She'd intended to spill the truth that day. Between the grief and the guilt, she'd wound herself into a mental frenzy that she couldn't snap out of and find her balance again. But that was a week ago. The bit of distance had grounded Gabby. Made her smarter . . . she hoped.

"You talked about the Foundation," Retta said. "It sounded to her as if you were trying to expose the group."

Smart woman. "Little did I know I was talking to the head of the group."

Retta's mouth flattened. "One of them."

Interesting. "Sorry. Did I offend you by suggesting someone else is in charge?"

"We had an understanding, Gabby." Retta's tone took on a scolding note. "We talked about this."

"You threatened me while I was standing in the room with a man who I knew had killed at least two people." Gabby gave the unknown man with them a glance, but he didn't have any reaction to the murder talk. "Pardon me for panicking and silently conceding to your Darren or Liam challenge."

"The police cleared Liam this morning." Retta counted out her list on her fingers. "The site that leaked the information about Kennedy and Liam being father and daughter was discredited last night. The story is now that an individual blackmailing Liam—"

"A person who doesn't exist."

"—framed Liam and spread information about Kennedy that may or may not be true in an attempt to extort money from him. This individual also planted evidence at Liam's home, which after being tested has no connection to Baines's death. So Liam is clear there, too." Retta wrapped her arms around her. "He looks like a victim. A man still grieving from his brother's death who became a target of someone looking for a quick payday."

"Is there a PR team at the Foundation that comes up with these lies, or is that part of your job?"

Retta shifted, suddenly sitting forward. "Don't underestimate Faith."

"She killed her best friend to protect a secret society. I'm quite clear about how dangerous Faith is." Gabby had spent five of the last six nights not sleeping. She had a bat next to her bed and a knife under her pillow.

Retta frowned. "Then why are you inviting her to be an enemy?"

This topic wouldn't take them where Gabby wanted to go. They could talk in circles, but she'd come here for a reason, and not the one Retta thought.

"We need a new deal," Gabby said, sounding more secure than she was.

Retta smiled. "You'd need leverage for that."

"Did I forget to mention I have this?" Gabby reached into her bra and pulled out a memory stick. "You stole Jessa's bag, but I had this. Well, not this one specifically. This one is a copy, because this isn't my first day dealing with you. I've learned a few things."

Retta glanced at the man who'd conducted the patdown then to Gabby again. "I don't know what you think—"

"Your files. Jessa collected them from the firm's top secret partner closet . . . or vault. I'm unclear on what it is. There's probably a technical name for it, but that's how she described it." Gabby set the stick on the table between them.

"Get to the point."

"Happy to. Do your fellow group members know you have a file on each of them? The information in there about Faith and what she did in the Young case to hide that mother and her kid and frame the dad for murder . . . how she lied to the police and the court." Gabby whistled. "Pretty damning stuff."

"What do you want?"

Gabby had more to spill first. "Then there's the files you kept on each of the Foundation votes. You handed down your special kind of justice a lot over the last three years." When Retta didn't say anything in response, Gabby continued, "Those folders don't have names on them, but I doubt it would be hard to connect the fact patterns with some of the mysterious deaths in the area."

Retta snatched the stick and closed it in her fist. "Congratulations. You played this game smarter than I thought you would. Actually, that's not true. I've always said you were one of my best students."

Gabby ignored all Retta's fake sucking up. She'd long ago lost the need to win over people she viewed as teachers and mentors. And she didn't think of Retta as either anymore.

Gabby stayed focused. She had a list of things she needed Retta to agree to. She'd gone over all of this, made contingency plans, and now it was finally time. "You're speaking on behalf of the entire Foundation?"

"Yes."

Gabby didn't fully believe that, but she pressed on. "To start, my family stays out of all of this, and no one goes near them. Ever."

"I already agreed to that."

She did. Faith hadn't, and that distinction mattered to Gabby. "Darren goes to prison for something he did and not for the murder. Jessa becomes an unsolved murder statistic and gets a shelter or something named after her that you fund. Most important, the Foundation immediately stops its nonpublic, behind-the-scenes pseudo–justice work."

Retta's eyes narrowed as she listened. "You're on dangerous footing."

"I could say the same about you. See, you don't know how many copies I have of that or where I have them." Gabby pointed at Retta's closed hand. "You should assume I have many copies and that some are being kept by people you would never suspect. People who don't know what they're holding."

"With the group's resources, we could bury you."

That was the fear. "Probably, but then I will take you down with me." Gabby tried to fake a smile, show more confidence than she had. "Are you really willing to take that risk?"

Please say no.

"And if I say yes?" The barking toughness of Retta's tone had slipped. She talked a good game, but she had to know Gabby would not back down.

"You're a very smart woman, Retta. You won't." Gabby felt some of the tension leave her shoulders. "Now, let's talk details."

Chapter Eighty-One

GABBY

GABBY READ THE headline a second time.

Legal Trailblazer and Highly Respected Appeals Court
Judge Announces Retirement

Four days after their meeting, and Retta made the move. Her self-punishment for her role in Jessa's death appeared to be losing the job she'd loved so much. Gabby could live with that.

She'd expected relief or at least an easing of the tension that had been twisting inside her since she found Jessa's body, but no such luck. More dominoes needed to fall. More time had to pass without a strange suicide or the death of a powerful male who'd recently escaped the justice system. Until then, *wary but hopeful* was Gabby's mantra.

"Did you know that was coming?" Liam asked as he sipped on his coffee.

Gabby pivoted around the stool in his kitchen and headed for the coffeepot. "The judge? Our paths don't cross that often."

"Earl used to joke that his wife would go out of her judge's chambers in a body bag." Liam lowered his mug to the breakfast bar. "Morbid, now that I think about it."

Gabby didn't want to talk about Retta and Earl or think about them. She'd played her biggest card and hoped it worked. She needed the threat to hold.

"The article talks about Loretta being impacted by Jessa's death." Liam scanned the article, clearly looking for the exact quote.

Gabby didn't need to hear it. She knew why Retta had picked now.

"Are you okay?"

Gabby heard Liam's voice but missed his question. When she looked up, she saw concern in his eyes. "What?"

"I know you and Jessa had a difficult history with the divorce stuff, but you'd been out for coffee and talking with her lately." Liam shrugged. "She was a friend, right?"

"She was." Gabby hadn't admitted that in years, and the word wasn't a comfortable fit now, but she owned it. Jessa's sacrifice needed to mean something. People would remember her but never know how brave she'd been at the end.

"I'm worried about you. Baines, then that reporter. The attack. Now Jessa. That's a lot to handle in something like two months." Liam closed the laptop. "Hell, I haven't grieved for Baines. There's been so much with the money issue and the police."

"And Kennedy." She noticed how he tiptoed around that. How he kept the peace.

She didn't deserve either. Some days she wished he'd let go, yell at her, make her pay for her terrible choices. She didn't want to be like Jessa and look back with regret, or whatever Jessa felt that made her act as if the hounds of Hell were at her feet.

"Is Kennedy talking to you yet?" He hadn't broached this subject at all. Until now.

Gabby waded in carefully. She leaned against the sink, hoping it would hold her up if the topic turned on her. "Barely."

"She'll come around."

She almost asked if he had, but she didn't want to know the answer. "We talk every day. Not about you or what happened. It's more like school gossip, but it's something. Baby steps."

"Speaking of strange things happening over the last few weeks . . ."

Gabby had to laugh. "Interesting segue."

Liam spun around on the chair to face her. "Earl contacted me. We talked about the bid paperwork you found. I expected him to stomp around and use it to have us disqualified from this project and a bunch of others, but he asked about us teaming up."

Liam coming clean about Baines's actions and the enormity of what that could mean for his business sank in right as he mentioned the team thing. "Wait, go back. A merger?"

"Not really. Under Earl's proposal, we'd combine for one job then see how it goes. Talk about more later." Liam didn't sound convinced about the plan. "Apparently, he and Retta bought a place in Florida and plan to spend a lot of time there now that she's retired and—"

"No!" Gabby didn't realize she'd screamed the order until she saw Liam's reaction. "Please don't do it."

His eyes widened, and he leaned away from her a bit. "Wow."

She needed to stay calm and be clear. "Sorry, but you don't want to get in bed with Earl."

"Want to tell me why?"

She needed him to hear her. She hadn't gambled and black-mailed only to have him undo all her hard work by walking into an arrangement with Earl. That man had an agenda, and a ruthless one. "I don't have a right to ask this, and I normally wouldn't. Not now. Not when things are uncertain, and you're barely tolerating me being in your house, but please. No deals with Earl. Be careful around him. He's . . . a problem."

He sat there for a few seconds then nodded. "For the record, I like having you in my house."

She couldn't go there or handle that. Not right now. Later, yes. They had to deal with all those balled-up, pushed-aside, ig-nored, and abandoned feelings. But they both had to grieve for Baines first. Be mad at him and miss him.

"I can't tell you why now, or go into details, but I promise I will soon. I will show you everything, tell it all. But we need distance from all the horrors of the last six weeks. We'll keep everything I say between us and agree to let it die there because we must."

"That's a hell of an ask."

"I know." This time she meant it. No more secrets. A lie about liking his tie or not was about as much falsehood as she wanted between them in the future. "Please, just trust me when I ask you to stay away from Earl."

"You make it sound like he's dangerous."

"He is."

Chapter Eighty-Two

NEW EVIDENCE IN CASE OF MISSING WIFE
AND CHILD—Bethesda, MD

The case of Penelope and Delilah Young is back in the news. Police state that the case was never closed, but the discovery of new evidence has given it increased prominence. The type of evidence has not been revealed.

The mother and daughter have been missing for almost four years. While no charges have been filed, Christopher Young has long been considered a person of interest in the disappearance of his wife and daughter, age 6 at the time she went missing.

Prior to their disappearance, Young had been arrested after the police received a 911 call from his wife in the middle of a domestic altercation. The court granted her a protective order, prohibiting Young from having any contact with her and limiting his contact with their daughter to supervised visitation. He filed to dismiss the charges, but his wife and child went missing before the scheduled court date.

The former residence of the Young family has been searched several times over the years, as have the residences of several family members. Young has denied any involvement and insisted that his wife and child are alive. He also accused Faith Rabara, a domestic abuse counselor, of assisting his wife in kidnapping their daughter and leaving the jurisdiction. Rabara has denied the allegations, and no charges were ever brought against her or the charity she runs, Safe Harbor Limited.

Both Young and Rabara have been questioned as recently as this week about the new evidence and case allegations. The investigation is ongoing.

Chapter Eighty-Three

GABBY

SUICIDE. THE OFFICIAL cause of death for Baines. Gabby had been notified this morning by someone other than Detective Melissa Schone, which was good because Gabby didn't want to see anyone affiliated with the Foundation or the group or whatever the hell the connection was for a very long time.

"Surprise."

She turned around at the sound of Liam's voice. He stood in the hallway with two duffel bags at his feet. One looked like his, and the other one looked empty. "I give up. What's this?"

"Your bag." He smiled. "Okay, more like a dramatization of your bag, because I wasn't about to go through your personal stuff and pack for you, but you get the idea."

She had no clue. "Am I moving?"

Seeing her bag sitting there, deflated and waiting, ticked off a punch of anxiety. She wasn't ready for any more change. Her house held horrifying memories she hadn't processed. Liam had inherited Baines's house and offered it to her, but she didn't want it because no amount of bleach would wash away the stench of death there. Then there were the job and money issues, and Kennedy's anger, which she hadn't tackled yet.

Gabby wasn't great at begging, but she would. Unless he needed her out. For all she knew, she'd finally trampled over his feelings for her, and he wanted to move on. She wanted him to be happy, but . . . Yeah, she wasn't ready to deal with that issue yet either. She was going to need a lot of therapy.

"New York trip," he said.

"Huh?"

He exhaled as he shot her a *why isn't she getting this?* look of frustration. "It's time to bring Kennedy home. Well, I guess that's your decision, but it's midterm break, and you got her a therapist, but we haven't done a great job of spending time with her and answering her questions. Not with everything else going on."

Gabby's body went into a defensive clench. She agreed . . . mostly, but danger still lurked, and Faith was a huge question mark, even with the news of her being under investigation in the Young case again. The idea of dumping Kennedy into the middle of that? No.

"She hates me right now. Not teen hate. Real hate," Gabby said, stating the obvious.

"She doesn't. Even if she did, she can hate you from her bedroom upstairs, while engaging in therapy and family dinners."

He made his solutions sound simple. He didn't know so much of what had happened behind the scenes or what she'd had to concede to save him. Gabby wasn't sure how she'd live with letting Jessa's death go unpunished, but she would. That deal with Retta wouldn't implode because of her.

"Look, you decide about the coming-home part, but I would like to see her," he said.

"You have a lot of work mess to untangle." But he sounded so . . . normal. She knew what he'd discovered about Baines weighed on him. She'd caught Liam searching for information on the fire, as if he wanted to find some tiny piece of information to contradict her beliefs on Baines's guilt.

"I'm taking one issue at a time," he said. "The easiest one is the money. Baines took it to go after Earl. That's clear now. There's a list of unforgivable things he did, but stealing to fill his own pockets and screw me and the business out of income isn't one."

"You're a good man." He hadn't forgiven her, and she didn't ask, but in quiet, subtle ways, he let her know he was trying. That was more than she deserved, so she grabbed on to it.

"Not really." He sighed. "But I have to make room for grief. There's anger and confusion, and I can't even deal with the idea of Baines intentionally hurting Natalie. Right now, I'm blocking the idea so I can survive it."

"I know."

"Part of me needs to think he didn't order her death or did and then tried to stop it." Liam exhaled. "He was my brother, and I can't wrap my head around him being evil. I know there's still a lot you need to tell me and aren't ready to do so."

"Not yet." She feared what he'd do if he knew the truth about Retta and her group.

"I'm not sure about your request that when I hear these horrible things that I then forget them, but honestly, not mourning who I thought Baines was might destroy me. So, I need to at least try to do that."

And she needed him strong, because all those emotions and feelings she'd been packing away and pretending not to have were going to rush over her one of these days. He wasn't the only one who needed to mourn. "It sounds like you already talked to a therapist."

"Not about the Natalie part, but about the rest." He shrugged. "I want to be there for you and Kennedy. Being pissed at Baines doesn't help any of us."

Hope. It flowed through him. She could see it, and it was infectious. He'd be okay. Eventually. Somehow.

"He made unbelievable mistakes and lost his way, but he loved you." She said it because she thought he needed the reminder.

"And he loved you." Liam's crooked smile returned. "Well, until you left him. Then he wanted revenge."

"He did a good job with that." Scorched earth. Baines didn't know another way. He was a hundred percent in, good or bad.

"About that." Liam exhaled as if he was expecting a fight. "I'm going to put part of the inheritance in a trust for Kennedy, and part will go to you."

No, no, no. That sounded wrong. Felt wrong. He was not her backup plan, and she needed to figure out her financial life on her own. "Not for me. You should—"

He held up a hand to stop her denial. "We'll talk about all of that later. Work out the details, and you can tell me the billion reasons why you'd rather get financially screwed as Baines's final act."

She couldn't help but laugh at that. "Sounds like you've thought this through."

"Right now, you need to get packed so we can go get your daughter and listen to her tell us how we've ruined her life."

Our daughter. "We do have a lot to talk about and work through."

He shrugged. "When we're ready, we will. Until then, we fake it."

Her specialty. "Agreed."

Chapter Eighty-Four

THE FOUNDATION

THIS FOLLOW-UP MEETING had been scheduled to vote on the Gabby situation and on other issues of concern to the ongoing functioning of the Foundation. Loretta would lead the meeting because all members agreed that Faith could not be present while she was under such prevalent media and law enforcement pressure.

The remaining members gathered on time, as always. The whispering and head nodding stopped the minute Retta entered the room. Without greetings and explanations, she sat down and started the meeting.

"While I have decided to retire from the bench, I will not be leaving the Foundation, either the actual Foundation or our group." Gabby would not win on that score. The group would be more careful, not issue death decisions except in specially defined cases, but the work would not stop.

Gabby had leverage, but so did Retta. They were locked in a battle where one could destroy the other. Retta was betting Gabby's need to protect her family would overcome her need to check on the group's ongoing progress. They would be careful. Not draw attention . . . and Gabby would never know.

Melissa Schone, who usually didn't say much, spoke up. "At our last meeting, Faith suggested you might take a temporary leave of absence."

"It's not her decision, it's ours." Retta had no interest in ceding control of the floor. She needed control over the agenda to keep questions to a minimum. "Our failure to abide by our own process and rules, even those not explicitly stated, increased the danger to all of us and cost lives. The new, clearer rules we agree to will prevent that level of collateral damage and potential discovery."

Dr. Downing's eyebrow lifted. "*Our* failure?"

The room went quiet. Retta pushed the conversation in the direction she needed it to go. "Is there a problem with the agenda?"

Dr. Downing flipped to the last page. "There's no mention of Faith or Gabby here."

Retta knew they needed this resolved as soon as possible. Four days of unrelenting press coverage was enough for Faith. "First, Faith. Melissa, do you have a status?"

"The police have two emails between Faith and Penelope Young, the missing mother in the cold case mentioned in the media, likely covered by privilege, that may support Christopher Young's claim about his wife and child being alive," Detective Schone explained. "We didn't turn them over, correct?"

We? No. "Correct," Retta confirmed, knowing she was walking a very careful line.

After setting Jessa up, Faith had needed a reminder of the

limits of her power. Being brought in for additional questioning on the Young case served that purpose, but now it was time to discredit the emails and publicly clear her.

"Christopher Young is very dangerous. Him being on the rampage threatens Faith as well as his family in hiding," Dr. Downing said. "We have enough deaths to answer for."

"Agreed. I suggest we handle the evidence against Faith immediately." And Retta meant that. She remained furious with Faith, but they'd started this group together. She didn't want Faith hurt. "Young needs to be neutralized."

"I'll handle it and will let Faith know," the detective said.

Dr. Downing nodded. "That leaves the Gabby situation."

This part might be tricky, so Retta stepped carefully. "In the spirit of limiting collateral damage, I suggest we postpone our vote on her indefinitely. If she stays quiet, as expected, fine."

"What stops her from continuing her hunt for information?" Detective Schone asked.

Mutually assured destruction. But the group didn't know about Retta's files or Gabby's blackmail. They knew the fake story Retta had planted about Gabby coming to her following Jessa's death and saying she wanted to get back to her life and her daughter, and now accepted Baines had killed himself.

"Self-preservation." That was the answer. Gabby was not a stupid woman. Retta was convinced of that. She looked around the room to gauge the expressions of the other women. "She has a lot to lose and a lot of secrets to hide. Those will keep her in line . . . so long as we're careful."

"We can't allow something like this to happen again," the detective said.

"Agreed." Retta heard some humming sounds and saw a few nods, so she quickly shifted. "I would also like us to think about long-term planning. While we all agree to a moratorium on new membership invitations to our group until we are comfortable trying again, that shouldn't prevent other types of expansion. Specifically, we should consider the possibility of starting a new chapter in Florida, where I will be living for part of the year."

No one disagreed. All seemed interested in the idea.

"We already have sister chapters in Philadelphia and New York City. Women in other regions need our protection as well." More nods. Retta appreciated the support. "Now, on to the rest of the agenda."

Chapter Eighty-Five

BREAKING NEWS: SHOOTING DEATH
IN BETHESDA—Bethesda, MD

Police have confirmed an altercation, leading to a shooting outside of a residence on Hampden Lane in Bethesda, Maryland, this morning. The shooting victim has been identified as Christopher Young. Young was pronounced dead at the scene. He had been the leading suspect in the disappearance of his wife and child for more than four years.

Witnesses at the scene say Young was armed when he threatened Faith Rabara, founder of the Safe Harbor Limited charity for victims of domestic and partner violence and resident of the address of the incident. A source who requested not to be identified said Young was heard shouting that Rabara needed to "pay for lying." It's alleged Rabara shot and killed Young in self-defense when he attacked her.

Police believe Young discovered where Rabara resided due to the recent news stories about the unrelated death of Rabara's friend and roommate, attorney Jessa Hall, at the same condo property.

Young's wife, Penelope, had visited Rabara's charity numerous times before her disappearance. Young alleged Rabara helped his wife kidnap their child and leave the jurisdiction. Rabara has denied those claims.

Following the discovery of new evidence in the case, Rabara and Young recently were questioned about the disappearance of Young's family and released. That evidence was discredited in a police statement two days ago. The nature of the falsified evidence has not been revealed.

Police say Rabara, who possesses the required license and gun permit for the firearm used in the shooting, is not expected to be charged. The investigation into the disappearance of Young's wife and child is ongoing.

Resources

National Domestic Violence Hotline
Expert advocates offer free support
24 hours a day, 7 days a week, 365 days a year
1-800-799-SAFE (7233)

National Suicide Prevention Lifeline
24/7 free and confidential support
1-800-273-TALK (8255)

Acknowledgments

I WROTE *THE LAST INVITATION* in a whirl of pandemic worry, grief over the loss of my dad, and fury over the ongoing disregard of violence against women and the seeming elimination of our rights. I was angry, frustrated, and exhausted, and somehow that translated into a book. So, if you're angry, frustrated, and exhausted, I see you and empathize. Know you're not alone.

Also know that while I did practice divorce law in the DC area for twelve years, and frequently was appointed as a guardian ad litem for children in their parents' horrible divorces, this book is pure fiction. I didn't cheat my way through law school. I didn't kill anyone. I was lucky enough to work with amazing, brilliant, and dedicated attorneys in two firms, some of whom have gone on to become judges. I am grateful for all of you.

I am also extremely grateful for May Chen, my patient and talented editor. When I pitch an idea and you get excited, then I get excited. Thank you for all your support and hard work, especially through an extra difficult last few years. My appreciation extends to everyone at HarperCollins and William Morrow, from my copyeditor, to the sales team, to the marketing and public relations people, to the production staff. You all make book miracles happen. And a special shout-out to the team at HarperCollins Canada for being such great advocates for my books.

Thank you always to my agent, Laura Bradford, for supporting my career and making the book deals happen, and to Katrina Escudero of Sugar23 for making dreams come true—multiple times.

Love and thanks to my husband, James, and to my dad, who would have loved this one.

About the Author

DARBY KANE is a former trial attorney and #1 internationally bestselling author of domestic suspense. Her books have been featured in numerous venues, including the *New York Times Book Review*, the *Washington Post*, the *Toronto Star*, PopSugar, Refinery29, Goodreads, the Skimm, and Huffington Post. A native of Pennsylvania, Darby now lives in California and runs from the cold. You can find more information at darbykane.com.

ALSO BY DARBY KANE

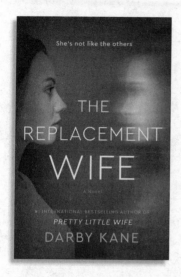

THE REPLACEMENT WIFE

The #1 internationally bestselling author of *Pretty Little Wife* returns with another thrilling domestic suspense novel that asks, how many wives and girlfriends need to disappear before your family notices?

PRETTY LITTLE WIFE

#1 internationally bestselling author Darby Kane thrills with this twisty domestic suspense novel that asks one central question: shouldn't a dead husband stay dead?

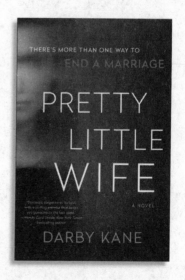

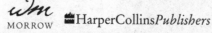